The Four Horsemen

A Novel by Mark Reimer

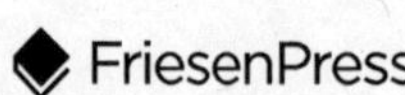

Suite 300 - 990 Fort St
Victoria, BC, V8V 3K2
Canada

www.friesenpress.com

First Edition — 2021

Cover Illustration: Ezra Jakob Reimer
Photographer: Paul Reimer

ISBN
978-1-03-910280-4 (Hardcover)
978-1-03-910279-8 (Paperback)
978-1-03-910281-1 (eBook)

1. FICTION, FAMILY LIFE

Distributed to the trade by The Ingram Book Company

What some readers are saying about *The Four Horsemen*...

I wish that I - and every kid who has and is and will grow up in a repressive, religiously abusive environment - could have had access to this beautiful, if hard, story when needed most; could have been given the hope that there is love for everyone, even if you are hurting and even if you don't fit the peg hole you've been assigned to by all the adults around you. That real love isn't perfect or even necessarily unconditional, but it always keeps trying anyway. For me, this message is the heart and the glory of *The Four Horsemen*, and why Reimer's semi-autobiographical tale is such a vital and significant addition to the growing library of Mennonite authors.

Cara Unger Hart, writer, at-risk youth support/mentor

While some people are torn from trust at too early an age, others of us are slowly tugged and ripped from belief systems over time. In *The Four Horsemen*, readers will find themselves immersed in their vested self-identities. The inevitable paradigm shifts of the book's characters reflect our own personal religious contemplations and experiences. The real events in each of Mark's "fictional" characters are treated with aching directness. The harshness of religious power is challenged by some unexpected sources of compassionate redemption.

Dr. Paul Loewen, BA, MDIV, DBA

It takes courage to explore and write about traumatic events in our personal and family lives. Especially so, when you're the youngest child born to the second and younger wife of a respected Mennonite evangelist/educator of a large, blended family, all of whom are suffering from post-traumatic stress following the sudden death of the first wife/mother. Then, instead of getting lost in the tragedy of such a beginning, you step back from it and seek to transform personal suffering into a work of fiction, which explores ***the*** suffering of many in a wider context, you may tap into a power which can become a gift of grace and redemption, not only for the writer, but for all who read it. I think cousin Mark (whom I used to babysit) does that in this novel; and I applaud him for it.

LEONA DUECK PENNER

In *The Four Horseman*, Mark Reimer presents an unflinching account of fundamentalist religion and family. As a pastor's son, I am grateful that my own childhood experiences did not match those of Mark's characters, but I appreciate Mark's focus on exploring the impact of fundamentalism, not only on communities and congregations, but on the oft-neglected families of its most ardent practitioners.

ANDREW UNGER, AUTHOR OF *ONCE REMOVED* AND *THE DAILY BONNET*

I think you're a person who hopes, who works for good, and you want that to come through. There's so much good in here, Mark. So many interesting characters, each going so many different directions in their personality, their voice on the page. I think you have the best approach you could have - speaking to today's world while using what you know of humanity through a variety of people you know.

STEPHANIE WARE, ENGLISH LITERATURE AND FRENCH TEACHER, AVID READER

Chapter One

(June 3, 2005)

"The Four Horsemen of the Apocalypse as promised by John in the book of Revelations are here!" Walter Rempel pounded his large fist onto the pulpit. "War has always been present, but fear of war, hatred leading to war, is not just about the fighting between countries. Our families are increasingly divided, with one sibling fighting another, children fighting with their parents." The preacher paused to let his words sink in. The low-ceilinged church was hot from an early-summer heat wave and the overflowing congregation, many of whom had travelled great distances to hear him.

Walter Rempel was not an imposing physical figure. He was rather short, a little stocky, with dark, brown, slightly dishevelled curly hair pasted against his head from the sweat he generated from his passionate preaching. His voice, however, was compelling. It was bold, rose and fell in volume, and held a sonorous timbre, his total conviction about the truths he was expounding sounding in every word. He waved and gestured with his large hands as he spoke, further drawing the crowd's rapt attention.

"Conquest is no longer just one country attempting to expand its borders by taking land from their neighbours, or the rich taking from the poor. Instead, it is about taking power over others, denying the authority of those rightly in charge and living only for themselves." Walter continued, his piercing gaze roaming around the room, letting each person know that he was speaking directly to them, imploring them to listen not only to the urgency of his voice, but to the importance of his message. He was living up to what people had said about his preaching as he attempted to connect with each person in the audience.

"In Africa and Asia there are more famines now than ever before. Food supplies in many parts of the world are dwindling, and people are lining up for food that simply isn't there. But famine is not only an absence of food for the body. What about when there is no satisfying food for the soul? A child's, a parent's, a person's soul withers when the love, the understanding, compassion from the surrounding community, is withheld from them. And with each of these abominations, the angel of death walks hand in hand! People are dying, emotionally, psychologically, as well as physically from the plague that is a lack of care, from the loss of love, from battles waged when one has no desire to understand the other." Walter's voice grew stronger with each utterance of death's many doors.

"Should we be afraid? Should we hide from this? Or can we answer the call of God to be a light shining in the darkness? Who will be the light to their family? Can we be the candle on the top of the hill, shining hope and spreading good news…" Walter glanced to his left as he caught sight of an usher almost running down the side aisle of the church. She paused for a moment with fear and hesitation carved on her face before timidly ascending the stage. The usher kept her eyes on the floor, allowing her long brown hair to fall forward, covering her face, as she approached the pulpit, where Walter's pause grew longer.

The usher leaned toward Walter, turning away from the congregation. He took a slight side-step away from the microphone and flinched upon hearing the message she whispered into his ear. Then she turned and fled down the aisle with tears streaming down her face. The congregation sat transfixed. What was important enough to interrupt a preacher?

Walter straightened himself, swallowed, and stepped back behind the pulpit. "Will you answer the call of God?" The keyboard player started playing the hymn "Just as I Am," very softly as once again Walter's voice rose in pitch and fervour. The audience knew the climax of the service was now upon them. They had heard the message, heard the invitation to respond, and now it was a question of commitment. "Will you stand with Jesus? Will you leave your sins behind and walk to the front to become a fisher of men?"

He paused, took a deep breath and continued. "Whatever you may be facing, Jesus is there with you. You do not have to face it alone. Come to the front. We have elders who will pray with you. There is nothing too big for God, he can save you from whatever comes..." Walter's voice cracked, "whatever comes your..." He sobbed, cleared his throat, and then cleared it again. "God has a plan for your life. Nothing just happens. Will you surrender yourself into his loving hands?"

Tears poured down Walter's cheeks as he stood behind the pulpit, both hands gripping its sides, knuckles white. Four people had already knelt at the front of the church, with an elder wearing a nametag standing behind each one. Another six repentant souls were walking down the aisles.

"Just as I am without one plea, I come, Lord, I come to thee... Fully surrender yourself." Walter's voice was weaker now, and he began swaying back and forth. "I come, Lord, I come." And then he stepped from behind the pulpit and joined the others kneeling at the front of the church, his face wet with tears.

An hour later all the prayer partners had finished recording personal information on their cards, most lights were turned out, and the parking lot outside the church had only a few cars left. Walter sat on the front pew, leaning forward, his head in his hands. The pastor of the church who had invited him to come speak stood at the back of the auditorium, tentatively looking at the back of Walter's head, at the clock on the wall, at the floor, and then at the pulpit. He shifted his weight from one foot to the other, and then took a step forward.

Halfway down the aisle the pastor stopped and looked at the pulpit again, turned to look at the clock over his shoulder, and then rested his hand on the pew beside him. "Chmmm, chmmm." He took another step before stopping once again. "Hhhmmm hhhmmm hhhmmm..." He hummed "Just as I Am" softly as he slowly took one step after another toward Walter, finally arriving and sitting down beside him.

"Walter," the pastor whispered. "Walter, the usher told me. She told me about Agatha. Do you want me to give you a ride back to Steinbach? I can have a brother drive your car behind us and deliver it to your house so you don't have to drive."

Walter didn't lift his head, his hands wet with tears. "God's plan. God has a plan that is His perfect will for each of us. He will never give us more than we can endure..." He sobbed through his hands. The pastor put his hand on Walter's shoulder for a moment, quickly removed it, and then slowly, deliberately put it back.

"All things work together for good to them that love the Lord and are called according to his purpose," the pastor quoted. Walter nodded. "And you, Walter, have been called, you have a purpose, the most noble purpose. You are bringing salvation to the lost. You are the shining light on the hill. Are you alright, Walter?"

Walter coughed, cleared his throat, and leaned back. The pastor removed his hand and shifted a little further down the pew.

"I'm fine. But I had better leave now. The children were with Agatha. I had better leave now." Walter hung his head as he lumbered toward the back of the church. A few lingering congregants moved toward him, beginning to extend their hands, but, seeing his face, they dropped their hands and took a step backward. Walter didn't look up as he took his coat from the hook beside the door and stepped into the night air.

It was still warm, and a breeze blew gently against Walter's face. He paused a moment with the door of the church still open behind him. Another tear rolled down his cheek, and he crunched over the church's gravel parking lot toward the navy-blue Dodge Durango waiting beside the road for him. Walter pulled open the door and climbed in before slumping his shoulders and head against the steering wheel. "God has a plan, has a perfect plan for you," Walter whispered, then shook his head a few times and sat up. He turned the key and the engine fired to life.

"I've anchored my soul in the haven of rest," came singing from the radio that was always left on in the car. "Ten bells and all's well..." Walter reached for the knob and turn off the radio. He turned on the car's lights, looked over his shoulder, and pulled onto the road. The sound of his tires rolling over gravel and the cloud of dust rising behind him automatically engaged Walter with the task at hand, and he steered the car south toward Steinbach.

"When I walk through the valley of the shadow of death, I will fear no evil, for thy rod, and thy staff, they comfort me," Walter recited, then sobbed. "What can I do now? Who will preach if I don't? Who will look after my children? Lord, I have spent almost my whole adult life sacrificing time with my family to serve you. I have missed their birthdays, their parent-teacher meetings, to hold revival meetings. How was that not enough for you? I thought that if I took care of your flock, you would take care of my family!"

Walter wiped the tears at the corner of his eyes as he drove. "What will I say to them? What if they are still there with her? What if they are there alone with her? Oh God, I need you! I need more than thy rod and thy staff to comfort me. My children need you. God's will for her life… this is God's will for her? God, please reveal your will to me!" He kept a steady stream of words directed at the heavens as he approached the north end of Steinbach.

Without thinking, he flicked on his right blinker and turned toward the Steinbach Bible School at the edge of town where he had his office and drove past it toward the house the school had provided for him and his family. There were three cars in the driveway and yard, but no ambulance or other type of emergency vehicles, and it looked like all the lights in the house were on. Walter stopped the car in front of the house and looked through the large dining room window into his house. Initially he only noticed the peeling paint from the cracked window frame. He shook his head and looked again and saw three of his children sitting at the kitchen table together with two ministers from his church.

Chapter Two

Walter leaned his head forward onto the steering wheel and swallowed. "God's will… God's perfect will… I will fear no evil." He wanted to believe it, and if he said it often enough, he might. Two minutes later the door nearest to the garage opened and Arnold Dueck, one of the ministers Walter had seen through the window, stepped out. Walter opened his car door and got out.

"Walter, are you alright? Are you coming inside? Your children have been wondering, have been asking for you for almost two hours. Wasn't your service in Landmark tonight? Do you have any idea of the time? Where have you been?" Arnold wasn't giving him any time to answer.

Walter closed the car door gently and took a few steps toward the house before stopping once more. "What do I say to my children, Arnold? Can I actually tell them that there is a God who has a plan for his children that looks like this? I don't know if I can do that." Walter's voice was almost a whisper by the end. Arnold quickly pushed the door to the house closed and stepped up to him, placing both his hands firmly on Walter's shoulders.

"Look at me. Walter, look me in the face. This is God's will! You cannot question that, you cannot ever question that. God knows all things. He knows why he does what he does, even when we don't understand. This is hard enough; you can't take away the certainty of God, who God is, how God works, from your children at this time. Remember God loves you and remember also that you love God. You committed yourself to serving God, regardless of the cost. All things work together for..." Arnold had started quoting from the book of Romans and Walter picked it up.

"...good to those who love God and are called according to his purpose." Walter finished the phrase. "I love God, and this is his purpose? My children love God, and this is his purpose?" Arnold tightened his grip on Walter's shoulders. He added a short but definite shake.

"It is not for us to question God. Doubting the authority of God, doubting his ability to make bigger plans than we might understand is a sin, Walter, a sin! This is no time to begin doubting and begin sinning! Your children need you. And tomorrow your church will need you. And next week the rest of the province will need you. There are souls that need to be saved! They will need you to know who God is if you are to provide them with comfort and guidance." Arnold's voice was hard and stern. "Do you understand me?"

Walter's whole body began shuddering involuntarily, sobs wracked his body, and he attempted to lean forward to support himself against Arnold, whose hands were still on his shoulders.

"Get a hold of yourself, Walter," he said as he stepped back and pushed against Walter's sagging body. "Take a breath, a deep breath. We have already begun praying with your children, but now that you are here, they need you to continue that. We called Elizabeth over from the dorm. She came to put the youngest one to bed. She is in the bedroom with him, telling stories and consoling him. But there are three who need you to be strong. Be strong, brother!" Arnold patted Walter on the shoulders, again pushing against them to help straighten Walter's body.

Dave Hoeppner, the other minister who had been at the table with Walter's children, opened the door and stuck his head outside. "Are you coming in? What's happening here? Walter, is everything alright?" Dave looked first toward Walter, then toward Arnold. "Arnold, is everything alright?" The light shining from above the door created shadows on Walter's furrowed brow and glowed off the sweaty forehead of Arnold Dueck.

"Walter just needed a moment to prepare himself, to remind himself of God's calling for his life, of his responsibility to his children, to his church, to the lost and to his God. Yes, everything is in order now," Arnold replied. He straightened his tie, adjusted his black suit jacket, took a step forward and put his arm around Walter's body, pushing him toward the door. "All things, Walter, all things. Remember that."

"Dad!" shouted Darrel as he leaped from the table, rushed to the door, and wrapped his arms around his father. At eighteen, Darrel was a full head taller than his father and had to lean down to embrace him. Eight-year-old Sonya and thirteen-year-old Anna were right behind him. Walter wrapped his arms awkwardly around his children. Darrel whispered, "Mom's…" he took a deep breath, "Mom's…"

"Dead," blurted Anna. "She's not…" Anna drew a deep breath, "here anymore." She took another deep breath. "The hospital took her away," her voice squeaked out between gasps. Walter brushed dark curls from her face, which was wet with tears. He stroked her head a few times before resting his hand on Sonya's head. A few tears welled up in Walter's eyes, and he quickly wiped them back.

"Why did they take her away? Where did they take her?" added Sonya, her face buried deep in Walter's stomach. She looked up toward Walter's face, hoping he would be able to offer a different response than that of her older brother.

Elizabeth appeared in the hallway, with a teary-eyed Benjamin in her arms. Six-year-old Benjamin was wearing only his pyjama bottoms, and his bare chest heaved with sobs. She hesitated a moment and then released Benjamin's wriggling body so he could squeeze into his father's embrace too. For a moment it appeared that Elizabeth would step forward and join the group, but after a hesitant step forward, she retreated back into the hallway once more.

"What happened to Mommy?" Benjamin looked directly into his father's eyes. "She was making supper when she fell down, and then she didn't get up again. Where is she now? Why did that big car take her? Where did they take her? When is she coming back?" Walter tightened his embrace around his children, unable to provide an answer to the questions.

"I don't think she's coming back," whispered Anna. Benjamin's sobs grew louder and stronger. Anna wrapped both her arms around him.

"Don't say that to him," Darrel hissed into her ear. "He's too young to know what happened."

Slowly Walter opened his arms. "Let's sit down at the table, everyone." He looked toward the hallway. "You too please, Elizabeth. I think I might need your help tonight." Walter avoided looking at Arnold Dueck and Dave Hoeppner as he directed his children toward the table. Arnold was quick to take a seat on one side of Walter and waved Dave toward the seat on Walter's other side.

Elizabeth, with her light-brown hair hanging loosely around her shoulders, sat across the table from Walter and pulled Benjamin onto her lap. He snuggled against her as his sobs subsided. Elizabeth wiped away his tears, stroked his back, and then kissed him on the cheek. He shifted his arms to give her a hug as she continued to draw circles and lines on his back. He closed his eyes for a moment, then pried them open. He blinked, closed his eyes again, and deep, rhythmic breathing took over his body.

"Children," Walter began. He took a deep breath, looked around the table at the young faces staring into his eyes, and at the adults carefully avoiding his gaze. "Children," Walter began again. "You know how… how the Bible teaches us that God has a perfect plan for our lives…" Darrel nodded. He sat perfectly still, his hands resting on the tabletop, keeping his piercing hazel eyes on his father.

Sonya gasped, looked up and then down at her shoes under the table. Her skinny arms gripped the chair and began to quiver. She took a deep breath, a sob breaking out, took another deep breath and used one arm to try and stop the other from quivering. Her sobs grew stronger and she put both arms on the table and hid her face in them. Elizabeth shifted Benjamin in her lap and placed her free hand on Sonya's shoulder. Gradually Sonya's sobs settled, but she kept her face hidden.

Anna squinted toward her father, shook her head, and closed her grip on the chair beneath her. She opened her mouth to say something but stopped herself. Her mouth hardened into a thin line, and she began kicking her heels against the legs of the chair. "You're not actually going to tell us…" Anna blurted out toward her father, blinking rapidly.

"Anna, this is no time to speak to your father like that," Arnold Dueck stated coldly anticipating where her comment would go. Anna glared across the table at him, biting her lip to keep from spitting out more words.

"Anna, Anna, please. This is a very difficult time, but God promises to never give us more than we can handle. Together, God walking with us, we can find our way through this too." Anna got up and walked toward the hallway. "Anna, please. We need to be together as a family now."

Sonya looked up, then quickly averted her eyes back down toward her shoes. Darrel stood up and took a step toward Anna.

"Anna, let me give you a hug." Darrel moved to put his arms around her. "We all love you too. It's not just God who loves you." Anna pulled away from Darrel at those words and stood in the entrance of the hallway, her back to the people around the table. Dave Hoeppner threw questioning glances from Walter to Arnold to Anna, and around the circle at the table, convulsively swallowing.

Walter stood up, stepped toward Anna, and placed his hands on her shoulders. She flinched at her father's touch. "Anna, come back to the table just long enough for us to pray together. Then maybe we all should go to bed. It is very late." Walter used his hands to turn Anna around and move her toward the table. He led her to his chair, then firmly put his hand on Arnold's shoulder and moved him out of his chair. "I'll take this chair, Arnold, beside my daughter. You can take her chair." Arnold stood up and moved around the table without looking at Walter or Anna.

Dave Hoeppner put both his hands, palms upward, on the table as if to hold hands with Sonya and Arnold, who sat on either side of him. Neither responded and he left one hand on the table while removing the other. Elizabeth gently rocked Benjamin, who was taking deep breaths, eyes shut tightly, no longer aware of what was going on around him.

"Let's pray," Walter said. "Lord, you have a plan for each one of us. Help us to understand, or at least accept what you have for us. Let us rest in the knowledge that you know best, you knew that Agatha needed to come home to you now, even though we… we… were not… ready for that." Walter's voice faltered before he continued. "Lord, keep us in your comforting hands as we walk through this valley of the shadow of… Amen."

No one looked up. A chair scratched on the floor as Elizabeth pushed back from the table. "I'm going to put Benjamin into his bed."

Walter looked at her, stood up as if to follow her, then stopped. "Thank you. Once he's in bed, would you help Anna and Sonya to bed? That was always Agatha's..." Elizabeth stood up slowly, allowing Benjamin's head to nestle against her shoulder, and then moved toward the last bedroom along the hall.

Darrel got up from the table and walked toward his father. "Dad, we're going to be okay. Don't worry. We'll just keep praying, and God will just keep taking care of us. Right?" There was a hint of fear in Darrel's question. He hugged his dad, and then sat down at the table again, his lips quivering for the first time. He rested an elbow on the table and let his forehead drop into his hand.

Walter took a step toward his daughters. "Goodnight, Anna. Goodnight, Sonya. I pray that God will give you a good rest and tomorrow, we will start on our new journey together." Sonya stood up and wrapped her arms tightly around her father's legs.

"Goodnight, Daddy," she whispered.

"I love you, Sonya, and God loves you," Walter said, leaning forward and rubbing his daughter's shoulders. "I love you, Anna. Tomorrow is a new day." Walter stepped toward Anna to give her a hug, but she stood up from her seat and side-stepped him before darting into the bathroom, slamming the door shut behind her.

Arnold Dueck stood and motioned toward Dave Hoeppner before turning to face Walter. "It's time for us to go. We called the hospital to come pick up Agatha as soon as Darrel called us to tell us about her fall. We will be back tomorrow. I'm sure we have many plans to make about the next few days and then your preaching engagements in Saskatchewan over the next few weeks." Arnold shook Walter's hand, then Dave gripped it with both of his and held it for a few moments before letting go. "I'm sure we can ask Elizabeth to look after your children while you are away. She's done that before, I think, but that too can wait until tomorrow."

"I'm so sorry, Walter. There is one thing you can count on—the Lord will take care of you and your family," Dave mumbled as he let go of Walter's hand and shuffled toward the door.

"Goodnight. See you tomorrow," Walter said toward the door, without moving to see his guests out. Elizabeth returned to the dining room and moved beside Sonya, who was leaning against her father.

"Sonya, let's go brush your teeth, and then I'll help you into your pyjamas." Elizabeth put her hand on Sonya's shoulder as she spoke. "And then I'll draw some pictures on your back and tell you a bedtime story. Any bedtime story you want."

Sonya kissed her dad on the cheek, and Walter kissed her forehead and placed her hand into Elizabeth's. "I want a story about my mommy. About when she and Daddy had Darrel and then got married." Sonya tightened her grip on Elizabeth's hand as they walked toward the closed bathroom door.

Elizabeth glanced at Walter, who showed no signs of having heard his daughter's request, or else simply didn't have the energy to react to it. Elizabeth knocked on the bathroom door and tried the handle. The doorknob turned, and she gave it a slight push. Inside she saw Anna sitting in the tub with her knees curled up against her chest, her whole body shaking as she cried, making no attempt to control the waves of pain. "Sonya, wait here for just a minute, okay?"

Elizabeth stepped into the bathroom, slid the door closed, and knelt beside the bathtub. Anna glanced up, threw her arms around Elizabeth, buried her face in Elizabeth's shoulder and wept. "Why, Elizabeth? Why did God do this to us? Why does he hate us so much? Why can't God just leave us alone? Why does he always mess up everything? I hate God! I hate him so much," she cried.

Elizabeth's eyes grew wide at Anna's questions and declarations. Questions she had never imagined asking, statements she knew were a sin. Elizabeth simply held Anna tight, rubbed her back with one hand while stroking her hair with the other. Elizabeth turned her head when she heard the door open. Sonya peered in and then rushed toward the two who were wrapped in an embrace. She draped one arm around Anna and one around Elizabeth, leaning her head on top of her sister's.

Elizabeth started humming while stroking Anna's hair and Sonya's back. This embrace lasted a few more minutes before Sonya opened her mouth wide with a yawn. "Anna, I'll be right back," Elizabeth said. "I'm going to tuck Sonya into bed." She stood, took Sonya's hand, and pulled her toward the door, then led her to the bedroom Sonya shared with Anna.

Elizabeth helped Sonya into her pyjamas and considered suggesting a night-time prayer, but left it unsaid. She tucked Sonya under a blanket, stroked her hair a few times, bent and kissed her on the forehead. "Good night, Mommy," Sonya murmured as she drifted into sleep. Elizabeth returned to the closed bathroom door and hesitated before brushing her hand against the door.

"Anna? Are you alright?" Elizabeth asked. "Can I come in?"

The door opened and Anna stepped out. "I'm tired. I'm going to bed. Goodnight, Elizabeth." Elizabeth followed Anna with her eyes, and when the door to the bedroom was closed, she turned and walked slowly toward the dining room. Walter and Darrel were still sitting at the table across from each other, both staring straight ahead without seeing anything.

Darrel broke his blind gaze first and looked at Elizabeth, at his father, then toward the hallway. "Thank you for putting the little ones to bed. Whenever I try to do that, they tell me I'm not their parent, and that they don't have to listen to me. It was a tough night, but you made it a little easier. Thanks."

Elizabeth wrapped her sweater around her and nodded toward Darrel. "You're welcome. Sometimes eighteen years are enough for your brothers and sisters to listen to, but not always. I guess tonight was one of those complicated nights. I was happy to help. I'm sorry for your loss. And Reverend Rempel," Elizabeth turned toward Walter, "of course I'm sorry for your loss too."

Walter nodded in Elizabeth's direction, while continuing to stare blindly ahead of him. "Dad, I think you should go to bed too. You've got a busy day ahead of you tomorrow," Darrel said while getting up from his seat and going to get Elizabeth's coat. "Perhaps, Elizabeth, you might be able to come over tomorrow to help out with Benjamin, Sonya, and Anna?" Darrel added handing the coat to her.

"Of course. I'll be here shortly after seven if that's alright with you. I'll be here on time to make breakfast for the children when they wake up," Elizabeth responded. She cast a glance toward Walter, who appeared not to have heard any of the conversation. She nodded one more time toward Darrel and then stepped out the door, gently pulling it closed behind her.

"Dad? Dad? Do you need anything from me? Are you ready for bed?" Darrel asked, moving behind his father and placing his hands on his father's usually strong, but now hunched shoulders. Walter crumbled into weeping under Darrel's touch. Darrel moved around his father's chair so he could kneel in front of him and wrap him in his arms. Walter grabbed his son in a tight embrace and continued to weep uncontrollably. Tears streamed down Darrel's face as he held his father.

"Dad, remember that God is with us, God loves us and never gives us more than we can handle, remember?" Darrel paused, then leaned into his father. Walter gasped, inhaling deeply, then wiped his tears from his face onto his pant legs. Darrel gave his father one more squeeze, then let go of him and stood up. "Are you okay, Dad? Should I call someone? Whom should I call?"

Walter took a deep breath and wiped at the last few tears still on his cheeks. "Darrel, you're a good son. Thank you. Thank you for your strong faith. Thank you for your words and reminders tonight. And thank you also for sorting things out with Elizabeth. She always does such a good job with the children. They really like her, don't they?" Walter stood up beside his son, put one arm around his shoulder, and guided him toward the hallway. Walter turned off the dining room lights and the hallway nightlight guided them down the hall. "Benji's sleeping? He should be sleeping. I'll just look in on him and then the girls. Will you sleep with Benji tonight, Darrel? So that when he wakes up he won't be alone?"

"Of course, Dad." Darrel eased Benji's bedroom door open, where a nightlight cast an orange glow across the room onto the bed where Benji lay. Walter sat on the edge of the bed, reached out and caressed Benji's forehead. Tears began to flow down Walter's cheeks once again, and he allowed them to flow uninterrupted. Darrel stood by the door and watched his father and brother. "I've got him now, Dad. I'll climb into bed with him."

Darrel pulled off his T-shirt, his socks, and then his jeans before getting under the blanket with his six-year-old brother. Walter stood by the door and smiled as his older son snuggled into bed with his much-younger brother. Darrel stroked Benji's short, dark hair a few times before he fell asleep, his arm falling naturally around Benji's shoulders. Walter smiled through his tears and closed the door before going down the hallway. He stopped at the bedroom door, the room he had shared with his wife for the past eighteen years, since he took the job as a bible teacher and they gave him this house to use as long as he worked there.

Walter reached out and stroked the door frame, opened the hallway linen closet, and pulled out a quilt. He took the blanket back through the dining room into the living room, wrapped it around himself and lay down on the couch. Walter tossed and turned on the couch for what seemed like hours before he finally dropped into a fitful sleep.

Chapter Three

(November 2008)

"You're not actually my mother! Why can't you just leave me alone?" nine-year old Benjamin shouted at Elizabeth, who was on her knees picking up toys. Benjamin violently kicked a little plastic car across the room just before Elizabeth's outstretched hand reached the car. "Besides, I didn't make this mess. Your little brat did that!" Benjamin looked at the almost year-old baby who was sucking on the corner of the blanket in which he was wrapped.

"Oh, Benjamin, you're telling me that little Jacob did that?" Elizabeth smiled despite Benjamin's tantrum. "Jacob isn't even one. How could he possibly dump all these toys across the dining room? Come on, help me put them back in the box. Then you can choose three toys to play with here in the dining room while I prepare dinner. The box with the other toys will be waiting for you in your room when you want them. Or, if you want to spread them all out on the floor, you can do that in your room, but not here in the dining room. The others will be here for dinner soon, and you don't want someone to step on them and break them."

"They won't break them! Only you break them," Benjamin burst out, and picked up a marble. He looked at Elizabeth, then turned and threw the marble at Jacob, just missing the gurgling baby.

"Benjamin! Stop it. Right now! Go straight to your room. Wait there until your dad comes to get you." Elizabeth put her body in front of Jacob. She placed her hands on her hips, biting her lip. Benjamin burst into tears and ran down the hall to his bedroom where he slammed the door.

As soon as the door was closed, Elizabeth slid down to the floor beside her baby, picked Jacob up and cradled him with one arm, the other hand reaching up to hold the small opal amulet hanging around her neck. "I need your strength, I need your wisdom," Elizabeth whispered over Jacob's head before looking down into his face.

"Oh Jacob, what kind of home have you been born into?" Elizabeth wiped her eyes on her apron, got up with Jacob and went into the kitchen. She placed the baby into a bouncy chair on the floor beside her, where he began rocking himself. Elizabeth washed her face in the kitchen sink, dried it on her apron, and then took a deep breath.

Three open cans of No-Name tomato soup sat on the counter beside an empty pot. Elizabeth poured them into the pot and placed it on the stove. *What else can I put in there*, she thought as she turned the heat onto medium. *Macaroni. Cook up some macaroni and add that. Tuna? Maybe a can of tuna? How would that taste? Maybe just the macaroni for now.*

Elizabeth pulled a bag of uncooked macaroni from the cupboard beside the stove, measured two cups into another pot and then filled it with water before turning the heat to high on another element.

"What did you do to Benji? He's crying in his bed and won't open the door for me. It's locked, you know," Sonya asked in a cold voice from behind Elizabeth. Elizabeth turned quickly and took a step closer to where Jacob was still rocking himself in his chair. "Well? What did you do this time?" Sonya's angry whisper hissed across the kitchen.

"Sonya, dear…"

"Don't call me dear. I'm just Sonya to you." Her voice was firm.

"Sonya, Benjamin tried to hurt Jacob and I sent him to his room until his dad comes home," Elizabeth answered quietly, taking a deep breath.

"He wouldn't have tried to hurt Jacob if you wouldn't have had him, you know. We already had four kids in this family. None of us wanted another one. You're not going to have more, are you?" Sonya paused, suddenly imagining more additions to the family. "Seriously? You're going to have more? How many babies do you think we need to have in this house?" Sonya screamed toward Elizabeth.

"Sonya! What has gotten into you? What makes you think we're going to have another one, or more babies? Jacob is nine months old. What are you thinking?" Elizabeth's perplexed voice shook. "Sonya, please. I have to finish making dinner. It's almost six, and your brother will be here with his girlfriend very soon. Do you know where Anna is?" Elizabeth turned back to the stove and saw a bright-red element in the corner of the stove and the still-cold pot of macaroni on the other element at the rear of the stove.

"Oh, please! What next?" Elizabeth's voice broke. She moved the cold pot over to the hot element, turned the now-boiling soup to low and stirred it a few times, scraping the bottom to peel off a thickened layer of soup. "Bread. There must be some bread left. And cheese? Please let there be cheese in the fridge." Elizabeth opened the refrigerator door and breathed a sigh of relief at the sight of a large block of bright-orange cheese.

Sonya tilted her head to the side and asked, "Why do you always talk to yourself? That's really weird."

Elizabeth smiled as she pulled the cheese from the refrigerator and turned to Sonya, who was still standing at the corner of the kitchen staring at her. "I'm just reminding myself of what is left to be done. Sometimes talking to myself helps me think my way through a situation. Do you want to help me? Would you cut some slices of cheese? Maybe a dozen, and put them on a plate, and then put the plate on the table?" Elizabeth tried hard to keep her voice calm as she placed the block of cheese onto a cutting board.

Sonya took an exaggerated step around Jacob's chair, making it clear she was avoiding stepping on him. She took a knife and started cutting the cheese into pieces. Each piece was a different size, thickness, and shape. She made a point of standing between Elizabeth and the block of cheese so Elizabeth wouldn't see what was happening. "Done!" Sonya announced as she took another exaggerated step over Jacob and placed the plate on the table.

"Thanks, dear. I mean, thanks, Sonya. Do you know where Anna is? Or did I ask you that already?" Elizabeth filled a basket with the whole-wheat buns she had bought that morning. "Okay, macaroni's almost ready, which means the soup is almost ready, bread is ready, cheese is ready. To drink? Oh, let me think. There must be some iced tea powder still in the cupboard."

Elizabeth opened another cupboard door and let her hand do the searching on the topmost shelf. She closed her hand on the desired container of iced tea and pulled it down. "That will do." She dumped some of the sugary powder into a large jug, then filled it with water. She caught herself just as she was about to use the tomato soup spoon to stir up the drink, and instead she opened a drawer and pulled out a long wooden spoon to mix the drink.

Elizabeth looked at the clock above the kitchen sink. "Ten minutes till Darrel's here. Where's Walter? Yes, Jacob, Darrel is coming home with his girlfriend, we finally get to meet her, not just hear about her. I think he is very serious about her. And I think Walter approves of her too. What about you, little one? Do you approve of your biggest brother getting engaged soon? Wouldn't that be wonderful for him!" Jacob gurgled toward his mother. "And what about Walter? Where is that father of yours, little one? He should have been here by now." Jacob gurgled again.

The door swung open and Walter came in, leading Anna ahead of him. She shook his hand from her shoulder and dashed to the bathroom. Elizabeth looked toward Walter with inquiring eyes. "Welcome home. What happened with Anna? Oh, and by the way, I need you to speak with Benjamin. He keeps shouting 'you're not my mother' at me, and just a few minutes ago, he threw a marble at Jacob's head."

"Of course you're not his mother. I thought we had all agreed to that when you and I married. And he would never try to hurt Jacob. I'll go get him for dinner. I see Darrel has arrived." Walter lumbered down the hall with heavy steps to the last bedroom door. He tried the knob, but it was locked. There was a knock on the outside door, and Darrel came in just ahead of Marigold, whom he had been dating for four months.

"Darrel, Marigold, welcome home, welcome here." Elizabeth smiled as she moved toward them. "Let me hang this up for you, dear," Elizabeth offered reaching for Marigold's coat. "And why don't you take a seat at the table? Oh my goodness, I guess we need some dishes, don't we?" Elizabeth ran back to the kitchen to find the appropriate bowls, spoons, knives, and cups for the meal.

"Let me help you, Mom," Darrel said as he walked up behind Elizabeth. She flinched at the sound of the title 'mom.' *Why did it sound so easy, even that it fit, when Darrel used that word, and seemed to create barriers for the three younger children?*

Walter returned to the table holding Benjamin's hand. Benjamin refused to look at or acknowledge Elizabeth. "Hi, Darrel," he said to the floor.

"Hi, Benji. Marigold is going to have dinner with us tonight," Darrel responded.

"Is she going to try and be my mother too?" Benjamin looked up at Darrel with tears in his eyes.

"Benji, that is not a good question," Walter scolded, gripping his son's shoulder.

Darrel knelt down in front of Benji, and then, with a look invited Marigold to kneel beside him. Darrel reached out a hand and tussled Benji's hair before pulling him into a bear hug. "Benji, before you had Agatha as your mother, and she'll always sort of be your mother, even though she isn't with us anymore. Now you are lucky enough to have Elizabeth be a sort of mother to you too. She's taking very good care of you, of Daddy, and of your sisters too. Marigold is going to be like a sister, but an older sister than either of Anna or Sonya are. That's all. A sister. Another sister. We're all going to keep on trying to be one big, happy family."

Benjamin dug his face into Darrel's chest and squeezed his arms around Darrel's neck as if planning to never let go.

"Oh, good grief. Little brother having another meltdown? My, that's so different," sneered Anna as she slid past the kneeling group and sat at the table. "What's for dinner, Elizabeth?"

"You mean 'what's for dinner, Mom?' don't you?" corrected Walter, applying downward pressure on Anna's shoulder with his big, strong hand. Marigold looked toward Anna, then toward Benji and Darrel, who were still wrapped in an embrace. She stole a glance toward Elizabeth in the kitchen and thought she saw her wiping her eyes with a tea towel.

Elizabeth sensed a gaze and quickly dropped the tea towel. She picked up Jacob in one arm and the pot of soup in the other hand and brought it to the table. "Oh my, I need a potholder. Please..." Walter dashed to the kitchen and returned with the recently discarded tea towel. He folded it up and placed it on the table, taking the pot from Elizabeth's hand.

"Here, let me finish setting the table," Walter said. He practically dashed to the kitchen to find the jug of iced tea. He brought it to the table before asking, "Is there anything else? Should we all sit down at the table now? Sonya, are you coming?"

Darrel lifted Benjamin in his arms and carried him to the table. He put him on a chair and sat down beside him, gesturing toward a chair on his other side, inviting Marigold to take a seat. Sonya appeared out of the living room door and took a seat beside Benjamin, nodding toward Marigold. "Sonya, this is Marigold. Marigold, this is my sister Sonya." Marigold smiled and held out her hand toward Sonya.

Sonya took it, looked at the table, and gave it a slight shake. "Hello." Sonya dropped Marigold's hand and tucked her hands into her lap. Elizabeth took the last open chair, holding Jacob in her lap.

"Who wants to pray?" Walter tried to sound cheerful about the prospect. There was no response from anyone around the table. "Son..."

"It's not my turn," Sonya shot out toward her father, then lowered her eyes again.

"Don't look at me. I don't ever pray anymore," said Anna, narrowing her eyes to glare at her father, daring him to call on her.

"I'll pray," offered Darrel. "It's been a little while since I've sat at this table and prayed with my family." Darrel swept the table with his eyes, casting smiles all the way around. "Let's pray. Lord, let this food to us be blessed, and let us use it as a source of nourishment for our bodies while we also seek nourishment for our hearts, souls, and minds in You. Amen."

"Please help yourselves." Elizabeth waved her hand across the table. "There's some bread and chee..." her voice drifted off and her face turned red when she saw the way the cheese had been cut. "And some cheese too." She swallowed, casting a glance toward Sonya, whose whole face was lit up, her eyes smiling and her mouth smirking back at Elizabeth.

"This soup sure smells good," said Marigold cheerfully. She took a bun from the basket Darrel offered her and then reached for the plate of cheese. "I always wondered about the best way to cut cheese. I see now that there are many ways to do that, and the cheese still tastes the same." Marigold had seen the brief visual interaction between Elizabeth and Sonya and thought she might be able to help diffuse some tension.

Walter served himself some soup before looking across the table at his oldest son sitting proudly beside his girlfriend. Walter smiled, remembering the first time he had sat at his girlfriend's table with her family. "Marigold, tell us a little about yourself. You're not from Steinbach, so we don't know your family."

Marigold smiled back at Walter. "Of course. My parents are George and Helena Barkman from Greenland. They are part of the Holdeman church there. They raised me in that church as well, but I left it when I was fourteen. The pastors came to tell me they wanted me to quit school and go to work on my father's chicken farm. I wanted to keep studying."

"I think I've bought some chickens from your father at the corner of Greenland Road and the highway. Does he ever sell his chickens there?" Walter asked.

"He used to, but not anymore. The government has rules against that. At first he said 'God's law is above man's law, so I don't need to listen to them,' but when they fined him for continuing to sell after he had been warned four or five times, then he stopped."

"And you said you stopped going to church when you were fourteen?" Walter asked. Anna rolled her eyes and groaned audibly at her father's question.

"I would quit going too if you would let me," Anna muttered. Walter acted as if he hadn't heard his daughter's comment. Elizabeth responded by offering Anna some more bread. "No, I don't want more bread, this bread or the bread of life, stuffed down my throat." Elizabeth put the basket of buns back on the table. Walter continued to ignore his daughter's comments.

Benjamin took turns putting a spoonful of soup in his mouth, taking a bite of bread, taking a bite of cheese, and taking a look at Darrel. He stole an occasional glance at Marigold too, and when he saw that she was resting one of her hands on Darrel's leg, he put one hand on Darrel's other leg. Darrel smiled down at Benjamin and patted him on the shoulder before continuing to eat.

"I have something to tell everyone here," Darrel announced. He coughed a little, wiped his mouth, and stood up. He stepped behind Marigold and placed his hands on her shoulders. "Last night I spoke with Marigold's father, asking permission to marry his daughter." He beamed around the table, and Marigold's whole face radiated her smile. "And after that, I asked Marigold to marry me, and she said yes!"

"Ahhh, I hate weddings! Do I have to go?" Sonya burst into tears and ran from the table, slamming the bathroom door behind her. Elizabeth got up quickly and placed Jacob into Walter's unsuspecting arms.

"Oh my, congratulations. This is indeed wonderful and exciting news, Darrel and Marigold. Please excuse me for a minute." Elizabeth followed Sonya to the bathroom and tapped on the door two times. "Sonya, it's me, Elizabeth. Can I come in?" She waited for a moment, tapped again, and tried the knob. It turned and Elizabeth opened the door just wide enough to allow herself in.

Sonya sat huddled in the bathtub, her arms wrapped around her legs, her face pressed into her knees. Elizabeth knelt down beside her and gingerly placed one arm around her shaking shoulders. Sonya didn't react, so slowly Elizabeth wrapped her other arm around her and gave her a tight hug. Sonya leaned into Elizabeth's shoulder and then turned to face her, wrapping both her arms around Elizabeth and pulling herself in close.

"I just don't know what to do with myself," Sonya blurted out. "When Daddy said he was going to marry you, I thought life was going to get better. I thought weddings were supposed to be beautiful," Sonya sobbed. "But before your wedding, I could only think about my mommy. Why did she have to die? I didn't want her to die. I cried the whole night, and Daddy got really angry at me." Sonya gulped in some air. "He keeps saying we're not allowed to cry for Mommy, that God had a plan, and that crying means we don't accept God's plan. I don't want to go to hell! What can I do? I cry so often. I miss my mommy so much. I don't want to sin 'cuz I know what happens to sinners. I'm sad almost all the time, and when I'm not sad, I'm so scared!" Sonya's whole body shook with her tears and fears pouring out.

Elizabeth stroked Sonya's back and caressed her hair before she said anything. "Oh, Sonya, life can be so hard to understand. I try to have the same faith as your father, but I just don't know how. What I do know is it's not a sin to be sad or angry. I think you can miss your mommy, you can cry, and you can tell me any time you are afraid or sad or just don't know what to do with yourself."

Elisabeth reached up and pulled at the thin chain she wore around her neck until the small opal amulet appeared. "Sometimes I don't know what to do with myself either. Sometimes I'm scared. Sometimes I'm sad, too." Elizabeth fondled the opal as Sonya shifted slightly to get a look at the stone. "I got this opal from my mother just before she died. I was sitting beside her, holding her hand, when she took this off and gave it to me," Elizabeth explained. "She told me her mother had given it to her as a wedding gift. My grandma told her, 'when you need to remember that you are loved and lovely, when you think you are alone, touch this stone and remember me. Know that I am always close to you because you are always in my heart, and I believe I am always in yours.' My mother then said those same words to me. Those were her last words." Elizabeth's hand closed around the opal for a moment.

Then she dropped the amulet and wrapped both arms around Sonya. "I think it's okay to be both sad and scared. Sometimes I don't know what God's plan is for me, for you. Or why He has such plans, plans for our lives that are so difficult." Sonya took a few deep breaths, her sobs slowing down.

"Really? It's okay to be scared? To be sad isn't a sin?" Sonya started, then continued, "I'm just afraid that I'll keep sinning if Darrel gets married. I thought I'd be able to forget my mommy now that you are here, but I can't, and I can't tell Daddy that. He doesn't want to hear that. I've heard what he says to Anna about her soul, and I don't want to go to hell, even if Anna will be there. I want to go to heaven, 'cuz that is where Mommy is. But if it's another wedding, I'm scared I'll just think about Mommy, I'll miss her again, and then I'll cry. And then Daddy will be angry with me again."

Elizabeth kept stroking Sonya's hair. "Let's make a deal, Sonya," Elizabeth offered. "When you are scared, when you are missing your mommy, when you think you need a good cry, you come to me. We'll tell each other stories about Agatha, the things we remember about her, the beautiful things we remember about her. We will find a way to be sad together, without sinning. Okay?"

Sonya looked up into Elizabeth's face. "Can we do that? What will God think? What will Daddy say?" Sonya's voice reflected a little hope, but a skeptical hope. Having someone to confide in when she felt sad had been lost for Sonya when her mother died, and Anna refused to talk about any sort of sin or 'such nonsense,' leaving Sonya alone with her fears.

"I'll talk to your daddy and let him know that sometimes you and I will share stories about Agatha. I don't think he'll be upset with that. But don't you worry, dear, I'll talk to him." Elizabeth pulled Sonya into a tight embrace before releasing her and standing up. "I've got to get back to the table to share this special moment with Darrel, Marigold, and the family. When you're ready, you come back and sit beside me at the table, okay?"

"Thanks, Mom," Sonya said, wiping away tears from her eyes. "I'll be there soon."

Elizabeth smiled at Sonya, placed a hand on top of her head for a moment and then closed the door behind herself as she returned to the dining room table. Walter handed Jacob back to her and then cleared his throat. "Darrel and Marigold are planning to get married next month, dear. And they will have their first child in just six more months." Elizabeth's smile twitched at the final statement. Anna grinned at the resigned tone of her father's voice and Elizabeth's twitching smile.

Darrel and Marigold smiled at Elizabeth and broke the brief silence. "We surprised Dad with our news about expecting a baby, before we're married and all, but we want to be honest with you. We wanted to get married right after we met, we knew we were right for each other, didn't we, dear?" Darrel looked at Marigold, who nodded.

"Like father, like son." Anna giggled. "God knows best and always has a plan, right, Dad? Nothing happens without God wanting or allowing it to happen." Walter looked at Anna briefly, opened his mouth to respond but decided against it. Both Darrel and Marigold blushed a little and briefly averted their eyes. Elizabeth ignored the statement and redrew the smile on her face.

"I'm so happy for both of you. Our Lord speaks about the sanctity of marriage, and how that is part of his plan for his people. And, of course having a baby, in time, is supposed to be a gift from God." Elizabeth's voice didn't sound like the coming baby was such a great gift.

Sonya re-emerged from the bathroom, a few drops of water still lingering on her face. She smiled around the table and realized she had missed something important. "What is it? Have you set the date for the wedding?" she asked.

Darrel reached out his hand and placed it on hers. "We want our wedding next month to be a very happy and special occasion. Do you think you would be willing to stand up with us? Would you be one of the bridesmaids?" Marigold looked across the table toward Sonya, and then at Anna.

"Anna, we would like you to be a bridesmaid too, if you would," Marigold said.

"You've got to be kidding me. You want me to be a bridesmaid? Oh my goodness! I don't know if I can do that. I don't like going into that church anymore. Or… where are you getting married? Maybe I don't have to go into that church." Anna sounded hopeful.

"We haven't worked out all the details yet, so we're not sure. Our church doesn't usually let people get married in it if they are already pregnant, so I don't think we'll get married there. But we don't know what our options are just yet. Marigold's family church is out. When she quit the church, that door was closed tightly. She isn't allowed back in unless she wants to repent and rejoin."

"And I don't want back in, and won't do that," added Marigold. "I don't care where we get married, I just want to get married to the man I love." Marigold kissed Darrel. Benjamin's eyes grew wide and he moved back a little in his chair. Walter coughed and blushed.

Sonya looked confused. "What do you mean 'if they are already pregnant?' That's a sin, being pregnant before being married. Who would do that? Darrel, who is 'they'?"

Walter coughed again before interjecting, "Enough talk about being pregnant for now. Let's just finish dinner and get ready for bed. It's been a busy day and we probably all need to get some rest." Walter reached for the plate of oddly cut pieces of cheese. "Does anyone need some more cheese? Some bread? More soup anyone?"

"I want a cookie," Benjamin said, shaking his head when the cheese plate passed. "Where's the dessert?"

"I didn't have time to make any dessert today, Benji. But there is some ice cream in the freezer. Who all wants some ice cream with raspberry jam?" Elizabeth stood up, cradled Jacob in one arm, and walked to the kitchen. She reached into the freezer compartment and found the pail of ice cream near the back. She brought it back to the table before turning toward the kitchen once again. "Anna, would you please clear the table? And Sonya, would you give everyone who wants some ice cream a bowl, please?"

"Okay, Mom," Sonya responded. Anna froze in her seat, staring at her sister.

"What did you just say? Did you just call Elizabeth 'mom'?" Anna's voice was incredulous. "Elizabeth, what did you do to her?"

Sonya started crying. "I'm so tired of being sad. Elizabeth said it wasn't a sin to be sad, and that I could be sad if I was sad. I just don't want to be sad or scared anymore. I want Elizabeth to be my mom, and I want to be happy again." Sonya hid her face from the others by wrapping her arms around her head and leaning it on the table.

Chapter Four

Early the next morning Walter was kneeling alone in the living room. His head was bowed, eyes closed, his hands clasped in front of him, leaning on the couch. "Lord," he began praying in a subdued voice, "what do I do now? Darrel and Marigold aren't married but are pregnant. Darrel was the one I was sure was walking most closely hand-in-hand with you, Lord, and able to resist temptation, to stay on the straight and narrow path. And in reality, that isn't my biggest concern. If Anna hasn't already committed the unpardonable sin, she's close, she will soon. I can't bear that thought! Benjamin, who used to love everyone, everything, is finding fewer and fewer things to enjoy and seems to be angry all the time. And Elizabeth, she seems afraid of the children, she doesn't seem to be able to see that she doesn't need to be their mother, she just needs to take care of them. Perhaps Sonya has turned a corner toward accepting Elizabeth in some way. Please, Lord, give me wisdom in knowing how to be a father to each of my children."

A knock interrupted Walter's prayer time. He wondered if Elizabeth was already awake and would hear the knock and answer the door. A quick glance at his watch shocked Walter. It was still before six. He stood up. "Sorry, Lord," he said, "there's someone at my door. I'll be back."

Walter rushed to the door to prevent any more knocking. He opened it to see Arnold Dueck and Dave Hoeppner waiting to come in. "Good morning, gentlemen. This must be very important for the two of you to come here at such an early hour. Please come in. Please come in all the way to the living room where I can close the door so the others won't wake from our conversation." Both guests kept their coats on, said nothing, and followed Walter into the living room.

Walter gestured toward the sofa and a chair and took a seat once his guests had settled. "May I get you a cup of coffee?" Walter offered. "I can wake Elizabeth and ask her to make some."

"Nothing for me, thanks," said Dave.

"We are here on a fairly serious concern, Walter. I don't think we want to waste time with anything else," said Arnold.

Walter looked at Arnold and saw no indication of concern, anger, excitement, sorrow or any other recognizable emotion. He then looked at Dave, who immediately averted his eyes, blushed, and looked down at the floor.

"Dave, will you begin?" Arnold didn't really mean it as a question.

Dave started by clearing his throat. "We had an important meeting with the ministerial yesterday night, Walter. An emergency meeting about something very important." Walter nodded and waited to hear more, as he still could not read any expression or direction for where this conversation was going.

"Some people seem to be telling stories… are wondering about… well, seem to think that…" Dave spluttered, his face turning a deeper hue of red with each bluster. Walter leaned forward, toward Dave, attempting to imagine the next statement.

"Marigold Barkman is unmarried and pregnant. Your son Darrel, also unmarried, is the one who put her in that condition," interrupted Arnold, impatient with Dave's wandering statements. Walter leaned back, suddenly realizing that the news Darrel had just delivered to his family yesterday was probably not news among the town's inhabitants, and certainly no longer a secret from the church. He took a deep breath.

"Yesterday Darrel brought Marigold here for dinner, and they explained their condition. They also explained that they intend to get married, next month, in fact. As soon as they can find a place that will allow them to marry and someone to perform the ceremony for them," Walter explained.

"Yes, well, that's all fine and good. If they can find some place other than in a judge's office, or a minister who will consent to marry fornicators. And Walter, do not consider performing that marriage." Arnold erased Walter's hopes for an easy marriage to come for his son. "And of course, none of that was our concern at the meeting yesterday. Dave, tell Walter what the ministerial has decided."

"But hold on," interjected Walter. "I'm part of the ministerial too. Why was I not called to this meeting? Why did I not have a say in any decision making?" Walter now understood what he was about to be told, what was about to happen to his oldest, only baptized, most church-faithful child. Walter looked at Dave, eyes pleading for Dave to change the words Walter knew were about to come from his mouth.

"Walter, I… I… voted against it. I know that Darrel was baptized many years ago, that he has sung at your services, has taught Sunday School, has never committed any visible sins in the community before. But…"

Once again Arnold interrupted Dave. "We have a full ministerial where we consider every voice. Even if you had been there and voted against it, there were seven votes against Dave, so your no vote would have made it two, if you would have in fact voted no against the most serious of sins your son has committed. If we don't hold our congregation to account, if we don't show that the consequences of sin are strong, who will believe anything we say? Who will believe in God's judgement to come if we can't pass judgement now?"

Walter looked Arnold directly in the eyes. "Let he who is without sin cast the first stone. Not an unfamiliar idea to you, is it, Arnold? Have you heard that before? Do you remember who said that? He also said 'do not judge, lest you be judged.' And also 'remove the log in your own eye before offering to remove the speck from a brother's eye.' Does that sound familiar?"

"How dare you quote scripture at me, Walter?" Arnold barked across the room. Walter flinched at both the loudness and the clear disdain in the voice. "Of course I know those verses, just as well as you do. As for being judges, every time you step into a pulpit and explain why the people listening to you are sinners, and that sinners, upon judgement by God, go to an eternal damnation in a lake of fire, that is no different." Arnold stared at

Walter while Dave looked at the floor, moving his feet closer together and then back apart and repeatedly wiping his brow.

"Walter, we are on the same side. We both read the same Bible, we both pray for the same things, and we both preach to achieve those same things. Just because this time it is your son who has sinned, that doesn't change the story." Arnold's voice softened a little. "We had no option, and you know that. We have excommunicated Darrel, and of course we hope he mends his ways. He can always come, with Marigold, to the ministerial to ask for forgiveness. And then we can arrange for them to apologize to the whole church for the bad example that they set and take them back into our congregation."

"I don't believe this is happening," Walter mumbled. "Only yesterday I heard my son was engaged, and yes, that he and Marigold were expecting a baby already, before they are married." Walter stood up, walked across the room, and leaned one arm against the wall. "It didn't used to be done this way, you know."

Dave looked up at Walter. "What do you mean?"

"Darrel isn't the first person to get someone pregnant before they were married. The church doesn't have to respond this way," Walter continued. "Why couldn't the ministerial just meet with them to express their disappointment? Why couldn't the church offer them forgiveness? Why is one sin bigger or worse than any other?" Walter sounded tired.

"We know Darrel was conceived out of wedlock as well, Walter. It seems to me that you might also know some verses that speak about the sins of the father, but enough of that," stated Arnold.

"However, neither of you were baptized or members of the church when that happened," offered Dave. "In fact, that was before you and Agatha were even professing Christians. If I remember correctly, was that not what brought you to the Lord? Was it not upon the realization of your sin that both you and Agatha gave your lives to Jesus? And was it not also then that you promised God that you would leave behind a life of pleasure, simply living for yourself, and serve God?" Walter nodded his agreement to all those details, turned, and sat down in the chair beside Dave.

"It's true," agreed Walter. "Agatha and I were married, and I began preaching. I was preaching in Saskatchewan when Darrel was born. I didn't see him until he was two weeks old. It seems I am always behind the pulpit when something important is happening somewhere else."

"Nonsense!" Arnold retorted. "What happens in a church, when people leave their life of sin behind, is the most important thing that can ever happen. They awaken to an eternal destiny in heaven. Nothing is more important than that! But enough, we have to decide who's going to tell Darrel and when he will be told. Do you want to be there?"

Walter flinched and turned to face Arnold. "Are you asking me to be there, with my very own son, when the church in which his father is a minister comes to excommunicate him? I suppose you are thinking I should be the one to tell him too?" Tears rolled down Walter's cheeks.

"Well, we had thought yes, that you should both be there and be the one to tell him," Arnold stated.

"Not everyone thought that," Dave chimed in. "Not everyone agreed to what happened."

"Enough, Dave," snapped Arnold. "The decision has been made. Now all we have to do is implement it. So, Walter, what do you say?"

Walter dropped his face into his hands while resting his elbows on his knees. "No, Arnold. No, I will not attend such a meeting, although I will call him to tell him it is coming. And I will not be the one to tell him anything about his standing in the church." Walter lowered his gaze to the floor.

"And perhaps I need to rethink much of what I have preached to so many people. What if what I told them isn't even true?" Walter leaned back in his chair with his eyes closed. "I think you can find your way out without me."

"Remember the night that Agatha died, Walter?" Arnold said. "You had some questions that night too. But with time you realized the way, the truth, the light, found in what you preach. And you kept preaching. This time too you may have some questions, right at this moment. But don't let doubt persist. Don't let doubt poison your mind, and angels of darkness lead you astray."

"We can let ourselves out," Dave said softly. "I'm so sorry that this has happened, Walter. I'm not sure how else we could have told you, or what other decision the church could have arrived at. I will talk to you soon."

Dave and Arnold crossed the dining room and exited the house, closing the door behind them.

Elizabeth appeared from the bedroom in her purple terry-cloth bathrobe. "Walter, has something happened? Something terrible? Why were Reverend Dueck and Reverend Hoeppner here so early in the morning? Are you alright?" Elizabeth sat on the armrest of Walter's chair and put one arm around him. She leaned against him, brushing his hair back from his face with her other hand.

"The church has decided to excommunicate Darrel for getting Marigold pregnant," Walter said, staring straight ahead. Elizabeth jolted upright. She leaned away from Walter, as if seeing him differently might provide a different response.

"The ministerial wanted me to be the one to tell him," Walter moaned. "What kind of church am I a part of, Elizabeth? What kind of church asks a father to excommunicate his son?" He put his head into his hands. Elizabeth stood beside Walter's chair for a moment, then moved to kneel in front of him. She took his head in both her hands and tilted it to face her.

"Walter, no one building, no one group of people, is the whole church. Did you say no? I mean, you did say no, right? You aren't going to tell him this, are you?" Elizabeth released Walter's face when she realized she wasn't sure what his answer to her questions might be. She stood up and took a step back. "You aren't going to be the one to tell him are you?" she whispered with her eyes wide, her voice further muffled by the hand she had clasped to her mouth.

"No!" Walter cried. "He's my son. He did nothing different than I did, and I wasn't excommunicated. How could I possibly be the one to tell him? What is happening to this church? Where is love? Where is forgiveness? All these years I've been preaching judgement and damnation. I suppose I have been telling Darrel all along that he is a sinner. Anna certainly has heard that message enough times and knows it. I have been telling everyone that God will excommunicate them from His presence if they do not follow the rules I say are His. Perhaps that is no different from what they asked me to do now."

Elizabeth sat down again on the armrest and put a hand on Walter's shoulder. "I don't know what to say. It's all too much for me to understand.

I understand that Darrel and Marigold love each other. Did you see the way that they looked at each other at dinner? Did you see the gentle caresses and touches they gave each other? The smiles in their eyes, on their faces? Or does love not matter? They are getting married, after all." Elizabeth looked out the living room window. "The church tries to make everything so complicated, don't they? Why can't they just let people live their lives in peace?"

"I'm beginning to realize it may be more than I can understand too. But it is what I know how to do. Does the truth change? What was sin when we were young, is it not still sin? And what will the people do if no one tells them the truth and warns them of God's disapproval? If I don't preach, if I don't teach what I know the Bible is saying, what do I do? More often now I begin to wonder if I am doing the right thing. The farm was sold when my parents died, so there is no farm to go back to. Or any money with which to buy a farm now." Walter leaned into Elizabeth and closed his eyes.

Benjamin stuck his head into the living room, yawned, then came over and crawled into Walter's lap. Walter opened his eyes and gave his son a hug. "I guess it is still a little too early to call Darrel. I don't want to wake him. Some breakfast, Elizabeth?"

Elizabeth stood up then put a hand on Benjamin's knee, "Good morning, Benji." He pushed her hand off his knee without looking at her. "I'll get some breakfast ready." Elizabeth took a step back from the chair and looked at the little boy wrapped in his father's strong embrace. She wiped a tear from her eye and turned to the kitchen.

She opened the door of the refrigerator, took out eggs and milk, and began preparing scrambled eggs. "Excommunication! What a terrible thing to do to a really fine person," she mumbled to herself.

She bent to get a cast-iron frying pan from the stove drawer and sat down on the floor. "Benji looked so calm when he sat with Walter," she mused. "What should I be doing differently?" She gazed across the kitchen and listened for any sounds coming out of the living room but heard nothing. Elizabeth grabbed the frying pan, stood up, and placed it on the stove top. *Sonya changed her attitude toward me and Jacob. What will it take for the Benji that used to love me to come back?* she thought.

Elizabeth retrieved plates, glasses, and silverware from cupboards and drawers and placed them on the counter. *And Walter, what will it take for him to not just ask some questions about the church's rules, but to stand up against them? To fight them to make changes? Will he ever just allow people to live and love?* As the eggs began to cook, she reached for a loaf of bread and began making toast before she let out a deep sigh. *And will I ever do anything other than cook and clean?"*

"Breakfast is ready, Walter, Benji. You can come to the table." Elizabeth took care not to shout too loudly as Sonya and Anna were still sleeping. She placed three settings on the table and left four others on the counter. She placed the milk on the table beside Benji's place and then filled and plugged in the kettle. As Walter and Benji emerged hand-in-hand from the living room, Elizabeth put a hot-pad on the table and placed the frying pan filled with eggs on it.

Walter's eyes opened wide when he saw the frying pan filled to the top with eggs. "Are we expecting breakfast company?" he asked, pointing to the pan.

"Oh my, I lost count of the eggs. I was a little preoccupied." Elizabeth blushed. "I guess there will be enough for us, for the girls, and for anyone who mysteriously appears at our door this morning. There is certainly enough for one more person. Perhaps two or three more." Elizabeth sat down across the table from Walter and Benji.

"I want cereal. I hate eggs. Where is the jam?" demanded Benji with arms crossed, refusing to sit. Walter reached toward his son and placed a hand on his shoulder. Firmly, he pushed Benji into his chair.

"This is the breakfast that is ready for us," Walter said. "You will eat this breakfast or none at all." The gentleness between father and son from a few minutes ago in the living room was replaced by a stern voice giving directions.

Benji started crying and banged his head repeatedly against the table. Walter put his hands around Benji's shoulders and pulled him upright. "Stop it, Benji. You can eat breakfast or go back to your room."

Benji bolted from the table and ran toward his room. "Why can't we ever have good food in this house anymore? She knows I hate eggs! That's why she made them! She hates me!" Benji slammed his bedroom door behind him.

Elizabeth bit her lip and clasped her hands in her lap. She took a deep breath, followed by another. She looked across at Walter. A tear formed and trickled down her cheek. "Walter, just a few days ago I'm sure he ate the eggs I made for breakfast."

Walter reached across the table and took Elizabeth's hands in his. "I think he likes his eggs fried, not scrambled. But that can't be all that is going on in that little head of his. Ever since we got married, he seems a little different. I'm just not sure why, or what has changed so much for him. He used to be so happy all the time." Walter squeezed Elizabeth's hands and then dropped them again.

"Dad! Elizabeth! Can't someone keep that little brat quiet! I was still sleeping," shouted Anna from the bedroom door she had just opened. "Next thing it'll be that baby howling. Can't it ever be quiet in this house? AHHH!" She didn't wait for an answer, but slammed her door shut.

At that very moment Jacob began crying from his parents' bedroom. Elizabeth leapt to her feet and rushed to pick him up out of his crib. She pressed him close to her body, rocked him gently, and then returned to the dining room table. She positioned herself, and then Jacob, so he could begin his breakfast at her breast.

Walter sat for a moment, as if determining what action to take, if any, or if it was simply best to have breakfast. He looked across the table at Elizabeth. "I guess Jacob began his breakfast without asking a blessing. Perhaps this once we will too." His hand wavered above the plate of toast, and he retracted it, bowing his head and folding his hands. "Lord, bless this food to our bodies and direct us along the path of righteousness throughout this day. Amen." He reached for the slice of toast and placed it on his plate. He covered it with scrambled eggs and began to eat.

Chapter Five

(May 2010)

Elizabeth hummed to herself as she stood by the kitchen sink washing dishes. Jacob was playing on the dining room floor with some wooden blocks. A school bus stopped at the end of their driveway and Elizabeth watched as Anna got off. Anna turned and waved at someone in the bus, then walked toward the house. The door didn't open for some time, but when Anna came in, the strong smell of tobacco followed her.

"Hey, Elizabeth. How was your day? What's for supper? Hey there, Jakey. How was your day?" Anna greeted them. Jacob grinned at his sister and pointed at his blocks.

"Hello, Anna. How was school today?" Elizabeth made a point of not mentioning the cigarette smell Anna brought into the house with her. All the necessary ingredients for a quick dinner were on the counter, but dinner had not yet been started. "Mac and cheese. It will be ready soon."

Elizabeth set a pot of water on the stove and turned on the heat. She cut open a package of wieners and chopped them into small pieces. She then cut up a large head of broccoli and put them in a bowl beside the wieners. As soon as the water was boiling, she measured three cups of macaroni into the pot. While it was cooking, she shredded some cheddar cheese and got the milk out. Elizabeth smiled approvingly and mused, "This is a lot better than the mac and cheese I used to make."

Another bus stopped at the driveway just as Elizabeth finished putting together all the dinner ingredients in the pot. She waved through the window with one hand while stirring the food in the pot with her other hand. Sonya smiled and waved back, but Benji kept walking with his eyes straight ahead.

The door opened and Benji shouted into the house, "Who's been smoking out here? There's a cigarette by the door." He climbed the steps and threw his backpack on the floor and then his jacket on top of his backpack.

"Hi, Mom," Sonya greeted. "Hi, Anna. I saw you walking with some boys today. I saw you from my classroom window. Why didn't you have classes this afternoon? Hi, little Jake." Sonya bent over her youngest brother to tickle him. Jacob giggled, and Sonya dropped to the floor beside him and began wrestling with him. Benji walked past them and kicked each block he could reach as far across the room as possible. Jacob's lips began to quiver when he saw his blocks disappearing around the dining room.

"Benji!" Sonya gasped. "What are you doing? Pick them up. Bring them back to little Jake, please."

"They were in my way. Besides, you're not the boss of me!" Benji retorted and went into the living room. "You're the one who was smoking outside," he directed at Sonya.

"I was not!" protested Sonya. "Mom, I was not smoking, and Benji just kicked Jacob's blocks all over the house." Sonya set Jacob on the floor. "Hey Jacob. Let's see who can collect the most blocks, okay? It will be a race. Let's collect the blocks and bring them here." Sonya scuttled across the floor on all fours in pursuit of one of the blocks, drawing giggles from Jacob. Soon he was crawling alongside her, laughing each time she grabbed a block and hurried back to the middle of the room where she was stacking them into piles.

"I want a snack. Why isn't supper ready? I'm hungry," Benji complained, coming back into the dining room. He saw the stack of blocks and changed direction toward them. He angled his body and then kicked the blocks directly at Jacob. One of them hit Jacob in the stomach, another on his arm, and the edge of a third block caught him on the forehead, just above his eye. Jacob screamed in alarm and then in pain. He reached up to his forehead with both hands to the place where he had been hit.

"Benji!" shouted Sonya. "You've hurt him!"

"Benji, you asshole!" shouted Anna, lunging toward her brother and pulling him away from the remaining blocks.

"Jacob, are you okay?" Elizabeth hurried to her son. She pulled his hands from his face to reveal a bloody gash across his forehead. Jacob wrapped his bloodied hands around his mother, wailing into her face. Elizabeth hurried into the bathroom where she filled the sink with warm water. She reached into the linen closet to retrieve a navy face cloth and dipped it in the water. Slowly and gently she brushed the moist cloth against Jacob's forehead. With each stroke Jacob's sobs grew louder.

"Mom, something's burning on the stove," Sonya shouted from the kitchen.

"Don't worry, Elizabeth. I've got this," Anna added. She went into the kitchen and over to the stove where smoke was rising from the pot holding their dinner. She tried to stir it but decided there was no saving what was in the pot. She lifted it, placed it in the sink and filled it with cold water, which turned the smoke to steam before it settled into nothing.

"You better head straight to your bedroom, Benji," Anna directed her brother. "And man, I wouldn't want to be you when Dad gets home." Anna mimicked taking off a belt, folding it, then applying it vigorously to an imaginary person. "That's going to be you tonight, you little brat," she mouthed in his direction. Benjamin stared at her for a moment, his eyes growing wider as she threatened him with what was to come.

"Dad would never use his belt on me. He likes me." Benjamin's voice quivered, not sounding as confident as his words. He stuck out his tongue at Anna, who merely laughed at him. "I'm going to tell him you were smoking, and then who do you think he'll hit with his belt?" Anna acted out taking a drag from a cigarette and blowing the smoke toward Benjamin, then offered him the imaginary cigarette. "Yuck. I don't like you," Benjamin cried as a parting shot at his sister before disappearing into his bedroom.

The door opened and Walter stepped into the house. "Oh my goodness, what is going on in here? It smells like something is burning!"

Benjamin burst from his room, pointing at Anna and shouting, "Anna was smoking in the house! And she called me an asshole."

At the same moment, Sonya tried to explain, "The dinner burnt on the stove. That's why it smells like smoke in here."

Elizabeth came out of the bathroom holding the damp facecloth to Jacob's forehead. Her voice was calm. "Walter, we need to take Jacob to emergency. I can't stop the bleeding on his forehead, and I don't want to press so hard on the cut."

Walter's eyes grew wide. "The hospital? The cut on his forehead? What is going on here? Someone please tell me."

"Anna, there is stuff in the fridge to make sandwiches. What else do you need? There's lots of milk in the fridge too. Please, Anna, can we leave you with Sonya and Benji?" Elizabeth implored her.

"Why can't I go with you, Mom?" Sonya whispered. "I can help you at the hospital. I can hold Jacob if you get tired."

Elizabeth handed Jacob to Walter, who wasn't sure how to hold his bleeding child. At first he brought his son close to him, but then held him at a little distance when he realized blood had dripped from Jacob's forehead onto his chest and was about to drip onto Walter's shoulder.

"Sonya, dear," said Elizabeth, putting her hands on Sonya's shoulders, "we never know how long we will be when we go to emergency. It may take only a few minutes, but it may also take an hour or two, maybe even three. Once we are there, it won't be so easy to bring you home to go to bed and get ready for school tomorrow." Elizabeth hugged Sonya. "You're offer to help is a beautiful offer. Thank you for that. You know how you can help me? You can help Anna get a new supper ready for you kids. And then you can help even more by cooperating with her to make sure everything is okay here while we go to the hospital."

"Anna," Elizabeth turned to face her, "what do you think? Can you handle taking care of your two siblings for a while? I don't know for how long you will need to be in charge."

"I've got you covered, Elizabeth. Leave it to me. The best peanut butter and honey, or jam, sandwiches coming right up." Anna smiled. "And you're going to cooperate too, aren't you little brother?" Anna's face was smiling, but her voice wasn't. Benji turned around and returned to his room, closing the door behind him. Everyone heard the lock clicking. "If that is what cooperation looks like, so be it. At least that means no trouble." Anna shrugged before waving her arms toward Elizabeth. "Go, go, go. Don't worry, Elizabeth, everything is going to be just fine here."

"Let me take him, Walter, so you can drive. I think my nerves are a little too shaken to drive." Elizabeth took Jacob, whose crying had settled into whimpering. "Oh, my little one, help is on its way. Soon you will know stitches, I think."

"I'm still wondering what is going on here. Will someone please explain to me what happened?" Walter asked.

"I'll tell you in the car. Let's go." Elizabeth, with Jacob in her arms, stepped outside to the car.

"See you soon, Mom. See you, little Jake. See you later, Dad." Sonya bid farewell and waved to each in turn.

Walter held the car door open for Elizabeth, who got in holding Jacob. He closed the door and went around to get in behind the steering wheel. "A cigarette beside the door to welcome me home. I step inside where kids are screaming at me, or each other. Jacob is in your arms bleeding from the head. There are blocks scattered all over the floor. Dinner was burning, then drowning in the kitchen. And now we're off to emergency where we hope we can see a doctor before falling asleep. What kind of a day is this?" Walter kept his observations going as he turned the car around and drove past the Bible School, turning right onto the highway. A car swerved to avoid him, blasting his horn and gesturing through his window at Walter.

"So, Elizabeth, is this a good time to tell me what was going on back there?" Walter ignored the other car but kept his eye on the street ahead instead of looking at her. *What was she going to tell him about his children? And what should he do about it?* Walter turned on his blinker to indicate a left turn onto Loewen Avenue. He turned left at the intersection continuing to keep his eyes only on the street in front of him.

"Where do I start, Walter?" Elizabeth sighed. "I'm scared for Jacob every day. When Benji comes home from school he finds some way of attacking him. Some days it is only taunting him, but other days, like today, he physically hurts him. This is the first time he has drawn blood."

"Attack is a strong word," returned Walter. "Children often tease each other. My other children teased each other too. That is normal for brothers and sisters to do." Elizabeth took a deep breath and started to cry. "What is it?" Walter asked in alarm, "What now?"

"What can I say? You asked what happened today. What happened today happens often, almost every day. I'm afraid I don't know how to protect Jacob from Benji. Sonya plays with him, Anna is fine, mostly ignores him, like her other siblings, but not Benji. And Benji doesn't listen to anything I say. His one response is 'you're not my real mother.' I have no idea what I can do to stop him from hurting Jacob, or to get him to listen to me." Elizabeth wiped her eyes and then wiped Jacob's forehead. "And it seems I don't know how to tell you what is happening in any way that will get you to pay attention." She sighed.

Walter drove in silence. He ignored the stop sign and turned right toward the emergency entrance of the hospital. He stopped at the door. "You take him in. I'll park the car and join you inside." Elizabeth opened the car door and stepped into the late afternoon air. She smiled in relief when she entered the empty emergency room and was able to go directly to the registration desk.

Walter arrived inside at the same time Elizabeth finished giving the young man at the reception the medical numbers, confirming the address, and giving a brief explanation for the purpose of the visit. Walter stood behind her with his hands on her shoulders. She leaned back into his strong hands, needing, wanting someone to take care of her.

"The doctor will be right with you," said the receptionist. "You are lucky. It is not often that this place is this quiet. Please follow me." She stood and ushered them into an area where curtains could be moved around to create examination spaces of different sizes. "Please just take a seat here for now." He pulled a curtain, enclosing them in a small room filled with screens and cupboards labelled with all manner of medical supplies.

"Elizabeth," Walter began, "I… I want to… I am trying to…" then paused. Elizabeth snuggled the whimpering Jacob against herself, humming in subdued tones into his ear. A woman wearing a tag identifying her as Dr. Klippenstein pulled the curtain back and came toward them.

"So your little Jacob has a cut on his forehead. May I please take a look?" Elizabeth offered Jacob to the doctor, who smiled. "Please, it is easier for me to check him if you hold him facing me."

The doctor placed a chair in front of Elizabeth and pulled on some blue sterile gloves. She touched Jacob's forehead near the wound and then slowly and carefully explored the skin around the wound. "First, I'll clean the wound. This might sting a little." The doctor opened a cupboard, pulled out some gauze, a brown bottle, and a small plastic bowl.

The doctor held the gauze to the top of the bottle and tipped it upside down. Gently she wiped the wound with the damp cloth. Jacob started to cry and pulled his head away from the doctor's hand. Elizabeth smiled at the doctor. "Sorry, I'll try to hold him tighter." The doctor nodded and returned the smile.

"That's fine. I flinch when something stings too. It makes sense that your son would do the same. He isn't wriggling so hard that I can't clean it. Just one more minute and I'll be done." The doctor wiped the dried blood from around the wound, then the fresh blood still appearing, until the wound was clearly visible.

"We have two options," the doctor explained. "The first option is four stitches. Two inside, with a special thread that will dissolve, without causing any problems, within a few days. Two more stitches outside to pull the broken skin back together. These two stitches will need to be removed in about one week. This option will result in a tiny scar that will appear as little more than a light-coloured dot on the forehead. If you choose the stitches, I can apply a topical anesthetic to help reduce the pain of the stitching, but it will cause some pain."

"And the second option?" asked Walter.

"The second option is a type of glue. I will apply the glue to the wound, filling the opening, sealing it to prevent more bleeding and to keep it clean. Of course, I'll cover it with a Band-aid too. The wound will heal, but there will be a more visible scar, possibly with a slightly changed skin tone around the edges. Initially the wound will be quite red but will eventually return to his natural skin tones."

"What do you think, Elizabeth? More pain with stitches, or no pain with ointment and bandage?" Walter indicated his choice with his voice.

"Perhaps you've had enough pain for one day, eh little Jake? I think you want to sleep more than anything. Yes, Walter, yes, doctor, I think we will go with the glue solution. I suppose the scar won't hurt in the future, will it?"

"A scar should not cause any pain in the future; it will just be a visible mark on his forehead. No more," the doctor assured them. She was sealing the wound and covering it with a bandage as she spoke. "There you go, good as new!" The doctor stood up, shook hands with Elizabeth, then Walter, and then touched Jacob on the shoulder. "You're ready to go, little man. Have a good night."

"I'll bring the car to the door," Walter said as he left the room. Elizabeth gathered herself and put Jacob's feet on the floor. He reached up for her hand and together they walked out of the emergency room toward the hospital entrance.

Walter pulled the car up to the emergency entrance and got out to open the back door for Elizabeth and Jacob. "There you go. We'll be home in time for some of those peanut butter and jam sandwiches Anna promised." Walter smiled, then leaned forward to kiss Elizabeth, who pulled back, turning her face away from Walter. Instead, she reached up and pulled the opal amulet from under her top and held it in her hand for a moment.

Walter straightened up, blushed, closed the door behind Elizabeth and Jacob and got into the driver's seat. He looked into the rear-view mirror and saw Elizabeth holding Jacob tightly to herself, tears silently rolling down her cheeks. Walter whispered toward the mirror, "I'll take you home."

Chapter Six

A small red car sat in their driveway when they returned home. "Darrel?" Elizabeth asked, with a puzzled expression on her face. "Could that be his car? What is he doing here? This is the middle of the week, and surely he has to work tonight in Winnipeg." Walter hurried to open Elizabeth's door, reached forward and took Jacob from her and hoisted him high above his head. Jacob smiled down at his father, and when Walter threw him up into the air, he burst out laughing.

"Again," Jacob blurted out, "again." Walter smiled and tossed Jacob into the air another time, and then again even before he was asked. The door to the house opened and Darrel stuck out his head.

"Welcome home, Dad, Mom. Benji told me Jacob had tripped with a block in his hand and cut his forehead. He said you had to take him to emergency. Must have been a nasty trip. Is the little guy okay now?" Darrel asked.

Elizabeth stopped and looked at Darrel. "Benji told you that? That Jacob had fallen and hurt himself?"

"Yeah, he seemed quite worried too. He was practically crying when he told me," Darrel responded. "I've never seen him quite so emotional about Jacob before. I know I would be quite worried if my little angel tripped, split her forehead open, and needed to go to the hospital. Speaking of which, my little angel is inside with Marigold. Come in and see them."

"I knew that there would be an explanation for what happened. Benji is such a sensitive little boy," Walter said, moving past Elizabeth, who was still standing in the same spot. "Come, honey, Marigold is inside with Abbi. I haven't seen her in a few months. I imagine she must have really grown!"

Elizabeth swallowed, put her hands on her hips, swallowed again, then gave her head a shake before she followed Walter, who was carrying Jacob inside. Once inside she managed to direct her attention to the visitors. "Marigold, welcome here. Darrel, welcome too, of course. And little Abbi. How beautiful she is." Elizabeth smiled at the child. She stepped forward and reached her arms toward Abbi.

Abbi lifted her arms to Elizabeth, who picked her up and twirled her around. "Gramma! Do it again," Abbi squealed. Elizabeth twirled around a few more times.

"Oh, that is as much twirling as I can do, Abbi. You're such a beautiful girl, but too big for me to keep twirling you. Tell me, when is your birthday? Soon you will be two years old. My goodness, you are growing up quickly."

Abbi held up three fingers and said, "Four more months. Three more months. Five more months." Elizabeth smiled and twirled around one more time.

"Darrel, Marigold, what a wonderful surprise to find you here. I think this is the first time you have come home in the middle of the week since you started studying at the university." Elizabeth looked toward her kitchen, where she saw the lip of a pot still rising above the edge of the sink. "I burned dinner earlier, so at the moment I have nothing substantial to offer you. Anna was going to make some sandwiches. Are you hungry? Come everyone, come sit at the table."

Marigold laughed as she picked up Abbi and took a seat at the table. "Oh, Elizabeth, you always offer us such good food. But Anna did beat you to it this time. She had sandwiches on the table when we arrived and was very quick to add some more. We each ate quite a bit of your brown bread. My, Elizabeth, your bread is getting better each time you bake. No more bought buns here. Darrel has an announcement, and he was too excited to make it over the phone. And no, Abbi is not about to get a baby brother or sister." Marigold smiled. "Darrel, are you going to tell them?"

Darrel went to stand behind Marigold and cleared his throat. "You all know that I started studying chemistry at the University of Winnipeg a few years ago, and last year I was offered a research job with one of my professors in the lab where he works when he's not teaching." He looked around the room, with all eyes focused on him. "Well, that lab has a sister lab in Saskatoon, and they have offered me a full-time job. At the same time, they will pay for me to finish my degree at the University of Saskatchewan, and then, in time, they will pay for my master's degree as well."

"I'm so proud of him." Marigold jumped to her feet, turned around and wrapped him in a hug. "We're moving to Saskatoon in May, just after Darrel finishes his classes and we celebrate Abbi's birthday together."

"That's the announcement." Darrel grinned. "As you can see, we are excited! It's not really a new beginning, because I'll be doing what I've been doing. But it's in a new place. And I've heard that Saskatoon is a beautiful city. You will all have to come and visit us there."

"What do we have to help us celebrate?" Walter asked. "Is there any ice cream in the freezer? Should I go pick up some donuts?" Walter scanned the faces for reactions or indications of interest.

"I want ice cream," piped up Benjamin, from where he was standing. Walter looked at Benjamin, who averted his eyes to the floor immediately.

"Me too, little buddy," said Darrel. "I love ice cream, and if there's one thing we can count on, there will be ice cream in the freezer of this house. Right?" Marigold smiled, still holding on to Darrel's arm.

"Elizabeth, would you get the ice cream, please?" Walter said. Suddenly he seemed to realize he was still holding Jacob, who had nestled into his arms and fallen asleep. "Oh my, I think you better take Jacob and put him to bed. He's had enough action for the day and must have fallen asleep. I'll get the ice cream if you take him." Elizabeth came over, took Jacob from Walter, and cuddled him in her arms. She carried him to her bedroom where his bed was set up in the corner of the room.

Elizabeth sat down on the bed and carefully undressed him. She lay him in the middle of his bed and went to the dresser to find some pyjamas for him. She came back and carefully pulled his arms and legs into place and then tucked a blanket around him. She stroked his forehead then whispered in his ear, "What do I do, Jacob? Walter doesn't seem to believe me, or any signs around him, that Benji is making your life difficult. I love you, and I love Benji too. What do I do?" Elizabeth asked the sleeping Jacob. "For now I'll keep looking for ways to try and keep you safe. And I guess have some ice cream with your tormentor."

When Elizabeth returned to the dining room, Benjamin was shoveling ice cream into his mouth, creating a white moustache with a touch of red in it. Elizabeth took a bowl of ice cream and deliberately took the open seat beside Benjamin. She looked at Benjamin, smiled, and whispered, "I like raspberry jam on my ice cream too." She put a spoon to her mouth.

Sonya picked up her bowl of ice cream and came to lean against Elizabeth. "Did you add chocolate chips too? I love chocolate and raspberry together."

"That sounds delicious! I didn't add any. Would you get some for me, Sonya?" Elizabeth asked, running her hand down Sonya's back.

"Yup, Mom. It's so good." Sonya skipped to the kitchen counter, took a handful of chocolate chips, and skipped back. She opened her hand to drop the chocolate chips into Elizabeth's bowl. "Oops, better clean these fingers." Sonya smiled and licked the residue of chocolate off her palm and fingers.

"Thanks, dear." Elizabeth smiled. "Benji, would you like some chocolate chips in your ice cream? I have so many, I could share with you."

Benjamin smiled. "Sure," he began, but caught himself. "Ah no, I don't really like chocolate so much." He looked around the table, saw an open seat beside Darrel across from him, and got up with his bowl. Benjamin walked past the kitchen counter, grabbed a handful of chocolate chips, and tossed them into his bowl before taking a seat next to Darrel. Darrel put his hand on Benjamin's head and tussled his hair.

"Even though we haven't been able to come home so often since we got married and moved to Winnipeg, I know I'm really going to miss this. You always make us feel so welcome, and so loved. Thanks for always having an open door for us." Darrel looked around the table. Marigold nodded her agreement.

"We have some new friends in Winnipeg, well, not new anymore," Marigold added. 'We've known them for almost two years now, and they are like family to us too. They drop in with cookies, or some cheese and crackers, and we do that at their place too. We are really going to miss them when we go to Saskatoon."

"You will probably meet some really nice people in whichever church you decide to attend once you get there," Walter said. He didn't notice everyone's eyes turning to him at the mention of going to a church.

Darrel looked at his father. "I don't know, Dad. I sort of lost faith in churches a few years ago. I know you and Elizabeth still go and take the three youngest with you. And if you find good company there, I guess that's good for you. Marigold and I are quite happy to find our way without church anymore."

"Who knows, Dad," Marigold added, "maybe we'll find a church that sees more than sin, more than sinners. Maybe there's a church in Saskatoon that believes in the power of, and the value of, love. We have no plans to raise our daughter with sets of rules for the sake of rules, or worse, for the sake of power."

"Three cheers to that!" shouted Anna, who had entered just in time to hear Marigold's statements. "I have no interest in any church that is more about rules than… okay, I'm just not into church at all. Any church, regardless of how they feel about rules." Anna saw the ice cream pail on the counter and changed her direction toward the kitchen.

Walter looked up. "I know our church isn't perfect. Probably no church is. But God can work miracles in our lives if we let him. And I also know that God can work miracles in someone's life even if they don't go to church."

"But what if someone smokes?" asked Sonya. "Can God still do miracles if someone smokes?" Sonya alternated her look between Anna and her father. "Or is smoking not a sin anymore?"

"What kind of a question is that?" Darrel said. "What does it matter if someone smokes or doesn't? If God is so powerful, how would something as small as a cigarette keep God from performing miracles? Or blessing a person?"

"Sort of confusing, isn't it?" said Elizabeth, slipping into the chair beside Sonya. "You've learned a long list of sins, haven't you? And you want to avoid sinning as much as you can, don't you? And you're doing a great job. I'm certain God is very pleased with you and the way you are choosing to live." Elizabeth patted Sonya's shoulder, then pulled her close to herself. "I think sin is not something that is confusing to just you, Sonya, but to almost all of us." Walter shot Elizabeth a dark stare, unconsciously shaking his head in her direction.

"God's word is clear about many things," Walter said, "but sometimes those things are better sorted out in the morning. It has become quite late. I think, Sonya, it's time for bed."

Elizabeth hugged Sonya again and whispered into her ear, "Let me know once you're ready to say your prayers you beautiful little girl, whose heart God loves dearly." Elizabeth helped Sonya to her feet. "Darrel and Marigold, would you like to stay for night? I see Abbi is beginning to look quite tired too. Our guest room is always ready for you. Will I see you in the morning? Or should I say good night and goodbye now?"

"What do you think, sweetie?" Darrel looked at Marigold. "I don't have classes until after lunch tomorrow. We could spend the night." Marigold smiled and nodded.

"In that case, I'll say good night now and take Abbi downstairs and put her to bed. Good night, everyone," Marigold said. "See you in the morning. Sleep well." Marigold nestled Abbi in her arms and disappeared down the stairs.

"Good night, Marigold and Abbi," Elizabeth added. "And good night everyone else too. Come, Sonya, brush your teeth and I'll meet you in your bedroom." Sonya went into the bathroom, while Elizabeth went into the second bedroom along the hallway.

Anna was headed toward the stairs when Darrel addressed her. "You're going downstairs? Did we take your bedroom? You don't share a room with Sonya anymore?"

"Nope. I'm all grown up and get my own room in the basement. The guest room is still where it always was, and now the room behind it is my bedroom. Don't keep me up with your antics tonight." Anna grinned.

"What do you know about that, little sister?" Darrel laughed. "Just you wait, you'll enjoy your antics too, soon enough."

"Soon enough." Anna giggled. "If only you knew all that I know!"

Darrel shot a glance toward their father to see if he would react to their conversation. Walter was oblivious to the siblings' conversation, as he was attempting to lift Benjamin's sleeping head from his ice cream bowl without waking him, or without getting too much ice cream on his shirt.

"Are you serious? Are you using protection?" Darrel whispered, shifting his glances between his father and sister.

"Of course I am, silly. I'm not going to get pregnant, like some other people I know did. Don't worry, Darrel, I'm fine. I'm not doing anything stupid." Anna smiled, hugged Darrel, and went down the stairs.

"Dad, good night. Do you need help with Benji? Do you want me to put him to bed?" Darrel offered.

"Oh, would you do that, Darrel? I'll get a cloth to wipe his face, and then if you put him to bed, that would be great." Walter went to the kitchen, wet a cloth, and came back to the table where he once again lifted Benjamin's face out of his ice cream bowl, wiped it clean, and then lifted him off his chair and offered his body, suspended in mid-air, to his brother. "Thanks, Darrel. Good night, Benji," Walter whispered into Benjamin's ear. Benjamin stirred a little, opened one eye, and then wrapped both arms and legs around Darrel's body.

Darrel disappeared down the hallway with his younger brother, pushing the door open into his bedroom. He wrestled off Benjamin's shirt, lay his brother down on the bed, and pulled off his pants. "Where are your pjs, kid?" There was no response. Benjamin simply rolled over onto his side on top of the bed. "Okay, tonight you sleep in your underwear." Darrel slid Benjamin forward on the bed and pulled his blanket out from under him. He tucked the blanket over and around him and then sat down on the bed beside him.

"Oh, Benjamin, what is happening here? The looks Elizabeth gave me told me that your story about tonight wasn't the real story. Anna has told me that you harass your little brother. Why? What has he done to deserve this? What has happened to the sweet little boy who loved everyone and everything? How do we get you back, Benjamin?" Darrel stroked Benjamin's forehead a few times, then leaned forward and kissed him. "Good night, Benji. I love you."

Walter was sitting alone at the dining-room table when Darrel returned. He took a seat beside his father. "Dad, you know that Marigold and I still believe in God, right?" Walter nodded. "You know that what the church did to me, to us, really hurt us, very deeply." Walter nodded again. "And you know that despite everything they did to us, we still have faith. We still live the same way you do, the way we always did. We haven't changed anything. We just don't go to church anymore."

Walter looked his son directly in the eyes. "They told me before they called you what they were going to do. I didn't know what to do, Darrel. I didn't know how to stop them. I know so many godly rules, but I didn't know how to protect you from their anger, their… their… I don't know their what." Walter took his son's hand. "Darrel, I know you are a good son. I know you are living right and are creating a good home for you, your wife, and child. God is clearly blessing you."

Darrel smiled. "I don't know about that word blessing, Dad. Anyway, thanks. We want a good home for our little Abbi, and for ourselves too." Darrel hugged Walter. "And what about your home, Dad? What kind of home are you living in?"

Walter looked surprised. "What do you mean? You know this home. You know who I am and how I live."

"Do you know what is happening in your own home, Dad? Did you see the look Elizabeth gave me when I recounted Benji's story about how Jacob was hurt?" Walter's eyes opened wide. "Did you see the expression on her face when you made that comment about how you knew there was another answer? Do you ever talk to her? Do you ever listen to what she is saying to you?"

Walter's eyes grew wider. "What do you mean? Of course I talk to her. Of course I listen to her. But sometimes what she says doesn't make sense to me. She thinks Benji is trying to hurt Jacob. Benji loves everyone. How could he hurt someone? How could he hurt his little brother?" Walter's voice faltered, his chin trembled, then he dropped his head into his hands.

There was a long silence. "Darrel, sometimes I just don't understand what is happening here. What if I haven't listened to her? What if I don't know what she is saying? I don't know if I want to know the truth. If I admit to the truth about my family, what will I have to do? If I admit to the truth about how the church behaves, the things it does to people, what will I have to do? I don't know what to think about God's plans for all of us and how they don't seem to be working out so well." Walter sighed into his hands and then looked up at his son.

Darrel sighed too and shifted his chair to sit in front of his father. He placed his hands on his father's knees. "Dad, for someone whom I've heard preach about being honest, or honesty as a virtue, or something like that, this is the most honest I think I've ever heard you be. And I believe everything I've ever heard you say about honesty. Being honest is important. Being honest is the right way to be, the right way to live. The only problem is that being honest doesn't always make things easier or clearer. Life can be a mess sometimes."

Walter sighed again. He placed his hands on top of Darrel's and smiled. "Perhaps you should be the one preaching, Darrel." Walter took his son's hands firmly in his own. "And now what? So life is messy. And maybe I'm realizing something about my life, about my family's life. But what does it mean? What do I do now?"

"Oh, Dad," Darrel said, leaning his head against his father's shoulder, "you'll figure it out. I don't think anyone else can tell you what you have to do next. You've got to make those decisions yourself." Darrel stood up. "I'm going to join my wife downstairs. I'm going to keep doing all I can to make her happy, all I can do to raise Abbi so she knows she is loved. And so are you, Dad. I love you. Good night."

Darrel put his hand on his father's shoulder for a moment before continuing downstairs. Walter went to his bedroom, where Elizabeth was already in bed. "Elizabeth, are you still awake?" She raised her head onto an elbow and nodded.

"We have some pretty amazing children, don't we? Darrel and Marigold are happy. Their baby is healthy and happy. Who could want more for a child?" Walter undressed and crawled under the covers with Elizabeth. "But I don't know about our other children. Are they happy? Are they healthy? Agatha's death was really hard on all of them. I don't know what to do for them. I don't know if I know how to be a good father." Walter rolled closer to his wife and put one arm around her shoulders. "What if I don't know how to be a good father, Elizabeth? I want to be a good father, and I want to be a good husband too."

Elizabeth lowered her head onto Walter's arm and allowed him to draw her closer. "I don't know, Walter. I don't know where to start either." Soft snores came back to Elizabeth, who sighed, rolled over, and got out of bed.

Elizabeth went over to her dresser, bent down, and reached for the bottom drawer. There was a creak as she pulled on the drawer, causing her to pause and glance over her shoulder toward Walter, who didn't stir. She pulled the drawer a little further and slid her hand over and around items until her hand settled on a tin box. Elizabeth lifted the box out of the drawer, slipped out of the bedroom, and went to the dining room where she placed the box on the table.

She lifted the chair, trying hard to not make any sounds that might disrupt the silence of the night. She pulled the chair just far enough from the table to allow her room to drop into the chair. She held the box in both hands for a moment and whispered into the night air, "I don't know how you did it, Mom, but I'm trying to follow your example. I've never forgotten how you lived, and I need your heart, your strength, more than ever."

Elizabeth opened the box and pulled out a stack of black-and-white photos that had become gnarled and browned with age. The top picture showed a woman in her late twenties, with three young children draped over her shoulders, wrapped around her legs, and lying leisurely in her arms. Elizabeth brushed her finger slowly across the picture, pausing a moment on each child.

"He gave you three children, Mom," Elizabeth mused. "And then went on to hurt them, hurt you." Elizabeth moved the top photo to the bottom of the stack, revealing the next one, a picture of a smiling six-year-old boy with a very bruised face and a cast on his left arm. Elizabeth gasped, instinctively reached for and pressed the opal amulet against her heart. "Only eight, and so careful to protect your little sisters, Jakey, no matter your sacrifice. What was it this time? Oh yes, Maggie didn't clean her toys, leaving them scattered all over the kitchen floor, and you said it was you."

"Oh Mom, how could you stay? Didn't you ever even think of leaving him? Of taking us away from his violence?" Elizabeth smiled ruefully. "Of course you didn't. Women didn't leave, weren't allowed to leave their husbands then, no matter what they did."

Elizabeth flipped to the next picture, which was of two girls, both under five years of age. A broken chair lay on the floor against the wall in the photo, a lamp on top of the chair, and a broken picture frame with an indistinct but clearly torn picture beside the chair. Both girls were smiling, with the younger of the two reaching her arms forward toward the photographer. "I miss you so much, Maggie. You are forever in my heart." Elizabeth wiped away the tear on her right cheek.

She leaned back in her chair, sighed deeply, then turned to the next picture, one of just her mother. Except in this picture, she didn't look as young as she did in the previous one. She stood tall, her long hair braided and wrapped around her head, a small bouquet of flowers in her hand. Her face was lined with a few wrinkles, but the same smile graced her lips. "Only two years later, but so much you had to go through in those two years. You smiled for us even as your heart must certainly have been breaking time after time. You protected us from him, at least most of the time, when you could." Elizabeth paused for a moment. "How many times did I hear you say 'children need a mother to take care of them, to keep them safe' and then watched you hide your own fear or sadness from us."

The final picture was very dark, with the outlines of four coffins barely visible. Two of the coffins were larger, for adults, and two smaller, for children. Elizabeth took a quick, deep breath. "Mom, Maggie, Jakey, you live in my heart. You give me strength. You give me direction. It is because of you that I can find love for Benji even when I am afraid that I can't protect my little Jake."

Elizabeth stared into the dark picture, traced the outline of the coffins with a finger. "I wonder, Dad, what happened to you to make you so angry. What made you so angry that day in the car? Why did you take out your anger on your wife, on your kids? Is there something that someone could have done for you? Mom was so kind to you, yet her kindness wasn't enough. Or was it? Did her kindness protect us from more, from what would have come if she hadn't been kind? Did you ever think you were being mean? Did you understand the fear we had of you?"

Elizabeth flipped back to the first picture again, the one of her mother with her three children surrounding her. "You did everything you could, Mom, to give us a good life. You are the reason I wanted to work with children, why I love children. Your words 'children need a mother' gives me the strength to keep trying with Benji. He needs someone who tries to understand him. I don't want him to become you, Dad. I will keep trying to understand him, to understand why he is so unhappy and if there is a way to change that for him before it destroys his life. If a little more love is what he needs, then I will find a little more love for him."

Elizabeth placed the pictures back into the box and took another deep breath. "And Walter, I will try to find a little more love for you to. I will keep encouraging you to see your children for who they are, to love them, no matter who they are." Elizabeth took her hands off the box for a moment. "I don't know if I can do what Mom did though, Walter, I don't know if I can stay if you don't want to know who your children are. Who we are." She picked up the box one more time. "Mom, I don't know if you ever got through to him." Elizabeth stood up, clutched the tin box to herself, and went back to the bedroom. She bent down, replaced it in the bottom drawer, and nudged it closed.

Elizabeth went back to her bed, crawled under the covers, lifted the opal to her lips, and kissed it. "Good night, Mom. Good night, Jakey, Maggie. The love with which you filled my soul keeps inspiring me to love my family."

Chapter Seven

Elizabeth sat down on the couch with the book *Dare to Discipline* in her hands. "Maybe you have some answers for me, Dr. Dobson," Elizabeth said to the book. "I try to love Benji, I try to be kind to him, and all he does is tell me how much he hates me, and how much he hates his brother." Elizabeth put the book on the coffee table. "I was up so late last night, maybe a nap might give me more energy to figure out how to deal with my family. I'm exhausted just thinking about what I might have to do tonight to keep Jacob safe." She pulled her legs onto the couch and stretched out on the soft green sofa. She leaned her head back and sighed.

"Elizabeth," a voice whispered into her ear. She moved her hand as if to brush away a buzzing fly. "Elizabeth," the voice repeated. "Elizabeth." This time it was more urgent, along with a hand on her shoulder. "Wake up, dear. It's five-thirty and there's no dinner on the table or on the stove." Walter's voice finally broke into her head and aroused her to consciousness. She sat up, rubbed a hand across her eyes, and looked at him.

"You're home early, Walter." Elizabeth smiled. "Did something happen at work today? Why are you home already?"

Walter sat on the couch beside Elizabeth, leaned his face toward her, and kissed her. "It seems like you might need a vacation. I've noticed that you've been tired lately, but I've never found you napping before," he said. Elizabeth jolted upright.

"What? Napping? What time is it, Walter?" Elizabeth was alarmed. She pulled his arm toward herself and turned it so his watch faced her. "Oh my goodness! It's five-thirty! Where are the kids? I haven't even started supper." Elizabeth jumped to her feet and dashed toward the living room door. She turned, darted back, kissed Walter on the forehead, smiled, and said, "Welcome home. I've got to start supper." She disappeared through the dining room and into the kitchen.

Sonya was sitting at the dining room table with her school backpack on a chair beside her. She had an open textbook and notebook in front of her. "Hi Mom." She looked up and smiled.

"Hi, Sonya honey." Elizabeth paused to put her hands on Sonya's shoulders. "What are you working on?"

"I had a bunch of homework—math, science, and social studies. The social studies questions are done, the drawing of where rain comes from… did you know that it comes down and then goes back up so it can rain again? Pretty cool, eh? And I have two more math questions before I'm done." Sonya leaned her head into Elizabeth's hand for a moment before leaning forward again. She turned and looked up. "Don't worry, Mom. Benji's playing with Jacob in their room, or at least they were playing when I last checked in on them."

Elizabeth shot a worried look in the direction of the closed bedroom door. "Okay, thanks, honey. I better get some dinner on the stove. I bet everyone's hungry already." She moved into the kitchen, opened a cupboard, and pulled out two tins of cream of mushroom soup and the large No-Name box of macaroni. She opened the faucet on the sink and reached for a pot from under the counter. "How about Anna? Has she come home already?" Elizabeth tried to sound casual as she put the pot of water onto the stove to heat.

"Maybe I'll just say hello to the boys," Elizabeth said toward the bedroom door. She smiled at Sonya, who had turned to face her.

"He's not always bad you know, Elizabeth. He doesn't always hate Jacob." Sonya's words stopped Elizabeth. "I know he's often real mean. But he's a little older now, and maybe he's growing up. I mean, I don't know what growing up means. But he hasn't pushed him down the stairs in a while, and I can't remember the last time he threw something at him."

"Oh, my little wise one. You don't know what it means to grow up, eh? Well, you will soon enough. It seems to happen very quickly for some people." Elizabeth smiled toward Sonya again. "And I just happen to think that you're going to be one of those for whom it happens that way. Actually, what am I saying? You've already had to grow up pretty quickly in this house, haven't you?" Elizabeth took a few steps toward the door covered with drawings of turtles, cars, and beaches taped to the bottom half and posters of the Ninja Turtles on the top half.

Elizabeth leaned her ear against the door, trying to hear what was happening on the other side. The door muffled the voices, but they sounded calm, so she knocked and opened the door. "Hi boys, welcome home," Elizabeth greeted the boys, stepping into the room before coming to an abrupt stop.

"Mom! We're playing ninja turtles," shouted Jacob eagerly from the corner of the room. His arms were spread eagle, away from his naked body, held against the wall by many pieces of duct tape. His pants were down by his ankles, which also showed pieces of silver tape peeking past the lowered pants. Benjamin, sitting on the edge of his bed, kept his eyes stolidly on the ground.

Elizabeth's hand shot to cover her mouth at the scene before her. Just at that moment Walter came up behind her. "Jacob! For goodness sakes! What are you doing? Pull up your pants. Where's your shirt?" Walter pushed past Elizabeth, right past Benjamin, and pulled Jacob's arms from the wall.

"Ouch!" Jacob started to cry. Walter pulled Jacob away from the wall and swatted him on the bum. A wail of tears burst from his lips and he started to run toward Elizabeth. His pants, still down, got in the way, and he fell to the floor. He curled into a ball and cried loudly. "Daddy, you hurt me!"

Elizabeth darted across the floor and sat down beside Jacob. She pulled him into her lap, stroked his back, and rocked back and forth. "There, there, Jacob. I've got you now. Everything is going to be okay." She stood him in front of her and pulled up his underwear and pants, zipping the zipper and buttoning him up before hugging him again.

Jacob's cries settled into a few gasps, a cough, and then just some shaking. He curled himself into a tight ball in Elizabeth's lap and pulled her arms close to his body. Walter stood and watched the exchange, and then without another word, left the room.

Elizabeth looked toward Benjamin, who hadn't moved and was still staring down at the floor. "What?" he blurted toward the floor. "He's the one who wanted to play Ninja Turtles. Someone had to be a prisoner so there was someone to be set free. He was the prisoner, and I was Michelangelo." Benjamin shot a look at Elizabeth. His eyes were narrow, his lips in a tight line, with deep lines etched on his forehead. "It was his idea, not mine." He looked back down at the floor.

"Perhaps we can continue this talk after supper," Elizabeth said softly. "I don't know what happened to me this afternoon, but I overslept and haven't finished making dinner." She placed Jacob on the floor in front of her and stood up. Jacob reached for her hand, which she held against herself. "Come, Jacob, you can help me finish preparing supper. Supper will be ready in ten minutes, Benjamin, and then we'll talk some more." Elizabeth turned toward the door and Jacob followed her.

"I hate your food," Benjamin whispered toward the floor, but loudly enough to be heard. "My mom was a real cook." A tear appeared in Elizabeth's eye and she quickly swiped it away with her free hand. She stopped for a moment, then continued toward the kitchen. "Probably tuna and macaroni again. Why can't we ever have pizza like other families do?" Benjamin continued to whisper toward the floor. He reached for one of the Ninja Turtles on the floor, picked it up, and shoved the toy's head into his mouth. He bit down hard, time and again, pulled it out, twisted it in his hands, and then bit it again. Finally, with one last mighty heave, he yanked off the head and threw both parts of the now-disfigured turtle against the wall.

Walter was sitting beside Sonya at the dining-room table. "This is very different math than I did when I was thirteen. I'm not sure what to say about this question." He looked up at Elizabeth and Jacob, who had gone into the kitchen.

Elizabeth put Jacob on the counter. "You sit here, Jacob. I'll tell you when you can help me." She stirred the pot of macaroni, which had been cooking while she was in the bedroom with the boys. She opened a drawer and pulled out a can opener.

Walter got up from the table and disappeared down the hallway. "Benjamin, which is Jacob's drawer? He needs a shirt," Elizabeth heard Walter say from the bedroom. A moment later Walter returned with a shirt in his hand.

"Here," he said, offering the shirt to Elizabeth. "He needs a shirt." She turned to face Walter, a can of soup in one hand and the can opener in the other.

"He needs more than a shirt, Walter." Elizabeth looked at him. "Did you see what was going on in there? And you think that Jacob needs a shirt? That is what you saw?" Walter looked at the floor. Elizabeth took a step toward him, took the shirt, and put it on the counter. Then she put the can of soup in one of his hands and the can opener in the other. She lifted his face toward hers. "Maybe they were simply playing out a Ninja Turtles game. I don't know. It didn't look so good to me, but sometimes playing doesn't look so good and it really is just playing. But more than anything, Benjamin needs to know about playing safely with a child half his age. Benji's eight, he's so much stronger than Jacob. I don't think this is actually about shirts."

Elizabeth turned and took the pot of macaroni off the stove. She poured the water and pasta into a colander in the sink before putting the macaroni back in the pot. "Are you going to open that can of soup for me, Walter, or just hold it? If you're not going to open it, I need it back so I can," Elizabeth said.

Walter opened the can and put it on the counter beside Elizabeth. Jacob flinched as Walter reached past him for the other can. Walter's hand stopped, and he looked at Jacob. He looked at the shirt on the counter and then at Elizabeth's back. She reached back to take the opened can of soup, which she emptied into the pot.

Walter opened the second can of soup, placing it on the counter beside Elizabeth. Once again, he looked at Jacob, who was looking at his mother's back and then at the kitchen floor. Walter moved right in front of his youngest son and reached out his arms. Jacob flinched again and gave a final look at his mother's back as Walter took ahold of him and lifted him up, pulling him toward himself.

"What do you think, little Raphael? Do you want to be a bareback turtle for supper tonight? Or would you rather have a shirt?" Walter picked up the shirt off the counter. "Look, Jake, it's a Ninja Turtle shirt. Which turtle is this one?"

Jacob smiled at Walter. "That's Donatello, Daddy. Everyone knows that."

"Well, it appears that maybe everyone but your daddy knows that." Walter carried Jacob toward the kitchen table. Elizabeth followed them with her eyes as she stirred the second can of soup into the macaroni on the stove.

"Is Anna home? Are we expecting her home for supper tonight?" Elizabeth asked toward the kitchen table. "Benjamin, dinner's ready!" she shouted toward the bedroom. Sonya cleared her books from the table.

"I'll set the table," Sonya said as she put her backpack on the floor in the hallway. She opened a cupboard and counted out six plates, which she placed around the table. She opened another cupboard and took out six glasses. "Dad, do you and Mom want coffee?" Sonya allowed her hand to pause by the cups.

"Not for me," said Elizabeth as she pushed six forks and six knives across the counter toward Sonya. "Thanks for helping, Sonya." They smiled at each other.

"Dad? How about you? Do you want a cup?" Sonya asked as she placed the silverware around the plates on the table.

"Not tonight," Walter replied. "Unless, well, no, no. Not tonight." Sonya grinned at her father.

"It's not supposed to be like that new math, Dad. It's not a hard question. You're allowed to have coffee if you want some, you know." Sonya reached up for a cup, which she placed at the end of the table. "There. Now if you want some, the cup is there for you."

"Benjamin," Elizabeth called as she came out of the kitchen with the pot of macaroni in her hands. She put a cork pad on the table and placed the hot pot on top of it. She turned back to the kitchen. "Benjamin, come and eat." She opened the refrigerator and pulled out a square Tupperware container filled with carrot sticks, which she brought to the table and set down beside the pot. "Walter, would you get Benjamin? I'll settle Jacob into his chair." She took Jacob from Walter's arms and placed him on a chair with a booster seat. She sat down beside him and rubbed his head first, and then his belly. "Is this turtle ready for some dinner? What is a turtle's favourite food? Fish?" She rubbed his belly again. "The fish is ready for you, mister turtle."

"Anna! I keep forgetting about Anna," Elizabeth remembered. "Sonya, do you know if Anna is at home? Is she in her room? Would you go check and let her know dinner is ready?"

"Sure, Mom, no problem." Sonya was halfway down the stairs by the time she finished her response. "Anna? Are you home? Anna? Are you down here?" Sonya rushed up to Anna's door, but hesitated to knock when she heard voices behind the closed door. She eased her ear up against the door to listen.

"Knowing you has changed my life," Sonya heard Anna say. "I was raised on everything being a sin and being scared of my own body. I tried liking boys, I did anything with any boy who wanted me." Sonya blushed at what she was hearing. "…And never enjoyed any of it. But you, Shelley, you make me feel alive. I finally feel like a complete person now that we are together."

"And all those sins? What about us being sinners and sinning?" Shelley asked. "All this sin stuff is totally new to me. I knew that people in Thunder Bay didn't like me because I came out ages ago, and that city is both racist and bigoted against anyone who isn't 'normal' like they are, but sin? I've never gone to church or known anyone who does." Sonya shivered upon hearing that Shelley didn't know about sin.

"Oh, don't worry about that sin stuff. I don't believe a word of it. My dad does, though. He's a preacher, after all, in one of those super-conservative, evangelical churches. They think anything that makes people happy is a sin cuz you should only find your happiness in Jesus, or something like that," responded Anna.

Sonya blushed, clapped her hand to her mouth, and looked at the door as if trying to see through it to the people inside the room. She tip-toed back to the bottom of the stairs and then shouted again, "Anna, are you down here?" Sonya approached and knocked on the closed door of Anna's bedroom. "Anna, supper time. Coming?"

"Let go of me, silly. You know you're invited for dinner too," Sonya heard Anna's voice say from behind the door. The door opened a crack, with Anna's head appearing in the opening while her body remained behind the closed door. Sonya's eyes grew wide when she saw a naked body on the bed in the corner of the room. Anna saw Sonya's eyes, closed the door and shouted through it, "Shelley and I will be right up. Tell Mom we need an extra plate for supper tonight."

Sonya stood staring at the door, mouth still agape. She turned and went back up the stairs. "Anna's home, Mom. And she's got a friend here too. She's also staying for supper." Sonya's voice was quiet. She sat down at the table and stared at her plate.

Elizabeth glanced at her. "Sonya, it's fine if Anna has a friend here. We just need another setting. Sonya? What's wrong, dear? What…"

"Hey, Elizabeth. How are you, sleepyhead?" Anna almost shouted from the stairs. "This is my friend Shelley. She works at the grocery store with me. I told her it was okay for her to stay for dinner, that you always made enough for a guest." Anna laughed and Shelley smiled toward Elizabeth.

"Hi, Elizabeth. I'm pleased to meet you. Hi, Sonya. And who's this little guy?" Shelley reached forward and tickled Jacob under the chin. He instantly smiled toward Shelley and then looked down at the table.

Anna was just opening the cupboard door where the plates were kept when Walter, pushing Benjamin in front of him, entered the dining room. "Hey Dad, hey Benji. This is my friend Shelley. She's joining us for dinner." Anna took a plate and set it on the table. She ruffled Benji's hair as she stepped past him into the kitchen to retrieve another setting of silverware. "Hey Benji, what's up? You alright?" Anna ran her hand through Benjamin's hair again as she motioned toward a chair for Shelley and took the chair beside her.

Walter sat down at the end of the table while Benjamin sat the other end. Anna was reaching for the pot of macaroni when Benjamin blurted out, "I'm not praying. If Anna doesn't have to pray anymore, I don't want to pray anymore either." Anna retracted her hand from the pot and looked at Benjamin. She looked at Shelley and shrugged.

"I forgot to tell you my family prays before meals. Actually, before meals, after meals, before bed, after waking up. Pretty much just prays all the time about and for everything," Anna explained to Shelley while rolling her eyes. All eyes turned toward Walter.

"Elizabeth? Will you pray?" Walter asked quietly. She nodded toward him. "Okay, let's pray."

"Lord, we place ourselves into your caring hands and thank you that you love each of us for exactly who and what we are. Help us to love each other and take good care of each other too. Amen," Elizabeth looked at each face in turn as she prayed. She put her hand on Jacob's knee when she reached the part about caring for each other.

"Shelley, welcome here. Thursday night is always our macaroni night." Elizabeth reached for Shelley's plate and served her.

"Thursdays?" muttered Benji under his breath. "Every day is macaroni night here."

"And our favourite veggie is carrots. Please help yourself." Elizabeth ignored Benji's statement. Walter passed his plate to Elizabeth to be served, followed by Sonya and Anna. Benjamin's hands stayed in his lap, so Sonya took his plate and gave it to Elizabeth. "Benji, do you want some carrots too?"

Benjamin kept his eyes downcast. "I'll take some when they come around," he said to the floor. Anna looked at Benjamin, then at Shelley, who was busy putting one forkful of macaroni after another into her mouth. She paused for a moment, realized that the carrots were closest to her, and passed them to Anna. Anna dropped some carrots onto her plate before passing them along. When the container reached Benjamin, he didn't touch it. He still hadn't lifted his hands out of his lap.

Sonya put the container on the table beside Benjamin's plate and turned her attention to her plate. She carefully avoided looking at Shelley. Walter looked across the table toward Shelley and began to open his mouth.

"Wait, Dad," Anna interrupted. "Let me help you out." She looked at Shelley with a mischievous smile. "Shelley's a Catholic, or used to be one. You don't know any of her family, because they just moved here from Thunder Bay, and they're not related to anyone in Manitoba. She doesn't smoke." Anna turned back to face Shelley and mouthed, "at least not tobacco!"

Shelley smiled throughout her introduction and then added, "I've been working at Superstore, which is how I know your daughter. We both work in the produce section and share a love of all those fruits and vegetables." Shelley smiled even more broadly. "Your daughter has made me feel very welcome here."

"Ahhh." Anna laughed. "See, I'm reaching out to newcomers."

"Well, Shelley," added Elizabeth, "any Thursday you need some macaroni with something added, you are welcome at our table. Maybe next week I'll just add veggies? Which ones do you think would work? Please, just don't say eggplant!" Elizabeth grimaced.

"I think pretty much any veggie you like, except apparently not eggplant, would work great," Shelley offered. "And maybe I can cull the shelves and come over early and make dinner for you next Thursday. I noticed today when I arrived you were in need of a little rest."

Elizabeth blushed remembering why she took a nap. "I… I… I don't know what came over me. I thought I'd rest for a few moments, and that was at two-thirty. I've never fallen asleep for that long before. I mean, I don't usually take naps. I don't know why I'm so tired." She looked around the table. She noticed that Benjamin had still not touched any of the food on his plate.

"Benji, maybe we've had too many Thursdays with macaroni. What do you say? Should I take you out to A & W for a burger?" Elizabeth offered. Benjamin's eyes grew wide, with a hint of a smile at the corners of his mouth. "Just you and me," she continued, and before anyone could protest, "don't worry, I'll take orders from anyone else who wants something."

Walter was staring at Elizabeth with a puzzled expression on his face. "I don't know Elizabeth, A & W is pretty expensive," he ventured in a subdued voice. "Do you think…"

"It's not like we do this so often. When is the last time we went to A & W, Sonya? When's the last time we took you out to a restaurant?" Sonya looked first at Elizabeth, not sure what to make of the offer of a hamburger, and then at her father, not sure what to make of his trepidation. "Benji, ready?" Elizabeth pushed her chair back from the table and stood up. "I'll clean up when I get back."

Benji didn't move from his place and looked back down at his plate. "I'm just not hungry. Not for macaroni and not for A & W burgers. Can I just be excused?" He looked up, his eyes not making contact with anyone at the table. He slid off his chair and went toward his room.

"Is the world ending?" Anna asked, feigning horror. "Benji not hungry for anything, especially a hamburger. I don't believe my eyes or ears." She smiled at Shelley and patted her hand. "My little brother could eat a horse, usually. Can't imagine what's going on in that little head of his for his stomach not to get messages of 'EAT' through to the brain." Anna looked at Elizabeth and shrugged. "Do you get it? Do you know what's going on with him?"

Elizabeth answered from the kitchen where she had already pulled out a bag of her whole-wheat bread. "I think I might have an idea. I think he's a little confused about something that happened this afternoon, maybe a little afraid of the talk that is still coming."

Anna looked at Shelley. "Always something going on around here that needs somebody's attention."

Elizabeth opened the refrigerator door and retrieved a jar of peanut butter and another jar of raspberry jam. "I'll make a sandwich for him." She cut two slices of bread from the loaf and started to spread the peanut butter on one slice. "Maybe he'll be hungry after a while, so I'll bring him something in his room. Just in case he needs a little space for himself." Elizabeth finished spreading jam on the other slice, put them together and placed the sandwich on a plate. She returned the jars to the refrigerator door. "I'll be back soon. Shelley, excuse me. It was so nice to meet you. Sonya, do you have any homework?"

"Finished it before dinner," Sonya responded. She shot a glance over toward where Anna was now holding Shelley's hand under the table. "I'll clean off the table, Mom." Sonya stood up and began collecting the plates from around the table.

"Although I don't have homework either, I should be going." Shelley pushed her chair back from the table and smiled at Walter before standing up. "Nice to meet you sir. Sonya, nice to meet you too. I hope you have a good evening. See you at work tomorrow Anna." Shelley nodded at Walter and waved across the room toward Sonya, who blushed and picked up a handful of silverware from the table before darting into the kitchen.

"I'll walk you to the street," Anna said. "Be back soon," she added toward Walter. He nodded before looking toward Sonya in the kitchen.

"Dad?" Sonya began, her voice faltering. "Can I ask you something?" She looked at her father before taking a chair beside him and looking down at her feet. Walter put a hand on her shoulder and gave it a gentle squeeze.

"Of course, Sonya. You can always ask me anything you like," Walter answered. He left his hand on her shoulder.

Sonya continued to look away from her father. "Can girls have girlfriends?"

Walter pulled his hand off Sonya's shoulder. "Oh my goodness. I don't know what kind of question I was expecting, but that wasn't it. I guess it depends entirely on what you mean by girlfriends. If you simply mean having girls who are your friends, yes. Why, you should have many girl friends, and it's probably good to have many boy friends like that too. The more friends you have, well, it seems it would be good to have many friends. But what you really want is at least one, maybe two, very close friends who will always stick by you. Why do you ask?" Walter looked at Sonya for any hint about why she was asking this question.

Walter's voice changed from a father's voice into a preacher's voice. "But if you mean a girlfriend, like Marigold was for Darrel before they got married… well, no, absolutely not. That is a sin, and the Bible is very clear that when a girl is old enough, she should have a boyfriend. God is very sad, actually very angry, if girls like girls or if boys like boys." Sonya cringed, blushed, and turned away from her father, looking out the dining-room window. In the distance she saw Anna and Shelley locked in an embrace. Shelley's arms were wrapped tightly around Anna's body while Anna's hands were holding Shelley's face while they kissed.

Walter looked at the reflection of Sonya's face in the dining-room window. While it was not a mirror reflection, it showed a look of fear in her eyes. "You're too young to be asking such questions, Sonya, or thinking about such things."

Sonya swept her hands over eyes, wiping away the tears that had sprung out hearing her father's reply to her question. She took a deep breath before getting up to clear the table.

"Thanks, Sonya," Walter said. He smiled at her. "Oh my goodness. Look at Jacob. He's fallen asleep on his chair. What a little sleepyhead that boy is." Walter looked at Jacob without moving. "Elizabeth will have to put him to bed before she washes up our supper dishes." Walter smiled at Sonya again. "No homework, you say? What a good evening." He was careful to lift his chair so as to make no sound when he stood up. "I'll go to living room to read the paper."

Walter got to his feet and went into the living room, picking up the newspaper from the coffee table on his way to his favourite La-Z-Boy recliner. He tilted the chair back, lifted the paper, shifted his hips toward the right-hand side of the chair, and opened the paper. Soon the paper was resting on Walter's face, his hands having dropped onto his belly, with light snores escaping from his nostrils.

Chapter Eight

Elizabeth knocked a few times on Benji's bedroom door. When she received no response, she switched the sandwich plate from her right to her left hand and reached for the door handle, then stopped before touching it. She leaned forward ever so slightly to place her ear against the door. Only silence. *Oh my*, she thought. *Should I just put the sandwich by the door for him? Is it worth trying to talk to him now, when he's so scared, when he knows what he was doing to Jakey was bad?* Her brow creased as she listened more carefully, hoping to find an indication, any indication, of either Benji's location in the room or his state of mind. Finally, she reached for the door handle again and turned it.

Benji lay face down and motionless across his bed. The curtains had been closed, and the automatic nightlight lay unplugged on the floor. Elizabeth took two slow steps toward the bed. She stopped and extended the plate with the sandwich, about to offer it to Benji, but didn't say a thing. For a long moment, she stood there with her hand and the plate reaching into the silent space of the bedroom. She took another step toward the bed, bending her legs to sit down, but again stopped herself before completing the action. Benji didn't move, didn't make a sound.

Elizabeth straightened her shoulders, stood up tall, and looked toward the curtained window. "What did I think I was going to say to him? What did I think I was going to find in here?" she wondered to herself. After a minute of gazing at the window, she relaxed her shoulders and took a deep breath. She leaned toward Benji and whispered, "Benji, I brought you a sandwich just in case you are hungry later on. I'll put it here on the nightstand beside your desk."

Benji continued to lie motionless and silent on the bed. Elizabeth placed the sandwich on the nightstand and then leaned over Benji's body. She placed one hand on each side of Benji and whispered into his ear, "Benji, I love you as much as I love Jacob. We have to figure out a way to make life work for each of us in this house, to be safe, to be kind." Just as she leaned further forward, he pushed himself up, smacking his head hard into Elizabeth's face, causing her to fall backward onto the floor.

Benji jumped off his bed, took a step with one leg over Elizabeth's body, placed both hands on his hips, and glared down at her. "You love me?" he shouted, "as much as Jacob? You want to be safe in this house?" Benji's eyes narrowed into slits and he swallowed two or three times before shouting down at her, "I hate you! I hate Jacob! I wish he had never been born! You want to be kind? Be kind then, move out with that little brat!" Benji turned and ran out of his room, down the hall, and out the door.

Elizabeth gasped, tried to take a deep breath, and sat up. Her eyes wide open, she braced her arms against Benji's bed to pull herself up. She stepped toward the door and grabbed onto the door frame to steady herself. "Walter," she said, trying to keep her voice calm. "Walter? Walter, where are you? I need your help," she called out. "Please, I need your help," she whispered desperately into the empty hallway. Elizabeth raised a hand to cover her mouth. "I just don't know what to do," she whispered into her hand.

Sonya raced around the corner from the dining room into the hallway, colliding with Elizabeth. "Mom? What is it? What happened? Where's Benji?" Sonya poured out one question after another. "Wait, I'll wake Dad." Sonya turned and disappeared around the corner. Elizabeth could hear her in the living room. "Dad, Dad! Wake up. Something happened. Benji ran out of the house. Elizabeth is crying in the hallway. Dad, do something!"

The door to the house opened and was slammed shut from the outside. Muffled shouts came from outside and the door opened again. "Let go of me, Anna! I hate you! Leave me alone!" Benji screamed at his sister, who held one of Benji's arms behind his back and the other one in front of his body. He was squirming, trying to kick backward to reach his sister's legs, and twisting and turning to get away from her.

"Look who I found outside using rocks to scratch the car." Anna's voice was halfway between a snarl and a laugh. Anna looked into the house and saw a wide-eyed, disheveled Elizabeth looking back at her from the hallway. Sonya took a few steps toward her, then dropped her arms and stood still, as Walter pushed a newspaper onto the floor and stood up from his favourite chair in the living room. "What's going on in here? I leave to say goodbye to Shelley, and it's as if Armageddon happened in here!" Anna gave Benji a hard shove, sending him forward into the dining room. He turned around as if to try and get out the door again, but saw Anna blocking it, legs apart, hands on her hips, as if daring him to try.

Walter took a few steps forward. "Where's Elizabeth?" He looked around the kitchen and dining room for her but couldn't see around the corner where she was leaning against the hallway wall. "What is going on here? Benji, answer me. What's going on here?" Benji turned toward his father, his face contorted by emotion.

"She hates me!" he finally managed to blurt out, pointing to where Elizabeth was standing in the hallway, hidden from Walter's view. Benji glared at her, set his chin, bit his lip, and narrowed his eyes. Then he turned and, as if on command, burst into tears that he directed toward Walter. Benji took a few slow steps, then a few more, toward Walter, never looking up into his face. "Elizabeth came into my room and tried to hurt me. She hit me once, she was going to hit me again, so I ran away." Benji wrapped his arms around his father's stiff body and wept into his stomach, tightening his embrace as he cried.

Walter turned his face downward to look blindly at the top of his son's head. He instinctively put his hands on Benji's shoulders, was about to hug him, but then pulled his arms away and looked at Anna with glazed eyes. Sonya dropped to the floor, wrapped her arms around the legs she had tucked up to herself, and buried her head in her knees. Anna moved further into the house, toward Elizabeth, who now leaned her whole body heavily against the wall.

"You okay, Elizabeth?" Anna went to her and touched her on the shoulder. Anna ducked her head so she could look into Elizabeth's eyes, which were pressed shut, her breaths coming in shallow gasps, her shoulders slumped. Anna took another step closer and wrapped one arm around Elizabeth's shoulder. "I never touched him," Elizabeth sobbed.

"So, Dad," Anna addressed her father from behind the hallway wall, "think it's maybe time for some more prayer meetings? Maybe you could use this as a sermon illustration. An illustration of what happens when, say, a father is dishonest with himself, his community, his church, about what is going on in his home. Maybe this could turn into a redemption story. A child lost in the darkness of despair places their hope in a loving father, or is that a loving Father, sees the light, comes to the light, changes his ways, begs forgiveness of everyone he's ever hurt and becomes zealous in becoming the best older brother in the world."

"I don't know what you're talking about, Anna," Walter began. He dropped his arms once again, one hand on the top of Benji's head, the other on a shoulder.

"Of course you don't. When did you ever know what was going on with your kids? In your own house?" Anna said this to herself as she took a step away from Elizabeth. She came around the corner of the hallway into the dining room. "Dad, wake up. Your son needs you to be a man, to be a father. Your wife needs you to be a man, to be a husband. Why the hell are you standing there as if you don't know what has been going on in this house for years? Wake up!" Anna turned toward the stairs and went down to her room.

Sonya looked up at the sound of her sister swearing at their father and placed her hands over her face. She turned to sneak a look at Walter, who still had Benji wrapped around his midriff. She pushed herself across the floor, sliding on her bottom, until her back reached the wall. Slowly she pushed herself into an upright position, stole another look at Walter, and then inched her way around the corner into the hallway before standing up.

In the hallway Sonya encountered Elizabeth, who had not moved for the duration of Anna's interactions with her father. Sonya wrapped her arms around Elizabeth's stomach, gave her a quick squeeze, and then rushed into her bedroom where she closed the door. Elizabeth heard the unfamiliar click of the door being locked.

"Okay, son, let's go to your room. I think it must be your bedtime, yes? When do you usually go to bed? After dinner, I think." Walter took Benji's arms with his hands and opened their grasp, which was still firm around his body. Benji resisted the end of the embrace for a moment before Walter physically turned him around, faced him toward the hallway entrance, and pushed him ahead. Entering the hallway, father and son came face to face with Elizabeth. Benji looked down and away from her, then practically ran the final few steps into his room. At the door, he turned around to look at his father.

Walter stopped beside Elizabeth, reaching out one hand to touch her shoulder. "I'll put Benji to bed tonight," he said before removing his hand and following Benji into his room and closing the door behind them.

Walter stepped into the middle of Benji's room, where he saw the sandwich on the nightstand. "Are you hungry? Do you need something to eat before you go to bed?" He looked at Benji, then back at the sandwich.

"I don't want anything she touched," Benji whispered, standing next to his bed.

"Do you use pyjamas?" Walter asked, dropping himself onto the bed. He gazed around the room. "Let me turn on the lights. I can hardly see anything." Walter stood up, crossed the room to the door, and flicked the switch. Both Walter and Benji flinched with the bright light filling the room. "Oh my, that is suddenly very bright." Walter moved back to the bed to sit back down.

"Do you use pyjamas?" Walter asked again, "or do you sleep in your underwear? I used to keep my pyjamas under my pillow when I was a kid." Walter slid his hand under the pillow looking for his son's pyjamas. There was nothing there. Walter was lost.

"Where do you keep your pyjamas?" Walter asked.

Benji sat down on the bed and then reached under the bed with one hand. He sat up with his Winnipeg Blue Bomber pyjamas in hand. Walter smiled. "You like the Blue Bombers? Do you like football? Maybe we should go to a game some time. Would you like that? Should just you and I, maybe Darrel when he comes to visit, go to a football game?" He almost chuckled. "What do you think, Benji? Will Darrel still be a Blue Bombers fan, or will he suddenly think he should cheer for the Roughriders just because he lives in Saskatchewan?"

Benji didn't respond to any of his father's questions. He made no move to undress or put on his pyjamas. Walter moved closer to his son. "Look, Benji… I mean… You know, Benji…" He faltered for words. "Benji, we have to…" Benji stared at the floor. "It's late, or at least it seems like it must be late. You have to go to bed. I mean, you have to put on your pyjamas and go to bed."

Walter dropped to his knees in front of his son, who continued to stare down at the floor. Walter reached forward and took the bottom of Benji's T-shirt in his hands and began to lift. Benji lifted his arms and allowed the T-shirt to be pulled over his head. Walter dropped the T-shirt onto the floor and reached for the pyjama top. Benji glanced at his father's face for a moment as Walter pulled the pyjama top over Benji's head, then looked down again.

"Your pants, son," Walter said. He reached toward them. "Do you need help? Or can you do this?" Benji stood up and pulled off his pants and Walter helped him step into his pyjama bottoms. "Come here, son." Walter pulled Benji into a hug, nuzzling his face into Benji's neck. Walter stood up and kissed Benji on the top of the head. "Good night, son." He stepped toward the door. "Do you have a nightlight? Do you leave your light on all night? Should I leave the door open, so you have some light?"

Benji crossed the room to where the nightlight lay on the floor. He plugged it into the wall, creating a soft glow. Walter turned off the room's light, which allowed the orange glow to envelop the whole room. "Aren't you going to tuck me in?" Benji finally spoke. "Aren't we going to say some sort of bedtime prayers?"

Walter nodded. "Of course, I'll pray with you. Do you want to kneel beside your bed to pray? Or do you want to be under your covers?" Benji knelt beside his bed. Walter knelt beside his son. "Is there a special night-time prayer you say each night? Or do you just sort of, you know, pray about something? About what happened during the day? Or about what you wish might happen?"

Benji got off the floor. "Maybe I'll get under my covers instead." He crawled into bed and looked at his father. It took a moment before Walter realized Benji was waiting for him to pull the covers around his son. Walter covered Benji and then tucked the edges of the blanket tightly around him. "Good night, Benji," Walter said. He stood up and stepped toward the door.

"Aren't you going to pray?" Benji asked from under the covers. Walter came back and sat on the edge of the bed.

"For what should I pray? Is there anything you would like to pray about?" Benji's lips started quivering. Soon his whole body was convulsed by sobs. Walter lay down beside his son. He put one arm under Benji's head and pulled his son toward him. Benji rolled up against Walter and snuggled his head into his father's embrace, then slid one arm over Walter's body. Two deep breaths turned into rhythmic breathing and Benji's body relaxed into the bed.

"Oh God. What is going on around me? What do I do now?" Walter murmured into the orange glow of the room, then rolled onto his back and closed his eyes.

Chapter Nine

Elizabeth inhaled slowly, wiped her brow as she exhaled, then pushed her hair away from her face. She stepped from the hallway into the dining room where Jacob still leaned heavily against the table, his head resting on his arms. Elizabeth smiled involuntarily and paused to gaze at her son. The last remnants of the macaroni dish spilled from Jacob's bowl were pressed against his arms and stuck to his chin.

"If only life where always this peaceful, eh, little Jakey? Eat, sleep, play, some hugs." Elizabeth directed her quiet, calm voice across the room. "Okay, maybe an occasional bath too, just to remove the leftovers from your face and arms." Elizabeth went to the kitchen and ran warm water over a towel before she went back to the table.

Elizabeth lowered herself into the chair beside Jacob and eased him up. She used the warm towel to wipe while supporting Jacob's body. When the evidence of dinner was cleaned away, Elizabeth lifted him off the chair and snuggled his body against her own. Jacob let out a contented gurgle but never opened his eyes. He nuzzled his head deeper into Elizabeth's shoulder and neck while she placed one soft kiss after another on his forehead, cheeks, and chubby arms.

She carried Jacob to her and Walter's bedroom, bent over the bed to lay him down, then reconsidered. Instead, she reached for the quilt at the end of the bed and wrapped it around Jacob's body and went to the door leading outside. She turned the knob and pushed against the door with a foot. She stepped into the cool night air, glad that she thought of the quilt for Jacob. She glanced at the growing collection of cigarette butts near the doorway before sitting down on the bench beside the garage.

Elizabeth had barely had time to reach for her opal amulet and look up at the stars when the door opened and Anna stepped out. She lit up a cigarette and took a step toward the bench where Elizabeth was seated with Jacob. "Oops," Anna blurted, dropping the cigarette. "I didn't know you were out here. I didn't know you ever came out here, at least not at night."

Elizabeth smiled at Anna. "I think this is the first time I've come out here at night. I often sit here during the day to watch Jacob play in the sandbox." She looked at the sandbox and added with a quiver in her voice, "He's always safe in the sandbox. He smiles, he giggles, he laughs, nothing to worry about."

Anna sat down beside Elizabeth and put an arm around her back, with her other arm reaching around Jacob. She squeezed just enough to add another layer of comfort to Jacob's body, as it was sandwiched between his mother and Anna's bodies. "I wish I knew what to say, Elizabeth, or what to do."

Elizabeth pressed her head against Anna's arm in a return embrace. "Dear Anna, just saying that is a gift to me!" A tear formed and slid down Elizabeth's cheek. "You are so thoughtful, it's easy to see why Shelley enjoys being with you." Elizabeth looked into Anna's eyes and again pressed her head against Anna's arm.

"I'd ask you 'what should I do?' but that wouldn't be a fair question. I think you are asking yourself that same question about many things too. What should I do so that Walter notices I am alive, if dropping cigarette butts at his door isn't enough to get his attention?" Elizabeth looked Anna in the eyes again. "What should I do if I'm not sure whether I like to be with boys or to be with Shelley?" Anna pulled her arms away from Elizabeth and Jacob and crossed them in front of herself, staring into Elizabeth's face.

"You didn't sound angry, Elizabeth. First about the cigarettes and then about Shelley? You knew about the boys? You never said anything." Anna kept her eyes locked on Elizabeth. "Aren't you scared for my soul? Don't you want to save me from hell? From my bad choices?" Anna's voice remained level, hints of surprise, curiosity, and wonder highlighting her words.

Elizabeth smiled, first at Anna, and then up at the stars. "Would it help you if I were angry at you, Anna? Would that give you something to either act against, or to confirm your suspicions that parents just don't get it?" Elizabeth looked back at Anna.

Anna's eyes were wide open, and she shifted her whole body so she could look more directly into Elizabeth's face. "You know you're blowing my mind, right? You're a preacher's wife, a Bible teacher's wife. Isn't even just saying what you're saying to me a sin?"

"I used to think I knew everything there was to know about sin, Anna. I could list all of them, I'm sure, just to be certain I would avoid all of them. I used to 'pray without ceasing' that God would forgive my sins, that he would save my soul." Elizabeth paused. "Now I'm no longer so sure about that list of sins, whether or not all of them are actually even sins. Is being who you are a sin? It can't be! And as far as being saved…" Elizabeth's voice drifted off. "Right now trying to save Jacob is the most important thing in the world to me. His body, his love of life, his innocence, his safety, those are the things that need saving. And I have no idea how to do any of that." One tear snuck down Elizabeth's cheek.

She extended her arm around Jacob's back and laid it on Anna's knee. "Anna, you make up your own list of sins, but only if that helps you be good. I think you are an amazing, wonderful young lady. I already said you are kind. You are so much more than kind. Your thoughtfulness around the house, toward your siblings, to me, yes, even toward your dad… we are so lucky to have you with us. I want you to be healthy, to make healthy choices, to make choices that make you happy, that fill your soul with joy and love. I'm so busy being scared for Jacob, trying to figure out how to be somebody, I'm not even sure who or what, to Benji, to keep the house going. I know I'm a terrible cook and wish I could make better food." Elizabeth smiled as Anna shot her hand to her mouth to stifle a giggle.

Elizabeth squeezed Anna's knee before readjusting Jacob's body against her own. "Anna, all I know is I love you. You are wonderfully made in God's image, and I'm just as certain God loves you. And I think the same is true about Benji. I just wish he thought the same thing about me." She sighed. Anna leaned forward against Elizabeth's shoulder and wrapped one arm around Jacob's body.

"No one has ever said anything like that to me before." Anna looked up at the stars. "All I've ever heard is sin, hell, more sin, a hotter hell, and then more sin. No one has ever suggested I'm made in God's image—more likely that I'm an abomination." Elizabeth shifted an arm and pulled Anna close to her, securing her body against her own with a hug. Elizabeth reached up and ran her hand through Anna's hair.

"I've probably done that to you, Anna, and I'm sorry. I used to believe with my whole heart, soul, being, that God hated sin, and obviously sinners too if he was going to toss them into a fiery hell forever. I used to explain those ideas to others, to try and change people, to save people, to make them believe like I did. I'm sorry for all the times I have given you that message, either with words or looks." Elizabeth stroked Anna's forehead.

"I don't know what to believe anymore. I think I want to believe something. I want to believe that there is more to this story than just you, me, and Jacob sitting on this hard bench late at night," Elizabeth continued. "Look at those stars! That huge sky! Thinking that my mother, my brother, and my sister are somewhere up there fills my soul with love. I think that love is the only thing that will change any of us. But I also know that because I don't know how to keep Jacob safe, I want there to be something, someone who can. I want there to be a God who cares about people and keeps them safe. Sometimes it's pretty hard to hold onto that way of believing when life happens the way it does." Elizabeth shifted her gaze from the heavens to Anna's face and smiled. "Don't worry about what you believe or don't believe, Anna. God doesn't need us to know, to be certain, about anything. If there is a God, surely such a God doesn't love us for whether or not we've understood all the confusing things taught about him and then sorted out what is the right thing to believe or to reject."

Anna pressed herself against Elizabeth's shoulder and smiled back. "I wish you came out here at night more often, Elizabeth." Anna stood up, took Elizabeth's hand, pulled it toward her face and kissed it before kissing Jacob's arm too. "I like listening to you. I think you are a better preacher than dad. Maybe I would find something to believe in too with more talks like this. Good night. I have to work an early shift tomorrow, so I better get to bed." Anna opened the door and disappeared into the house.

Elizabeth's gaze followed Anna as far as possible, then she leaned her head back against the garage wall and smiled into the night sky. Without looking down, she adjusted the quilt, making sure Jacob's arms were snuggled inside the blanket. "Anna, dear Anna. Why on earth did we ever come up with the idea that we could make someone better by calling them sinners? You are a wonderful, delightful, beautiful person. You don't need to change anything about who you are," Elizabeth whispered to the stars. She reached up and felt the amulet against her chest and placed a hand over it. "Love, right, Mom? Your love saved us, even gave us life, but it couldn't stop the accident from happening."

Chapter Ten

"Elizabeth?" a whisper came from the door. "Are you outside? Are you out here somewhere?" Walter's voice was filled with worry. The door closed and footsteps crunched across the gravel. "Elizabeth? Please be out here."

"I'm on the bench, Walter," Elizabeth responded. "Here, beside the garage." She looked toward the corner of the garage, where she saw Walter peering around the yard. He hesitated a moment and then stepped around the corner, where he seemed to be waiting for an invitation to come closer.

Elizabeth motioned to the bench with her left hand, keeping her eyes on Walter's face. He waited a moment longer, and then, looking at the ground, sat down beside Elizabeth. He folded his hands in front of him and stole a glance at Jacob, then at Elizabeth. She was again looking up at the stars, deliberately taking one deep breath after another.

"You've never not been in the bedroom at night, Elizabeth. I was afraid. I didn't know where you were." He finally looked at her, then turned his body toward her. "Why are you out here? Why are you out here with Jacob? Shouldn't he be in bed?"

"Walter, you came outside to find me so you could scold me? To tell me how to take care of my child?" Elizabeth's voice was soft and clear. She looked at Walter, who tried to hold her gaze but soon looked down at the bench. "You said you were afraid. I'm afraid too. I don't know how to keep Jacob safe from Benji."

"But Benji is young. He doesn't mean…" started Walter.

"Walter, please listen to me. Let me finish, then you can say anything you want." Walter looked up for a moment, then looked at Jacob. "You don't want to hear about what Benji does to Jacob, about why I don't feel I can keep him safe. Because I can't keep my baby safe, I don't feel safe here either. You don't want to hear what I try to tell you about what is happening here."

Elizabeth looked up at the stars for a moment, then back at Walter. "I think you don't listen to either of your daughters either. There is much you could learn about how wonderful your daughters are, if you paid attention to them."

Walter sat very still. "I was afraid you might have taken Ja…" Walter started sobbing. "I don't know what I would do if you weren't here." His body shook with sobs. "When Agatha died, I almost died. I don't know how to be a father to my children, I need help. I need your help." Elizabeth put her hand on Walter's shoulder.

"Elizabeth. I don't know what to do differently. Anna told me to be a man, to be a husband, to be a father. What does that even mean? I heard that, and I don't understand it. It's not that I don't want to listen." Walter tried to steady the quiver in his voice. "Oh God, what do I do now?"

Elizabeth smiled at him. "Pray, Walter. Pray just like that. But don't stop there. Think about what you might do, think about what you can do. You might even try talking to me, try listening to me, to your daughters, and to your other son too. We all need you to love us. Love us in whatever ways you love people. Benji is hurting. He's hurting so badly all he knows how to do is to hurt back, trying to get even with the universe by getting even with whoever is within arm's reach. Unfortunately, too often it is Jakey who is within arm's reach."

"Get even with the universe? What does that mean?" Walter asked. "Are you trying to tell me that he is angry at God? Is that it? He's angry at God for taking his mother. Maybe he's angry at me for telling him it was God's will that his mother died and left him alone with his sisters and me. Do you think he's angry about Agatha's death?" Walter's voice showed that new ideas were beginning to flood through his mind. "And Anna? Is it the same thing with her?" Walter looked at Elizabeth, appealing for her to confirm these new thoughts.

"I think you are beginning to understand Benji." Elizabeth nodded while Walter was listing his questions. "I think you might want to have a few more conversations with Anna, to maybe find out a little more about what motivates her. Just love her too. And let her know you love her." Elizabeth rubbed Walter's shoulder, then opened her mouth wide with a yawn. "Oh Walter, this is late for me. But I want to hear you out. What else are you wondering?"

"I don't know if I know how to either talk to, or to listen to, my children. Maybe I don't know how to listen to anyone," Walter confessed. "How do I learn to do that?"

"Try it, Walter. Try to talk to Benji. Be honest with him. What do you see? Ask Benji what he sees."

"What if what he says scares me, Elizabeth? He said he hated you. He said you hate him, that you hit him. What do I do if he says that again?" Walter begged. "I don't know what to say to him when he says things like that."

"I heard him say those things too." Elizabeth's voice was a whisper. "I don't know what to do either, Walter. When he accused me of hitting him, that was new. That scares me more than him saying he hates me. I'm afraid I won't know how to protect Jacob, to keep my little boy safe." Elizabeth paused, took a deep breath, held it for a long moment and then exhaled. "I wonder if I should take Jacob away from here..." she looked at Walter.

Walter jolted upright. "Leave? What are you saying, Elizabeth? You would leave with Jacob? Leave me with the children? Leave me alone? You know you can't do that! Leaving your husband is a sin! It is strictly forbidden in the Bible! Elizabeth..." Walter was now standing in front of her, his voice rising in volume. His face was flushed, his whole body quivered. He stared down at Elizabeth, then at the ground, then up at the sky, uncertain of where to look.

"Walter, quit it! I am not your congregation. I am not asking you to preach to me. I am asking you to listen to me for a change." Exasperation poured from her voice. "You just said you didn't know how to listen to, to talk to someone. So learn! Here's your chance." Walter sat down again.

"What are you saying? What are you trying to tell me, Elizabeth?" Walter's tone was totally changed. His voice was quiet, although not quite calm.

"I'm telling you I'm scared, Walter. I love you, I love your children like my own. And I love Jacob as much as the other kids. And I'm scared about what is happening. Benji is so angry, and he doesn't know what to do with it. I don't know what to do either. I want you to know I'm afraid, and why I'm afraid, that's all." Elizabeth put her hand on Walter's knee. "I want us to find our way through this together. I need your help to keep Jacob safe. I don't want to do it alone. And I'll do whatever I can to work out whatever needs to be done for Benji. I don't want you to do it alone."

Walter slowly put his hand on top of Elizabeth's hand. He gave it a soft squeeze. "Together? Right, together. We're in this together."

"And now, maybe together we should take Jacob inside, put him to bed, and go to bed ourselves, dear," Elizabeth said, leaning forward and kissing Walter on the cheek. "We don't have to figure out everything tonight. We do have more time to find our way. And yes, we are in this together."

Chapter Eleven

Elizabeth yawned, stretched her arms, and rolled over in bed to smile at Walter, but he wasn't there. "What? Walter's up before me? What time is it?" she asked herself as she rolled over to look at the clock on the bedside table. "Eight o'clock! Oh my! No wonder Walter's not here. My goodness, I've never slept until eight." She swung her legs over the side of the bed and pulled her hair back from her face and tucked it into a quick roll at the back of her head. She changed out of her pyjamas and slipped on a pair of jeans and a hoodie.

Elizabeth stepped out of the bedroom toward the kitchen. She stopped when she saw Walter sitting next to Benji at the table. Walter's left arm was draped over the shoulders of Benji, who was putting the last spoonful of something into his mouth. Empty bowls sat in front of them. Walter looked up and smiled at Elizabeth. "Good morning. I thought I'd make some porridge for breakfast this morning. Benji and I just finished but there is more on the stove for you. I don't think there's enough for the girls. And I don't actually know if they'd eat it anyway if they knew I made it." He smiled again, rubbed Benji's shoulders, and stood up.

"Good morning. Thank you, I'd love some porridge. Good morning, Benji," Elizabeth said from the kitchen where she was emptying the last of the porridge into her bowl.

Benji dropped his hands from the table to his lap and kept his gaze directed at the floor. "Benji." Walter nudged his son's leg. "Remember?" He left his hand on Benji's knee.

"Morning," Benji whispered to the tabletop. Walter patted Benji's knee. Benji looked up at Elizabeth. "I'm sorry Eliz… Mo…" the words stuck in his throat. He looked down again.

Elizabeth sat down across the table from him. "Thank you, Benji. I love you, and we will all work together to find a way to make today a good day."

Benji lifted and turned his face toward Walter. "Can I go back to my room now? Please?"

"Get dressed, son, and have a good day. I have to leave for my school but will be home early today. Elizabeth, don't make supper. Tonight we will go out for a family meal to Chicken Chef. They have the best chicken and pizza in town!"

Elizabeth stared at him, her eyes wide open. "Going out? The whole family? Are you sure, Walter? I can make chicken, or pizza, or both. I'll send Anna to the store. Oh, she's probably already at the store. I'll call her and ask her to bring the ingredients we need when she comes home. She said she had to start early, so I think she'll be home early too." Elizabeth stood up.

Walter took her hands in his. "I think you have earned a day off, at least from cooking. I don't remember the last time our family ate out. Maybe when we did that preaching tour and had to move quickly from Hepburn to Saskatoon. But that wouldn't have been the whole family, just a few of us. Oh my goodness. I wonder if we have ever gone out to eat as a family."

"It's okay, Walter, really," Elizabeth interjected. "Restaurants are so expensive. I can try to make chicken the way they do at Chicken Chef. And I can try to make pizza too." She winced a little thinking about the last pizza she had tried making. She looked at the kitchen for a moment before turning her face back toward Walter.

Walter dropped her hands and lifted his to the sides of Elizabeth's face. He smoothed her hair with one hand. "I want to try to learn some different ways, new for me, to try and interact with my family. I don't think I know my own children." He leaned forward to kiss Elizabeth. "Maybe I don't even know my own wife." He took a small step backward. "And I want all of that to change. If I want that to change, I have to try to change too. Yesterday night really scared me, and I think I might be responsible for all of what happened. Please help me?"

Elizabeth took Walter's hands and squeezed them in hers. "Of course, my love. We agreed last night that we are in this together." Elizabeth kissed both of Walter's hands and then wrapped her arms around his waist. "What a gift you have given me this morning." Then she smiled. "And I'll be very happy not to cook supper today. I'm sure the kids will be super happy to have something other than macaroni and wieners for dinner too." Walter chuckled, kissed Elizabeth one more time, and then headed toward the door.

"I'll be home early. I hope you have a good, safe day." Walter closed the door behind himself. Elizabeth sat down at the table, looked at her bowl of porridge, and wiped at the tears that were forming at the sides of her eyes. "Thank you, Walter. Thank you so much. I don't know if I could have imagined a morning like this," she whispered to her bowl.

Chapter Twelve

"You're serious? Dad said that?" Anna queried. "He's taking the whole family out to Chicken Chef? What happened? Who died and left him some money? Did you finally smack him on the head, Elizabeth?" Anna laughed. "I'll be in my room. Need to tell Shelley I'm busy over dinner tonight and will have to see her later." Anna skipped toward the stairs and disappeared down them faster than usual, whistling as she went.

Elizabeth sat down on the floor beside Jacob, who was turning pages in a book. Every once in a while he would point at a picture on the page, identify a shape, a colour, an animal, or number before turning the page. "Too soon you are going to be in school too, Jakey. This will be a quiet house when that happens." Elizabeth picked up three books that lay on the floor near him.

Benji opened the door and stepped inside, mud on his face, his hands, his clothes, and his shoes. "Oh my goodness, Benji! What happened to you? I didn't notice you going outside, I didn't even notice the rain," Elizabeth declared, moving her gaze between her son and the sunny view through the window.

"It didn't rain. I used the garden hose to make the mud. It was awesome!" Benji exclaimed, leaving a trail of mud behind him as he stepped further into the house.

"Wait, please, Benji! I just washed the floor. I can wash that part again, but please, go back to the door and take off all your muddy clothes." Benji stopped, took another step forward, then stopped again. The muscles in his face twitched, his jaw moved from side to side. "I'll bring you a towel or some clean clothes. Of course, you will need to take a bath before dinner. Did your dad tell you we were all going out for dinner tonight? We're all going to Chicken Chef when your dad gets home. No macaroni for you tonight." Elizabeth smiled.

Benji stood still for a moment longer. "A towel, I guess." He turned around and retreated to the door where he proceeded to take off all his clothes and throw them in a pile. Elizabeth hopped up and dashed to the bathroom. She opened the linen closet and pulled out a large, dark-blue towel, remembering that was Benji's favourite colour. By the time she stepped out of the bathroom, a naked Benji was walking toward her. She took a step sideways to allow him to pass and handed him the towel.

"Here you go, Benji. This towel is so big you'll be able to wrap your whole body in it two or three times." Benji flipped the towel over his shoulder and went directly to the bathroom from where the sound of water filling the tub soon filtered into the dining room. "No fights, no mud thrown at me. It's a start," Elizabeth whispered into the air.

"I'll bring you some clothes, Benji." She got up again and went to Benji's bedroom. She stepped in, flicked on the light, and walked across the room to the dresser. "Underwear, socks, T-shirt and shorts, that should do," she muttered to herself as she pulled open one drawer after another to collect clothes for Benji. She turned back to the door and gasped.

Duct taped to the wall was Jacob's T-shirt from the previous day. Three headless Ninja Turtle toys lay on the floor directly in front of the T-shirt. Shreds of shiny paper lay scattered over the headless turtles. Elizabeth bent forward and saw the remains of what had been some of Jacob's Ninja Turtle card collection.

"And I thought we were having a good day," Elizabeth murmured. She leaned her head against the wall for a long moment, took a few deep breathes and straightened herself. "What do I do with this?"

Walter entered the house and shouted a greeting from the door. "Hello, everyone. Who's ready to go out for dinner?" His voice was more cheerful than Elizabeth had heard it for some time. "Hey, where is everyone? No one going to say welcome home to their dad?"

"I'm down here," Anna's muffled voice drifted up from her basement room. "Just let me know five minutes before we're ready to go."

Sonya dropped her book to the living room floor and ran to embrace Walter. "Hi, Dad! Chicken Chef! I'm going to love it, right?" She wrapped her arms tightly around her father's waist.

"I've never heard of anyone not loving it, sweetie." Walter laughed. He bent forward and gave Sonya a quick embrace. "Hi Jakey, where's your mom? You're reading all alone?" He disentangled himself from Sonya and took a few steps across the dining room before leaning forward and picking up Jacob. He tossed him into the air a few times, each toss eliciting more giggles. Walter dropped a kiss on Jacob's forehead and placed him back on the floor.

"Where's Elizabeth? Where's Benji?" Walter gazed around the room and then rested his eyes on Sonya.

"She was here a minute ago," Sonya responded. "She sent Benji to take another bath."

"What? Another bath? What does that mean?" Walter looked confused.

Sonya laughed. "He took a mud bath outside with all his clothes on. Mom said he needed to take a bath before you came home, before we went for supper." Sonya dropped to the floor, made faces at Jacob and crawled toward him. Jacob erupted in giggles and started crawling toward Sonya.

"Hi, Walter. I'm getting some clothes for Benji. I'm in his room. Can you come here for a moment?" Elizabeth called out.

Walter stepped into the hall and knocked on the bathroom door as he passed. "Hey, Benji. Good and clean now! I have a surprise for you this evening." Walter saw Elizabeth's face inside Benji's room and stopped. "What now?" He took three quick steps and extended his hands toward Elizabeth's shoulders, but then stopped when he saw her eyes welling with tears.

"What?" Walter bent to look into her eyes. "What?" he whispered again. She motioned with her head to the wall behind Walter. He turned to see what was causing the alarm for Elizabeth. "Jacob's T-shirt? Is that it? You think it is damaged or something because it is taped to the wall? Here, I can take it off." Walter turned toward the wall and reached out his hand. He stopped moving when he saw the pile of rubble on the floor.

"Are you bringing me some clothes or aren't you?" Benji's voice came from behind the bathroom door. He followed up his words with some loud, impatient knocks against the door.

"I'll bring Benji his clothes," Elizabeth said. She placed a hand on Walter's motionless shoulder, stepped past him, entered the hallway, and knocked on the bathroom door. "I'm putting your clothes just outside the door, Benji." She bent to place his clothes beside the door. The door opened, Benji stepped out, took the clothes and went toward his bedroom. He paused when he saw Walter looking at the pile of decapitated toys, then pushed past his father and entered the room.

"I was tired of those toys," Benji tried to sound casual, but looked nervously toward his father. Walter avoided looking at Benji and followed Elizabeth to the dining room where Sonya was playing with Jacob.

"Look! I'm a seal. Arp, arp, arp," came Sonya's voice from around the corner, followed by gales of laughter from Jacob. Elizabeth entered the dining room and saw Sonya flopping on the floor, her arms pinned to her sides, her face contorted into as pointed a face as she could create, and her mouth opening and closing, more like that of a fish than a seal. Jacob rolled onto his stomach and tried to imitate Sonya but only succeeded in laughing some more. A smile crossed Elizabeth's face.

Chapter Thirteen

Benji tried to slide closer to Anna, who was sitting beside him in the booth at Chicken Chef. Walter reached out an arm, dropped it to Benji's waist and pulled him close. Benji wriggled a little, but Walter's arm now draped around his shoulders made it clear escape was not possible.

"I've never been here before," said Sonya at everyone, smiling. She looked at a painting of a pastoral scene, her smile growing. "I love that picture," she added, then pointed at the photographs of the local museum hung on the wall. "When are we going to visit the museum? I've seen so many pictures of that windmill, but I've never actually seen it from up close. And do they really give you a ride in a wagon? Pulled by those Clyde's horses," she giggled, "they're called something like that." She was already pointing to the dessert counter, about to open her mouth again, when a server appeared at her side.

"Do you need another minute? Have you decided what you would like?" The voice was friendly, sweet, and soft in the quiet restaurant. By arriving at 5:00, Walter's family appeared to be well ahead of any evening rush.

"Uhm, well, a Combination One with eight pieces of chicken, a medium pizza, and a bottle of pop looks good to me," responded Walter. "Elizabeth, what do you think? Is that enough for five of us?"

"Actually sir, Combination One is for takeout only." The server blushed and looked at the menu. "But, if you look at family specials, there is an early-bird dinner, served until 5:30, that is almost the same. You get six pieces of chicken, a medium, two-topping pizza, large fries, large coleslaw, and a pitcher of your choice of pop, for only two dollars more than Combo One."

Walter looked at Elizabeth, around the table, and then at the photograph of the Family Special in the menu. Sonya was eagerly nodding. Anna smiled up at the server, who blushed some more and looked at her notepad. "We can each have a piece of chicken, a piece of pizza, some fries, coleslaw, and pop, and still enough for seconds for someone who wants more. I think that sounds good. Elizabeth?" Walter looked across the table.

"Sounds absolutely right. That should be enough for all of us. Plus, we are here, if we need something else, we can probably order something else too. Isn't that right?" Elizabeth looked at the server.

"Of course. I'll come back during your meal to see how the special is, if it is enough, or if you need anything else." She looked at her notepad and wrote down the order. "What kind of chicken would you like? Crispy or Original? Pizza toppings? And what flavour of pop would you like?"

"Crispy, please," blurted Sonya.

"Pepperoni and mushroom," added Anna.

"Dr. Pepper," whispered Benji, looking down.

"There you have it." Walter smiled at the server. "And maybe a water for each of us to start."

"I'll be right back with your waters," said the server before turning and going through the swinging doors into the kitchen.

Walter leaned back into the bench and cast his gaze around the table. He smiled at Elizabeth, then Sonya, glanced quickly at Anna, then he paused, looking at the top of Benji's head. Aside from requesting the pop flavour, Benji had not said a word and had not looked at anyone at the table since leaving the house.

"I have some pretty big news for all of you," Walter started. Elizabeth snapped her head up to look at Walter, who was looking at her and then Benji. "Girls, Benji, I don't know if you knew that I am booked to go to Saskatoon next week."

"Do we get to go with you? Will we get to visit Darrel and Marigold?" shouted Sonya.

"And what about Abbi?" Anna poked Sonya under the table. "Don't you want to see your little niece too?" Anna teased.

"And of course Abbi," Sonya added.

"Well, initially I was going to take Elizabeth along, just Elizabeth, so we could get a little mini-vacation. You know, something we haven't ever taken since we were married," Walter continued. Elizabeth tilted her head to the side, looking at him.

"Initially?" she asked. "What does that mean?"

Walter swallowed, took a deep breath, and swallowed again. "I called Darrel this afternoon, just before we left the house, and made this decision." All eyes turned to Walter. He coughed and looked at the kitchen door. "Where's that water?" He looked around the circle of faces one more time before continuing.

"Darrel and Marigold invited Benji to come for a short vacation, to spend some time in their home. School is out right now, at least for you kids, for another few weeks, so it is the perfect time for Benji to go." Benji's eyes grew wide; he wasn't sure if he should be excited or scared. "Darrel also said that there is a camp there, near Saskatoon…"

"For delinquent kids," interrupted Anna, laughing.

"Anna, what's that got to do with anything?" Sonya asked. Anna shook her head toward her sister while motioning her thumb toward Benji. Sonya's eyes grew wide for a moment before Walter continued. Elizabeth sat motionless, staring at Walter.

"Please, Anna. I want to find something special for each one of you, something special to enjoy for your summer vacation. You'll all be going back to school real soon. Anna, your final year of high school. When Darrel mentioned this, I thought this was a good fit for Benji. What do you think, Benji? Do you want to go to Saskatoon with me on Sunday? Spend some time with Darrel and Marigold? And, of course, Abbi too?" Walter tousled Benji's hair and looked at him.

"For how long will I go?" Benji asked.

"I think three weeks in total. One week at Darrel's place, one week at camp, and then another week at Darrel's place before coming home," Walter responded. The server returned with a tray of water glasses and set one glass in front of each person.

"Thank you." Elizabeth nodded to the server. She picked up her glass and was about to offer Jacob a drink when she noticed he had fallen asleep in his highchair. She stood up to pick him out of the chair. She hugged him to herself and then glanced across at Benji. He had been staring at her, but dropped his gaze the moment she looked at him.

"This is a big surprise indeed," Elizabeth said. "What do you think, Benji? Would you like to go to Saskatoon for three weeks? If that is too long for your first time away, I'm sure we can make it a shorter time."

Benji kept his eyes on his plate. "I think three weeks is good. I like Darrel. I like Marigold." Walter dropped his hand to Benji's knee and gave it a squeeze.

"Then it's settled. Tonight we'll enjoy our dinner. Look, here it comes, and then tomorrow Benji and I will get ready to go to Saskatoon."

Chapter Fourteen

"Good night, Benji," Walter said from the doorway. "Your night-light is plugged in. I'll leave the door open just a little. Sleep well. Tomorrow we'll pack what you need for your time in Saskatoon with Darrel and Marigold." He eased the door toward himself, leaving a small gap open. He turned and walked to the dining room with a self-satisfied smile on his lips.

Elizabeth sat at the dining-room table, a cup with only a few drops of coffee in it in front of her. She looked up as Walter dropped into a chair across from her. "What a day," he said. "Highs and lows with Benji, make that lows and then highs." Elizabeth sighed. "What? Aren't you happy that Benji will be in Saskatoon for a few weeks? You and Jacob will be safe!"

"Oh Walter, I don't know." Elizabeth dropped her head into both hands. "He's leaving, we're not resolving anything. So he goes to spend three weeks with his brother, with whom he feels safe. That part is good. And maybe he grows up some while there. But didn't you hear his response? 'I like Darrel and Marigold.' In some ways it feels like he's being rewarded for hating me." Elizabeth looked up, across the table at Walter.

"I thought you'd be so happy." Walter breathed hard. "So, now that he thinks he's going to his brother's place, you want me to tell him it's not going to happen?" He ran a hand through his hair. "I don't know what to say. I don't know what to do."

"I don't want to make it hard, or harder, for you. I'm grateful, honest I am, that you are thinking about what is going on here, thinking about how to help me be safe, how to keep Jacob safe. I just wish you would have discussed this with me first, rather than announcing it to me the same as to the kids. We were going to be in this together, remember?"

"Yeah, but isn't this together? You just said you and Jacob would be safer, didn't you? Isn't this the perfect way to get rid of him for three weeks?"

"Walter! I don't want to get rid of him!" Elizabeth almost shouted before clapping her hand over her mouth. "I'm exhausted, it's true. I took an afternoon nap a few days ago because I feel so worn out trying to deal with all of this. I slept in this morning because I'm still exhausted, but I want to learn what will work for him, for me, for us, when we are all together in the same place." Elizabeth gasped, and tears began to trickle down her cheeks. She swiped at them with the back of her hand before taking in a deep breath. "I don't know. Maybe it is the right thing to do. I just wish we had talked about our options and made a decision together." She shook her head, looking at her feet. "No, I don't want you to take the trip away from him now. You put him to bed, you know whether or not he's looking forward to going with you." Elizabeth lifted the cup to her lips, tried to take a sip, but found only the final cold drop.

"I tried," Walter said. "Honest, I want to learn to listen. I guess I'm not so good at that. I'm used to just making decisions about everything. I'm used to just knowing answers for everything, knowing God's will for all of us. That sort of thing." He looked across the table at Elizabeth and slowly inched his hands forward and took her hands in his. "I'm trying. I want to do better. I'll do whatever you say, whatever you want me to." He looked directly into her eyes.

"I don't want to tell you what to do," Elizabeth whispered. "Together, remember? Together means we talk, we argue, we beg, we cry, we might even pray together, but I'm not telling you what to do. And I don't want you to tell me what to do, either." She pulled one hand from under Walter's and stroked the back of his large, strong hands.

"Help me, then. I don't know how to do this," Walter begged. "You've told me that you're scared because you don't know if you can keep Jacob safe. The other night when you weren't in bed, when you were outside,

I was afraid I might already have lost you because I don't know how to keep you safe. Please believe me, Elizabeth. I want to do this right. I want to learn how to do this together." Walter turned his hands palm upward. Elizabeth smiled and placed her hands on top of his.

"Ok, of course I believe you. Obviously you had a plan in mind, you had the idea that taking Benji to Saskatoon, to be with Darrel and Marigold, was going to do something good for us. Right?" Walter nodded.

"So then let's try your plan. Tomorrow you help Benji pack what he needs for three weeks. Or rather, you and I help Benji pack what he needs. We prepare him together. I am there beside you when you explain what you expect from him. You were planning on giving him at least something to think about while away weren't you, Walter?" Elizabeth squeezed Walter's hands.

"Uh, sure. I can do that," Walter said. "What do you think I should say?" He looked into Elizabeth's eyes. She smiled and held his gaze.

"How about something about being kind to Abbi? About treating Abbi like she's his little sister and the same way that he should treat Jacob when he comes home again," Elizabeth started. "Maybe something about watching how Abbi behaves toward her parents, especially toward Marigold, and somehow using that as an example of how he might respond to me once he gets home. What else?"

"What kind of punishment should there be if he doesn't behave properly?" Walter asked.

"Oh, Walter." Elizabeth grimaced. "No punishment, no talk of punishment, please. Let's just aim toward what to do. I feel like all the kids know too much about punishment, too much about hell already. Let's keep it to being kind."

"But Elizabeth, the Bible is clear…" Walter started.

"Clear? The Bible is clear? Which part of it? The Old Testament says that disobedient children should be stoned to death. That's clear, yet who follows that command of God? What exactly is a parent supposed to do with that? Forgive your offenders seventy times seven, but God will never forgive sinners and send them to an eternal torment as punishment? What kind of God even says such things? Who finds that clear?" Walter stared in disbelief at his wife. "Please, whatever else you tell me, please don't tell me the Bible is clear."

"I've never heard someone argue that the Bible isn't clear unless they don't believe in the Bible. Do you even believe in the Bible, Elizabeth?" Walter's voice was incredulous.

"Believing in the Bible isn't what this conversation was supposed to be about, Walter." Elizabeth sighed. "We're working together to find a way to help Benji." She dropped his hands and looked into his eyes once again. "Can we deal with the Bible some other time? I don't know if we can figure that out tonight too." She took a deep breath.

"Okay," Walter responded. "Benji, we're working on the Benji problem. Right. Saskatoon. Talk to him together. Tomorrow." Walter leaned back, as far back as he could, and pulled his hands off the table to place them in his lap. "Do you want to pray together? Now, before we go to bed?"

"Oh, Walter, really? You want to pray, pray. Pray for us to do right by Benji tomorrow," Elizabeth clasped her hand.

"Maybe I'll just pray in bed," Walter said. He stood up and turned toward the bathroom. "I'm going to go to bed. Are you coming to bed too?"

Chapter Fifteen

Elizabeth sat on the bed beside Benji, an open suitcase between them. "You've packed your underwear, your socks," she paused, pointing at each item to count them, "that should be enough. You have three pairs of shorts… T-shirts, Benji, you need some T-shirts. How about five T-shirts? Choose your five favourite ones." She smiled at him. "Let me guess – the purple one with red stripes across the chest, the Winnipeg Blue Bombers shirt, the Winnipeg Jets shirt, and… oh yeah, the Elm Tree School one and… the dark-green one, it has something written on it too, but what?" she mused.

Benji rifled through the middle drawer of his dresser. He deliberately put aside each of the shirts Elizabeth had identified before pulling out an unmarked brown T-shirt, then a yellow T-shirt with the DHL Express logo in the center, then two more plain white ones. He turned and gave them to Walter who was standing beside him. "I need one or two more?"

"Two more, son," Walter responded, passing the four T-shirts to Elizabeth to fold and place into the suitcase. Elizabeth glanced at Benji, who was staring straight at her. "Dress clothes for church? What does he need for that? Oh," Walter's voice drifted, "that's right. Darrel and Marigold don't go to church." He turned to Benji, who had another T-shirt in his hands and had already pushed the drawer closed.

"Do I need anything special for that camp?" Benji asked.

"Oh, good, you remembered!" Elizabeth exclaimed. "You need a swimsuit or two, a beach towel, a sleeping bag, a flashlight, and I think that is it. Right? Walter, can you think of anything else?" She stood up. "I'll go get the sleeping bag and flashlight from the basement. You find some swimming shorts. There are a few beach towels in the bathroom towel closet. Choose any one you want Benji," Elizabeth said over her shoulder as she disappeared down the hall and then down the stairs.

Walter sat down on the bed. "Do you know where your swimsuit is, Benji? Do you have a swimsuit? Do you like swimming?" Walter looked across the room at his son, who was pulling open the bottom drawer of the dresser. "We should go swimming some time. I hear the town pool is really nice. There are actually a few pools right there in the same building." Walter smiled to himself.

"Here, Dad," Benji said, handing his father two pairs of brightly coloured shorts. "I think these are new. I hope they fit." Benji pulled the shorts back before his father could take them and held them up to his waist. "Looks about right." He tossed them back toward Walter.

"Try them on when you get to Darrel's place. If they don't fit, ask him to buy you some that do, and I'll pay him for them," Walter said, crumpling the shorts together and pushing them into a corner of the suitcase. "And a towel. Go choose one and bring it back to me, okay?"

Benji took a few steps down the hallway, disappeared, and reappeared a few moments later with a large purple towel in his hand. "I want the purple one. Purple is my favourite colour." He held it to his face, inhaled deeply, smiled, and handed it to Walter.

Walter took the towel from Benji, rolled it up, squeezed it into the suitcase, and closed it. "You don't think your mother will want to put that sleeping bag into the suitcase too, do you?" He looked toward Benji.

"She's not my…" Benji started then stopped and looked down. "I mean, I don't know what she'll want to do with that. It would be pretty stupid to put it in the suitcase. It's full already."

Walter shook his head at his son. "Benji, I think one of our conversations needs to be about kindness. Elizabeth is getting you your sleeping bag from downstairs, she's not putting it into anything yet." Then Walter sighed. "I guess we should also figure out what you should call her. Anna calls her Elizabeth, Sonya, Darrel, and Marigold call her Mom. What's the right one for you?"

Benji just stared at the floor. "If she left, I wouldn't have to call her anything," he mumbled under his breath. He darted a look in the direction of his father, wondering if his comment had been heard, but Walter was rifling through the suitcase again and scratching his head.

"So, do we have everything?" Walter looked up and asked.

Elizabeth reappeared at the top of the stairs with a canvas bag in her hand. "I put the flashlight into the sleeping bag, which is in this bag. I also put a sheet and a small pillow into this bag. I didn't think it would all fit into your suitcase, Benji. This will be your second piece of going-to-camp luggage," she said. "Okay, it looks like everything is ready. I'll go make some sandwiches for you to take along on the drive. Is there any kind of sandwiches in particular that either of you want?"

She looked from Walter to Benji, waiting for any suggestions. Walter glanced up at the ceiling. "Ummm, I think I would like some… do we have cheese? Some cheese and raspberry jam sandwiches." He looked at Elizabeth, who nodded a confirmation for cheese.

"We have two kinds of cheese, Walter. I'll make you one with each type of cheese. Or do you want more than two? And you, Benji? Any special requests from you?" Benji looked at the wall, then at his suitcase, then at Walter.

"Couldn't we just stop at McDonalds, Dad? Or some restaurant and get a hamburger? I'd only need one hamburger," Benji said. "We don't ever go to restaurants like other people. Why can't we just stop this once?"

"Your mother asked you about sandwi…" Walter started, then stopped. He looked at Elizabeth, shrugged, and raised his hands. "Just a moment, son," he said as he stood up and motioned to Elizabeth to follow him down the hall. "What do you think, Elizabeth? Should I make an issue of him ignoring your question? Should I tell him what kind of sandwiches he is going to get? Or could we stop at a restaurant?"

Elizabeth twirled a few strands of her hair in her left hand. "I hate to keep making a big deal out of everything he says or does… Maybe it is the easiest thing for today, just before you leave to let him have his way. It doesn't hurt to stop for a hamburger. When school starts there will be lots of sandwiches to have for lunches," she responded.

"You're sure? Do you want to send something, anything else, along? That way we could stop for a burger, but you've also sent something for us," Walter continued. "If we want him to learn to listen to you, to respect you, in time to like you, maybe this is where we start? I'll try to not make an issue out of everything too, but sometimes I just don't know what I should say or do. This is still difficult for me."

Elizabeth leaned forward and kissed Walter's nose. "You're wonderful, Walter! You're learning, you're trying. Thank you." Walter wrapped his arms around Elizabeth and lay his nose against hers. "I'll put some fruit in a bag. Sonya baked cookies a while ago. I'll get them from the freezer." Elizabeth kissed Walter on the lips, twisted herself out of his embrace, and went to the kitchen.

Walter returned to Benji's room. "Good idea, Benji. Stopping for a burger makes it easier for Elizabeth. She doesn't have to make us any sandwiches then." Walter patted the top of Benji's head. "Right, you're packed and ready to go. Now I have to pack my bag. I'll have a few more suits than you do." Walter laughed, tousled Benji's hair, and left the room.

Chapter Sixteen

Benji's laugh and Abbi's giggles drifted across the living room to the kitchen where Walter was sitting at the small table with Darrel and Marigold. The smell of coffee filled the small space. "I haven't heard Benji laugh so much, so freely, in I don't know how long." He smiled across the table, taking the mug of coffee from Marigold. "Do you have any milk?"

Darrel nodded. "He is so gentle with Abbi. Usually I won't let her out of my sight if she's playing with someone new. You know what I mean, right? Benji's not totally new, but mostly. She hasn't played with others too much since we moved to Saskatoon." Marigold passed a jug of milk to Walter, then handed a mug to Darrel before sitting down with her own half-full cup.

"Do you need milk?" Walter asked, looking at Darrel, then motioning the jug toward Marigold. Darrel shook his head, so Marigold took the jug and returned it to the refrigerator. "It's so good to see Benji smile. And to make eye contact when he talks. Even his shoulders look different here than when he's at home."

Marigold smiled across the kitchen into the living room where Benji was playing dress-up with Abbi and her dolls. "He seems totally comfortable, doesn't he? And this is a different Benji than the one you know at home?" Marigold looked at Walter. "What do you suppose it is that has changed him so suddenly?"

Walter's face tightened, and he bit down on his lip. "The obvious, at least to me, answer is that Elizabeth isn't here," he said to the tabletop. He looked up. "I don't want that to be the answer! But what else can it be? Right up to the moment we left he said things like 'she's not my mother,' and although he hasn't used the words in the past week, his eyes certainly tell her 'I don't like you.' Elizabeth knows it all too, and he doesn't even pretend to hide that."

Darrel reached for his father's hand and held it in both of his. "Wow, Dad, that can't be easy. Not for Elizabeth, not for Benji, or for you." He looked toward the two playing, giggling children and patted Walter's hand again. "So what happens next? I mean, when he gets back home in a few weeks?" Marigold put her hand on top of Darrel's and gave Walter's hand a squeeze.

"I've been praying about that for ages," Walter said. "I just haven't received any answers. I don't know what to do with Benji. I want to spank him every time he is mean to Elizabeth." Darrel and Marigold simultaneously gasped and pulled back their hands. "I won't do it!" Walter added quickly.

"Have you considered counselling for him? And maybe a few sessions with the whole family? You know that family therapy is available, right?" Marigold offered.

"I don't know if I can do that," Walter said. "The Bible says we should bring our problems to the Lord in prayer. Do you still know that hymn? 'What a friend we have in Jesus, all our sins and griefs to bear, what a privilege to carry, everything to God in prayer.' That one." Walter looked at Marigold and then at Darrel. "It seems like a lack of faith to go to a counsellor, as if Jesus isn't enough."

"Still? To this day finding help from a counsellor is a problem?" Darrel winced. "Oh, Dad, you use medicine when you're sick. Why on earth wouldn't you use a counsellor to help you, and your son who is seriously hurting, find some help? I mean, there have to be 'Christian' counsellors available in Steinbach by now, if them believing like you is important."

Marigold added, "And there are counsellors who specialize in grief counselling, family therapy, everything, anything counselling. I will pray that you will become open to using the help that is right before your eyes,

Dad." Marigold got up, reached for the coffee pot on the counter, and held it toward Walter. "Another cup?"

Walter nodded. "Yes, please. I'll get the milk." Walter stood up, stepped across the kitchen, and opened the refrigerator door. He stood there a moment with the cool air from the open door pressing against him, then he closed the door without taking the milk and turned toward the table. "Do you really think it's okay to talk to a counsellor? What about praying? What about trusting in God? The Bible says God won't let you down, won't give you more than you can handle." Walter sat down, reached for his coffee, and took a sip. He gagged and almost spit onto the table. "Yikes! No milk."

Darrel laughed. "Dad, think of a counsellor as milk. You can't handle the flavour of coffee without milk. It seems to me, to us, you can't handle Benji, or Elizabeth either, just as they are. Add a counsellor to help you find the flavour that works for all of you." Marigold cringed and rolled her eyes as Darrel spoke, and then smiled at him.

"Wow, Darrel. Nothing like turning milk into a counsellor." She laughed. "But seriously, Dad, you pray for healing, then go see a doctor or get medicine. You believe that is within God's will. You say you're praying to understand your son and your wife and your own situations, so why not take the answer God is putting right in front of your eyes?"

"Maybe." Walter nodded. "I'm sorry, I can't drink this coffee." He stood up and pushed his chair under the table. "I wanted to make it all the way home today, so I better get going." He walked to where Benji was waving a flamboyantly dressed doll in front of Abbi's extended reach and knelt beside him.

"Okay, Benji, it's time for me to leave for home. Darrel said that he or Marigold would bring you back home in three weeks, just before he has to start his university classes again, and you have to go back to school." Benji looked over to his father and let Abbi take the doll from his hands.

"Remember what we talked about on the drive here. Kindness. That's the one word I want you to think about and work at. Also, remember to listen to both Darrel and Marigold. They are going to be in charge for the next three weeks. Whatever instructions they give you, you listen carefully." Walter put his hands on Benji's shoulders. He looked into Benji's eyes, then pulled his son toward himself and enveloped him in a bear hug. Benji returned the hug and buried his face in his father's shoulder.

Marigold brought a brown paper bag to the front door of the house. Darrel came from the bedroom with Walter's suitcase and opened the door, stepped outside, and went to Walter's car. Darrel opened the back door and lay the suitcase on the seat. Marigold went to stand beside the driver's door.

Walter gave Benji one more squeeze, then stood up. "See you soon, son," Walter said. "Have a good time. Remember, be kind." He tousled Benji's hair and went outside. Benji didn't say a word to his father. He sat down on the floor across from Abbi again, picked up a bright-green doll dress and held it in front of Abbi's face. She giggled and handed the doll to Benji so he could change its clothes.

"I packed you a lunch, Dad," Marigold said, handing him the paper bag. "There are a few sandwiches, some cookies, and an apple. I hope that's enough." Walter hugged her and then turned to hug Darrel, who had come up beside them.

"Those are my favourite cookies, Dad." Darrel smiled. "I almost stole them from your lunch when I saw Marigold put them in there. Drive safely." Walter lowered himself into the driver's seat, closed the door, and rolled down his window. "Most of all, don't worry about Benji. He's going to be fine. He's going to enjoy the parks we will go to here in Saskatoon, the camp will be something new and wonderful, and then more good times here with us before we deliver him back home." Darrel reached into the window and patted Walter's shoulder.

"Thanks, son. Thanks, Marigold. This is a huge gift to us," Walter acknowledged. "I hope it is a good time for Benji. And I hope the time also allows me to have some good conversations with Elizabeth about what we might do once he comes home again." Walter looked up at Darrel and Marigold. "I know, I know. I'll talk to Elizabeth to find out what she thinks about counselling. Maybe there is a place for a counsellor for Benji." He offered another large smile. "Maybe some counsellor has an opening for me too."

Chapter Seventeen

(Three Weeks Later)

Benji slammed the car door, ran to the house, left the house door ajar upon entering, and ran directly to his room without saying a word to anyone. Elizabeth came out of the kitchen, Sonya looked up from the table where she was drawing, and Walter put down his newspaper and stood up. Darrel came in through the open door a moment later, Benji's suitcase in one hand and his sleeping bag draped over his shoulders.

"Hi everyone, he's home!" Darrel exclaimed with a grim frown on his face. He set the suitcase down, dropped the sleeping bag on the floor, shrugged, and pointed toward Benji's bedroom door. He was about to say something when Sonya rushed to him and wrapped him in a hug.

"Welcome home, Darrel. I miss you so much. Can I come up for a visit next year?" Sonya asked. With each statement, she pressed herself into his chest, then withdrew to look up into his face.

"Hi, Darrel. I'm glad you made it here safely. How was the drive?" Elizabeth came from the kitchen to give Darrel a hug. "And Benji, what's going on?" She looked quizzically down the hall toward Benji's closed bedroom door.

"Hi, son," Walter said. "Long drive, huh? Where did Benji go?" He looked around the room. "I'm sure I saw him come in."

"Hi Dad, yeah, you saw him come in. Although he made it to his room in record time. I have no idea what is going on with him. Can I have something to drink? We haven't stopped for over three hours and I'm parched!" Darrel left Benji's luggage on the floor and took a seat at the table. "Where's Anna?"

"What would you like, Darrel? Coffee? Milk? Water?" Elizabeth went back into the kitchen. "I can make you some coffee, but it will take a few minutes." Elizabeth waited for Darrel's response.

"Water's good. Thanks," Darrel said.

"Anna went out for coffee with Shelley after work. They both got off work at eight-thirty this evening. I imagine she'll be home soon." Elizabeth brought a glass of water to Darrel, then sat down across the table from him.

"Walter, come sit down with us," Elizabeth invited. "Let's hear some stories, Darrel, about Benji's time with you." Walter turned his blank stare from Benji's suitcase to the table and took a seat beside Elizabeth. He smiled across the table at Darrel.

"I don't know how to describe the past week," Darrel started, "especially in comparison to the first week." Sonya dropped into a chair beside Darrel.

"What do you mean? Dad said he thought Benji really liked being at your place," Sonya said.

"For sure, those first few days when Dad was still there. In fact, the whole first week, he was the Benji I knew when he was young," Darrel explained. "He laughed, he played with Abbi, he offered to wash dishes, he offered to mow the lawn, he followed every instruction, request or suggestion we made. We couldn't have asked for a friendlier, more cooperative kid. It was such a delight to have him with us."

"So that sounds very positive," Walter offered. "It gives us a standard that we can hold him to. We can remind him of his excellent attitude and behaviour if he continues acting like he did before he left for Saskatoon. Right, Elizabeth?" Walter looked at Elizabeth, who hadn't taken her eyes off of Darrel.

"It sounds as if something is about to change in your story," Elizabeth ventured. "What happened in week two, or in week three?"

"Week two, well, that is when he went to camp, remember?" Darrel looked from Elizabeth to Walter. "I don't know what all they do, but they keep doing stuff every day for a week. It sounded like a week of heaven to me." Darrel smiled at Sonya, and then looked back at Walter and Elizabeth.

"On Monday morning, just before we dropped Benji off at the camp, he sounded super excited about going. For each activity I said they had, he cheered and said 'I love that' and then cheered again,' Darrel continued. When we arrived at the camp, I found the welcome person, and that guy took Benji's suitcase and away they went. Benji turned to wave at me with a huge smile and said 'See you Saturday' and walked away. We didn't hear a thing all week because who does hear from someone at camp?"

Darrel swallowed and his eyes grew dark. He let go of Sonya's hand and folded his hands in front of himself on the table. "The following Saturday when I arrived, I hardly recognized him. Or at least his face. His eyes were red, his hands were stuffed deep into his pockets, his knees were pressed together and when that greeter guy, I think his name was Fred… ahhh, Fred… Fred something-or-other, put his hand on Benji's shoulder and said goodbye, Benji burst into tears."

Elizabeth's and Walter's eyes grew wide. "Like, what do you mean, Darrel?" Sonya asked. "Was he so sad to leave because he had such a good time?" Sonya looked at her parents but didn't recognize the expression on their faces.

"I don't know," Darrel said. "He was so excited about arriving, I assumed he'd have a good time there. But I couldn't figure out his response to leaving. And then we got back to our place." Darrel dropped his chin to his chest for a moment before looking up again. "I thought we'd have another week of playing, laughing, helping, whatever. Lots of good stuff. But that didn't happen. Just like here, he went straight to his room and wouldn't come out unless we called him. And sometimes even then he didn't want to come out." Darrel looked perplexed. "After a few days of that is when I called you, remember? I knew something was wrong."

Elizabeth looked at Walter. "We talked about maybe getting him to see a counsellor once he got back. Your phone call made a counsellor sound like a really good idea."

"What's a counsellor going to do for him?" Sonya asked. "Shouldn't we just pray for him? Or pray about this first?" She looked at her parents, not understanding the conversation happening around her.

"Marigold tried to coax him out of his room, and sometimes, when I was standing outside his door with her, I could swear I heard him banging his head against his bed, or the floor, or something," Darrel went on. "Even Abbi's invitations to come out and play didn't get a response. Mostly he just stayed in his room. When he did come out, he didn't make eye contact, he didn't say anything, he wasn't hungry. He just wasn't himself anymore," Darrel finished.

"When you told us how he was behaving, I wondered about what might have happened at camp," Elizabeth said. "I mean, sometimes stuff happens at camp. An older, or bigger camper, bullies a younger one. Or he sees something. With all those activities maybe someone had an accident, and he saw someone get injured. I don't know. But it sure sounds like something happened."

"It was very thoughtful of you to call the camp to see if something happened. Did the person you talked to notice anything that might explain the changes in Benji?" Walter's eyes appeared hopeful with his question.

Darrel nodded his head. "When I called the camp, the same guy who first greeted Benji, and then came to say goodbye to him when I arrived, answered the phone. Fred Pinkerton was his name! I asked Fred if he had noticed anything about Benji while he was at camp. Fred said he hadn't seen any changes at all, that he was friendly, active, and participated in everything the camp offered. It just didn't make any sense at all." Darrel looked at Walter, then at Elizabeth. "From what Fred said, and from what we experienced that final week, well, it just couldn't have been two more different kids. I don't get it. I was so busy getting ready for my classes, that well, I just didn't push trying to get him out of his room or to go play."

"Now what?" Walter asked Elizabeth. "He's in his room. I, we, we need to go say hi, to welcome him home. Let's give that a try. Plus, it's sort of late. He probably just needs to get a good night's sleep."

"And speaking of sleep, I need that too," said Darrel. "I'm going to take my usual bed downstairs." He got up, swallowed the last few mouthfuls of water, and set his glass on the kitchen counter. "I'll see you in the morning. Good night. Still want to come next summer, Sonya?" Darrel smiled at Sonya, who had also gotten up and was heading to her bedroom.

"Yes, I want to come!" exclaimed Sonya. "But I just want to hang out at your place. I don't like all those outdoor activities. If they had swimming, then I'd want to go, but that other stuff you said, nah, not for me." She smiled. "Good night Darrel, good night, Mom and Dad." Sonya closed her bedroom door behind her, leaving Walter and Elizabeth alone at the table.

"Oh my, Walter, how confusing this is," Elizabeth started, fingering her opal amulet. "Of course, you are right, we need to go welcome him home. And I think you're right too, he needs to get a good night's sleep. Sometimes they just don't get to sleep enough at those camps because there is so much going on all the time. Not getting enough sleep can leave someone upset, but this sounds like something more than just being upset." She stood up and gave Walter a nudge.

"Yeah, a good night's sleep. Tomorrow we can figure out whatever else we have to figure out, right?" Walter took Elizabeth's arm, stood up, and the two of them walked side by side down the hallway to Benji's closed door. Walter tapped on the door and waited for a response. A few moments later, he tapped again, looked at Elizabeth, and shrugged. "Do you think he fell asleep?"

Elizabeth nodded. "Maybe." She reached for and turned the door handle. The door slid open, sending a shaft of hallway light into the darkness. From the door, Elizabeth and Walter could make out Benji's form, already under his covers, his face turned away from the doorway. They looked at each other, looked at Benji again, and then pulled the door closed, leaving it slightly ajar to allow some light into the room.

"I guess that answers that question," Elizabeth whispered. "And after hearing Darrel's confusing story, I'm tired enough to go to bed too." Walter nodded in agreement, flicked off the dining room light as they passed it, and entered the bedroom right behind Elizabeth.

Chapter Eighteen

(Three weeks later)

"Could I please speak to either Walter or Elizabeth Rempel?" the voice at the other end of the phone asked.

"This is Elizabeth. May I ask who's calling?" Elizabeth responded. She pushed hair out of her face with one hand and cocked her head to hold the phone against her other ear.

"Oh hello, Mrs. Rempel. You are Benjamin's mother, yes?" There was a slight pause on the line, but not long enough to allow either a confirmation or a denial. "I am the secretary at Benjamin's school. The principal is wondering if you, or preferably both you and your husband, have time to meet with her in about twenty minutes. The principal, Ms. Elgin, says it is quite urgent, and equally urgent that both parents attend, if at all possible."

Elizabeth moved the phone from her ear to in front of her face and stared at it for a moment before moving it closer to her face again and saying, "I know I can be there in twenty minutes. I'm not sure about Walter, but I'll check with him to see if he can come too. This is very short notice, you know." She looked at the phone again, confusion furrowing her brow.

"Alright. Twenty minutes, then. You can park in the visitors parking and enter through the front door. The office is immediately to your right when you come in. See you in twenty minutes." The call ended abruptly, leaving Elizabeth holding a silent phone to her ear.

Elizabeth shook her head a few times and then pressed Walter's number into the keypad of her phone. She heard the phone ringing on the other end as she put on shoes and reached for a sweater. The answering service gave her permission to leave a message. "Walter, this is Elizabeth. It's 1:40 and Benji's principal wants to meet with us at 2:00 this afternoon. Yes, that's in twenty minutes. The secretary only said it was urgent, nothing else. I'm going to walk. Please, if you can, meet me at the school office as soon as possible. Jakey is still with Anna, so he's in good hands." Elizabeth ended the call, pulled on her sweater, and stepped out the door.

"Urgent," Elizabeth mused out loud. "Hmmm, Benji has certainly been out of sorts at home since coming back from Saskatoon, but he's been out of sorts at home quite a bit. No teacher or principal has ever said anything about him misbehaving before." She gasped as a thought occurred to her. She held a hand to her mouth and almost broke into a run. "Oh my, he must be hurt. Something terrible must have happened at school and he must be badly hurt." She slowed down again when she realized her fear was probably unfounded. "Surely if he had been hurt she would have said something over the phone and asked us to come immediately, not in twenty minutes. Oh dear. Benji, what is happening now?"

Elizabeth was entering the school yard when she saw Walter's car pull to a stop in a visitor's parking space. He got out of the car, his face flushed, his eyes showing fear. He ran up to Elizabeth and panted out, "I heard your message right after my class and came immediately. What is going on?" Walter put one hand on Elizabeth's shoulder and then turned to walk with her.

"I'm so glad you could make it. The secretary sounded quite alarmed, but not willing to say anything on the phone. I'm so worried," Elizabeth told Walter. "For a few moments I thought he must have been hurt, but then making an appointment for two wouldn't have made any sense, right?" Walter nodded his agreement and opened the door, allowing Elizabeth to enter the school in front of him. "There," was all she said as she pointed to where the secretary had instructed her to go.

"Hello," the secretary greeted them with a smile. "How may I help you? Are you here to pick up a student?" She reached for a phone. "In whose class is your child?"

"Ah, well, Benji is in Mr. Klassen's class. But we're actually supposed to meet with the principal for something urgent," Walter explained while Elizabeth nodded. The secretary's expression changed in an instant. Her eyes narrowed, and her smile was replaced with a stern frown.

"Please take a seat. I'll let Ms. Elgin know you are here." The secretary picked up the phone and tersely barked into it, "They're here," and hung up. "Go ahead, take a seat. She'll be out as soon as she can." Before they had a chance to sit down, a door down the hall opened and footsteps approached.

"Hello, I'm Ms. Elgin." The woman smiled as she extended her hand first to Elizabeth and then to Walter. "You must be Walter and Elizabeth Rempel, Benjamin's, I believe you call him Benji, his parents. Please follow me." She wore flat-soled shoes that made soft patting sounds against the floor with each step. Walter and Elizabeth walked behind her, still quieted by the shock of being called to the office.

Ms. Elgin held the door open for them to enter, waved them to two chairs at a round table, and then seated herself in another. She smiled again before she started. "I apologize for the possible surprise, or shock, with the request for an urgent meeting without giving you more details. First of all, I want to assure you that Benjamin is physically safe, nothing has happened to him. He is not hurt."

Walter noticeably exhaled and allowed his shoulders to relax. Elizabeth took a deep breath and held her hand to her chest. "So that is the good news, but clearly something did happen. Something urgent," Elizabeth commented.

Ms. Elgin nodded. "Indeed, yes, something that is quite unusual at our school for someone Benjamin's age." Ms. Elgin pushed her chair forward and rested both arms on the tabletop. "Benjamin was exposing himself to the girls in the girls' bathroom." Walter and Elizabeth gasped. Elizabeth shot both hands over her mouth.

"I'm sorry, there is no gentle way to tell you what happened," Ms. Elgin said. "But now we need to talk, not just about what happened, but to somehow try and figure out why it happened. Although I've been here only a year, I've read Benjamin's file, and in all the years he has been here, never, never, has there been any sort of trouble. He has never misbehaved in any way, nor given any indication that he might even be capable of, or interested in, exposing himself to the girls." Ms. Elgin paused.

Walter's cheeks and forehead turned crimson, then he stammered out, "I... I...really don't... don't... understand." His eyes fell.

Ms. Elgin continued, "Can you think of anything, anything at all, from the past month, few months, that might somehow be linked to this? It may not necessarily look the same, but has he shown an interest in anyone else's body? Has he asked questions or made comments that seemed more than just normal childish curiosity? I know it is normal for children his age to wonder about and ask questions about their bodies, the opposite gender's bodies, sometimes they play at..." her voice trailed off, inviting a response, indicating there was no shame awaiting the response.

Elizabeth looked directly into Ms. Elgin's face. "I'll tell you two things that happened in our home over the past few months, and then a confusing story that also took place this summer." Elizabeth repositioned herself in her chair.

"How long ago, Walter, did Benji undress Jacob and tape him to the wall?" Elizabeth looked at Walter, then continued before he could respond. "Jacob is Benji's younger brother. We came into the room to see Jacob without a shirt, with his pants and underwear pulled down to his ankles, duct taped to the wall. Benji was standing across the room from him, so it was not clear what was happening. Benji claimed that Jacob had wanted to play Ninja Turtles and wanted to be rescued from some danger. Benji was going to rescue him. Forcing Jacob to undress to play had not happened before."

"We dealt with that, though," Walter interrupted before Elizabeth continued.

"Not much later, again in Benji's room, we found Benji had duct taped Jacob's T-shirt to the wall, had ripped the heads off of some Ninja Turtle toys, and shredded Jacob's Ninja Turtle cards." Walter nodded. Elizabeth looked at Walter for a moment, then added, "We didn't think it was actually directed so much at Jacob as at me. Benji has had some difficulty accepting me as Walter's wife, as his stepmother, since his mother, Agatha, died.

We're trying to figure that out. But how could this be related to Benji not liking me? We're trying to figure out whether he needs some counselling, or perhaps we all need some family therapy."

"Those are the two incidents in your home. You mentioned that there was a confusing story from this summer too?" Ms. Elgin inquired, leaning forward.

Walter cleared his throat. "I brought Benji to Saskatoon to spend three weeks with my older son, Darrel, who lives there. Darrel told us that during the first week Benji was there, it was the same old Benji he knew before Agatha died. He laughed, he played, he helped out with household chores. He was a regular, happy kid. Then in the second week he went to an outdoor activities camp. He arrived at the camp very excited about all the activities. Then, a week later, when Darrel returned to pick him up, Benji had changed. The final week in Saskatoon he hardly left his room. He appeared miserable. And quite frankly, that is how he has been since coming home. He spends most of the time in his room. When he comes out, he doesn't make eye contact, he's quiet, he doesn't even insult Elizabeth or make comments wishing she wasn't his mother anymore." Walter looked over at Elizabeth. "Does that sound right? Am I missing anything?"

Elizabeth shook her head. "No, you're not missing anything. Oh, maybe one thing. Darrel did say he called the camp to ask if they had noticed anything about Benji, if they had seen him change from being excited about being there to being angry and lost. Darrel spoke to some camp staff person who knew Benji, and that person said there had been no problems." Elizabeth took one of Walter's hands in hers. "We just keep wondering if all of this acting out, in all these different ways, is just him trying to deal with his mother's death, his father's remarriage, and how much he doesn't like me or his little brother."

"We've talked about finding a counsellor for Benji," Walter interjected. "It sounds to me like that might be more necessary than ever." Walter looked at Elizabeth, then back at Ms. Elgin. "I don't know. Do you, at the school, have a counsellor? Or can you recommend one to us, because frankly, we don't know any, and I wouldn't even know where to begin looking for a good one."

"What do you think, Ms. Elgin? Is there a connection between what he was playing with Jacob and this bathroom incident? Or is the acting out of something that clearly is bothering him part of this? Although, if he's really angry at me, or really angry at having a younger brother, exposing himself doesn't really make any sense to me. Does it to you?" Elizabeth looked to Ms. Elgin for a response.

"Oh dear, it is all so complicated, isn't it?" Ms. Elgin responded. "I wish I could say 'yes' or 'no' to your questions, Ms. Rempel, but I can't." She turned from Elizabeth to Walter. "I think your desire for a counsellor is a very good, and a very wise one, Mr. Rempel." Walter nodded.

"And to your question about a school psychologist, that one I can answer with a 'yes.' It seems I already have your consent to complete a referral, which is what I was going to ask of you at this meeting. I have the referral documents ready in my desk, because like you, I believe that counsellors can be an invaluable resource. Sometimes they can find a way into a student's story that others can't, and suddenly so much about what they are doing, or ways in which they are acting, make more sense." Ms. Elgin opened a side desk of her drawer and pulled out a large manila envelope. She pulled out two documents and placed them in front of Walter and Elizabeth.

"Thankfully our school district does provide a variety of personnel with varied expertise, as we try to meet whatever needs our students have. We have many good teachers, many good resource teachers, to help those with reading or math difficulties. But those are far from the only difficulties our students have. Here, let me explain the referral process and what will happen next."

Chapter Nineteen

"See you next week, Benjamin." Earl Tilitson waved as Benji stepped out of his office door. "Excuse me, Ms. Rempel, could I have just a few moments of your time, please?" he added when he saw Elizabeth through the open door.

Elizabeth nodded to the counsellor before addressing Benji. "Please wait for me here, Benji. I'll see what your counsellor wants, and then we'll head home." Benji didn't look up as he took a seat in the waiting room. Elizabeth walked toward the door, looked back at Benji, then entered the office. It was spacious, with a variety of chairs, loungers, and cushions on the floor, with a desk in the corner and three shelves against the one windowless wall filled with books, baskets of toys, drawing supplies, games and items Elizabeth didn't recognize. She stood in the center of the room and looked at the counsellor.

Earl motioned toward a seat. "Please take a seat, Ms. Rempel. I won't take much time, I promise. You will be able to have Benji home very soon." Elizabeth sat down on the nearest chair while Earl walked toward her and sat on the chair closest to where she was. "I just want to make sure you know that I have read the referral, the information from the school. No problems before, an out-of-the-ordinary event at school, and the background information you and your husband provided. In addition, I want to invite you to ask me any questions that come to your mind at any time while I'm seeing Benjamin. Often parents wonder what a school psychologist is doing, saying, asking, and while respecting client confidentiality, one of the stated goals by both you, as his parents, and the school, is to develop collaborative strategies to work with your son. So, that means we will have occasional conversations and dialogues about strategies to try and then later debrief about their effectiveness. How does that sound?" Earl smiled at her.

Elizabeth smiled back. "This is all so new to me, but yes, it does sound good. I'm particularly grateful for any conversations and suggestions you might have for what I might try at home with Benji. I've been worried about him for some time, as well as for my youngest son, Jacob. We need to find better ways to live together in safety." She swallowed. "How soon will you have some ideas about what is going on with Benji?" Elizabeth's desperate desire for change was evident in her voice. "I'll try anything to make Benji happy, and to keep Jacob safe." She looked at the clock on the wall and stood up. "I do need to get home now. But is there anything else I need to know before going?"

"No. Thank you," Earl said. He got up and walked to the office door, opening it for Elizabeth. "See you next week, Benji." He waved toward Benji as he stood up. Benji didn't look up and didn't return the greeting; he just waited to follow Elizabeth out of the door. They walked in silence to the car, where Benji got into the back seat, leaned his head far back against the headrest, and closed his eyes. Elizabeth slid in behind the wheel and started the car.

"Benji, do you want anything on the way home? A drink of some sort? A milkshake?" Elizabeth looked at him in the rear-view mirror. Benji kept his head pressed back and his eyes closed and offered no response. Elizabeth waited another moment, then started the car and headed for home. She drove slowly, alternating her glances into the rear-view mirror to make sure Benji was alright and then at the street. The town was small enough, the traffic light enough, that she arrived home without incident in a matter of a few minutes.

The moment Elizabeth turned off the car, Benji picked up his backpack and got out to enter the house. By the time Elizabeth could follow, he was in his room with the door closed. Sonya got up from the table where her schoolbooks lay open in front of her. "Hey, Mom," Sonya greeted.

"Hi, Sonya," Elizabeth said, returned the greeting. She hung the car keys on a key hook near the door and entered the kitchen. "Want to help me with supper, dear?" Elizabeth opened the door to the refrigerator and looked at the contents. Sonya pushed her books into a pile, picked them up, and placed them in the corner of the dining room.

"It's time I learned to cook, right?" Sonya smiled and entered the kitchen. She stood beside the refrigerator, alternating looks at Elizabeth and the fridge's interior. "What are you thinking, Mom?" Elizabeth extended an arm around Sonya's shoulders.

"Well, let's see," Elizabeth started. "We've got lettuce, tomatoes, some cucumbers, and… maybe that's it. Will you put together a salad? I'll cook up some spaghetti and make a hamburger and mushroom sauce. How's that?" Elizabeth took a package of ground beef from the refrigerator and placed it on the counter beside the stove.

"Delicious! Except for the mushroom part," Sonya groaned. "It has to be mushroom? Even Anna doesn't like mushroom stuff. What about you make it with some sort of tomato sauce?" Sonya moved the vegetables she had gathered for the salad to the sink and began to wash them.

Elizabeth laughed as she handed Sonya a cutting board, a knife, and a large glass bowl. "Here, you put the salad stuff in this bowl, and I'll find some tomatoes to make the sauce instead of some mushrooms. Thanks for reminding me that I'm probably the only one in the house who likes mushrooms." Elizabeth patted Sonya's head as she stepped around her and went back to the refrigerator.

Sonya finished washing the vegetables and began cutting the tomatoes and cucumbers into small pieces before tossing them into the glass bowl. She tore the lettuce into small pieces, then used a spoon to mix them all together. "What kind of dressing are we having? Is there something in the fridge, or do you want me to make one?"

"Your choice, sweetie," Elizabeth said, keeping her focus on the frying pan where the ground beef was beginning to sizzle. "There are two or three different dressings in the door of the fridge, but if you'd rather…" She was cut off by the sound of the fire alarm screaming in the hallway near the bedrooms. She moved the frying pan from the heat and stared frantically around the kitchen then dining room. "Where's Jacob? Sonya, where's little Jake?"

Elizabeth was already entering the bedroom hallway before Sonya could respond. "Anna's got him in the backyard. They're playing something out there. He's fine." Smoke was coming out from under Benji's door as well as from the opening at the top.

"Benji! Benji, are you okay?" Elizabeth shouted, reaching for the door handle. She turned the knob and yanked open the door, allowing even more smoke into the hallway. She coughed, lifted the top of her shirt up over her mouth and nose, and entered the room. She attempted to protect her eyes from the smoke with one hand while looking around the room for Benji as well as the source of the smoke.

Benji was sitting naked and motionless in the middle of the floor with a garbage can in front of him. Flames were still dancing around the inside of the garbage can but the amount of smoke coming out was diminishing. Benji stared into the garbage can, tears streaming down his cheeks. "Benji, what's happening? What's burning?" Elizabeth went over to the bedroom window and pulled it open, coughing again when she turned back into the room.

She grabbed a pair of Benji's jeans that had been tossed onto the floor, wrapped them around the garbage can, and held it as far from her as she could and ran to the bathroom. She put the still-flaming garbage can into the bathtub and turned on the faucet. Water, smoke, steam, hissing, and crackling all mixed in the bathroom around her. Soon it was steam and water pouring into the garbage can and then only the running water. Elizabeth turned off the water, dropped onto the floor, and leaned her back against the wall just as the screaming smoke alarm went silent.

"Mom? Mom, are you okay? What was that fire?" Sonya asked from the bathroom doorway. She inched into the bathroom and leaned over the bathtub. "Is that underwear? Why was Benji burning his underwear?" Sonya looked at Elizabeth. Elizabeth swiped at her hair with her right hand, then sat up enough to look into the garbage can.

"You're right, Sonya, that is underwear," she said, then dropped back against the wall. "I'm sure if I could think of any reason for burning underwear, I'd tell you, Sonya. I don't get it. I have no idea why Benji would do this." Sonya sat down beside Elizabeth.

"Hey, what's going on in here?" Anna came barging into the house with Jacob on her hip. "Elizabeth? What are you doing in the bathroom?" Then Anna smiled. "So this time the fire didn't happen in the kitchen, eh?" She put Jacob onto the floor and he came bouncing into the bathroom and dropped himself into Sonya's lap. He looked up as if expecting to be told why they were all sitting on the bathroom floor.

"I better check on Benji," Elizabeth said, using the bathtub to help push herself up. She reached down and patted Jacob on the head. "Everything is okay, little one. Sonya, are you good with keeping him for a while?" Elizabeth stepped past Sonya and Jacob, then draped an arm around Anna. "You know you are always a life saver for me, right?" She leaned her head against Anna's for a moment and then entered the hallway and took the few steps to Benji's bedroom. "Benji, can I come in again?" Elizabeth paused at the open bedroom door and saw Benji still sitting at the same place in the middle of the room. She took a step into the room, hesitated, and then took another one.

Elizabeth knelt down on the floor in front of Benji. "The fire is taken care of. The windows are open, and soon the smoke smell will clear – at least, I hope it will clear out of here. The fire is out, at least in the garbage can. Can you tell me why you needed to burn those underwear?"

Tears started to trickle down Benji's cheeks. He bent his head forward, nestled it against his raised knees, and wrapped his arms around his head. Elizabeth moved closer, put a hand on his shoulder, felt sobs shake his body, then sat beside him and put her arm fully around his shoulders and pulled him against herself. Sobs convulsed Benji's body as he pressed himself against Elizabeth.

Elizabeth stroked Benji's cheek, at which he tightened his body, pulled away from her, and wiped his eyes. Benji looked at Elizabeth sitting on the floor beside him and stood up. "Why did you come into my room?" Benji demanded with both hands on his hips, leaning forward and over Elizabeth's head. He balled his hands into fists, narrowed his eyes to slits. "You just wanted to see me naked, didn't you?" he screamed. Tears poured down his face as he repeatedly gasped for air.

Elizabeth grabbed a blanket from the bed, wrapped it around Benji, and moved him to the bed. He threw himself backward onto the bed and rolled his body away from Elizabeth. She reached out to touch him but pulled her hand back. "There was a fire. I wanted to make sure you were safe, that's all." Tears rolled down Elizabeth's cheeks. She lowered her head into her hands, wiped her eyes, and pushed her hair from her face.

"Benji, I think right now you don't want to talk to me, and that is okay. Your dad will be home soon, so if you want to, you can tell him what happened here. Or maybe the next time you see Mr. Tilitson you can explain it to him." Elizabeth sat for a moment longer, lifting an arm toward Benji's back, then pulling it back again. "I'm going to check on Jacob and the girls, unless you want to talk. I'll stay with you if you want me to."

Benji didn't stir, didn't say a word nor make a sound. Elizabeth got off the bed and took a step toward the bedroom door. She stopped when she saw a box of matches resting against the wall, went to pick them up, and scanned the room to see if there were any more matches she hadn't seen. When she didn't see anything else, she left the bedroom.

Anna stared at Elizabeth in the hallway, her eyes wide open. "Yikes, Elizabeth! What was that screaming about?" Sonya and Jacob were pretending to take a bath, Sonya pretending she hadn't heard any of her brother's screaming.

"Oh my, Anna, I really don't understand what just happened. Burning underwear, crying, actually letting me sit with and hold him for a moment, then yelling at me." Elizabeth shook her head. "He's wrapped in his blanket now, face against the wall, and back to silence."

Anna took a step closer to Elizabeth and put an arm around her shoulders. Elizabeth leaned into Anna. "I wonder if he has said anything to that counsellor at his school. Does he have any clue what happened to Benji, why he's behaving the way he is? What is going on in that head of his? It's clear he's in some sort of pain, but why? This seems like something other than wishing Jacob and I weren't here, but what?" Anna nodded but didn't offer any response.

Elizabeth gave Anna a quick hug and smiled at Sonya and Jacob before continuing. "Will you sort of look into Benji's room now and again? Just to make sure he is at least sort of okay? You don't have to go in or ask him to get ready for dinner or anything, just see that he isn't burning anything else. I'll finish making supper. Walter should be home soon."

Anna nodded. "Sure, Elizabeth. I'll make sure Jacob is occupied too." Elizabeth nodded thanks and went back to the kitchen. Sonya appeared at her side a moment later.

"I'll finish that salad." Sonya peered around the counter, saw no vegetables left, and looked into the bowl. "Oh, the salad is finished." She smiled. "I'll put it on the table. Anything else I can do to help?" She put a hand on Elizabeth's shoulder. "Plus, ummm, can I ask you something?" She leaned her whole body against Elizabeth. Elizabeth put an arm around Sonya's shoulders. Sonya looked at the ceiling, then at Elizabeth before quickly dropping her eyes to the floor again.

"You can always ask me anything you want, sweetheart. What is it?"

"Did something happen to Benji in Saskatoon?" Sonya looked back into Elizabeth's eyes, tears beginning to roll down her cheeks. "I know he wasn't so happy before he left and all, and that he had done some really mean things to Jacob, but doesn't this seem like something else?"

"You are as observant as you are wonderful, my little helper." Elizabeth lifted Sonya's hands upward and pressed them against her own heart. "Do you feel my heart beating?" Sonya nodded. "That's the thing I am most certain of right now. My heart is full of love for my children, full of pain and hurt for the troubles my children have to face, but it's still beating. And as long as it's working, I'm going to love you all, and I'm going to keep trying to figure out what is going on around me, in your life, in Benji's life, in all of my kid's lives. I don't know what else to tell you, Sonya." Elizabeth gave Sonya's hands a squeeze. "I don't think I gave you the answer you wanted, I'm sorry about that. But I wonder the same thing you do, dear. Did something happen to Benji in Saskatoon? And if something happened to him while he was there, what was it? And what should we be doing about it? Surely there must be something that we can do now to make him a little happier about his life."

"I could ask him," Sonya offered, removing one of her hands from Elizabeth's and twirling a strand of hair.

Elizabeth smiled. "Of course you could, dear. Somehow I think Benji might not give you any better an answer than I did. But, you know, there's no harm asking. If you are with Benji some time, and you think the time is right, you go right ahead and ask him anything you want to." Elizabeth hugged Sonya and stood up. "Now, I better finish frying up that hamburger and boiling the water for those noodles."

Elizabeth busied herself in the kitchen while Sonya went back to the bathroom where Jacob was still playing in the bathtub. Anna was leaning against the door frame, looking down the hall toward Benji's open bedroom door and then back at Jacob. When Sonya arrived, Anna draped an arm around her shoulders. "Nice little family we have here, eh?" She smiled and pulled Sonya close. "Us sisters, though, we're doing alright, aren't we? I mean, I'm doing okay. How about you Sonya? You doing okay with all of this happening around you?"

Sonya responded by putting her arms around Anna's waist and squeezing. "I love you, Anna. You make it seem as if it is possible for a person to stay calm in the middle of a storm. How do you do it if you don't pray anymore?" Anna smiled and kissed Sonya's ear.

"What do you think praying is?" Anna asked, glancing down the hallway.

"You know," Sonya laughed, "even if you don't pray anymore, you can't have forgotten what it is."

"So you talk to God," Anna began, "and I talk to Shelley. She's so smart, so wise. She makes me feel like I can be smart..."

"But you are so smart," Sonya interrupted.

"Awww, you're so kind, little sister." Anna hugged her again. "Maybe my talking with Shelley is like you talking to God. When I'm frustrated, sad, angry, happy, it really doesn't matter which of those, I like talking to her, hanging out with her. She makes me feel special."

"But God isn't my girlfriend or anything like that," Sonya responded.

"Your what?" Anna gasped. "Did you just say God isn't your girlfriend?"

"Well, isn't Shelley your girlfriend?" Sonya looked up at Anna's face. "I've seen you holding hands, and kissing and... well, stuff that I thought people did with their boyfriends, but she's a girl, so your girlfriend."

"Have you told Dad about this?" Anna grabbed Sonya's shoulders.

"No, of course not," Sonya said. "Dad only says what the Bible says, so there's no point in talking to him about anything. I hate it when he says things like 'then they go to hell' or something like that." Anna looked down to try and hide her smile from Sonya. "You only asked if I'd told Dad. How come you didn't ask if I'd told Mom? I haven't talked with her about it either, but I guess she wouldn't say the same thing as Dad. What do you think? What would Elizabeth say?" Sonya looked into Anna's eyes.

"Elizabeth knows all about me," Anna revealed. "She says Bibleish sort of stuff too, but it's so different than the kind of stuff Dad says. She told me that I was made in God's image, that I was beautiful just the way God intended me to be. She told me I didn't have to change anything about me. Yeah, Sonya, I think you can talk to Elizabeth about anything you want to and she won't give you weird answers." Anna leaned her forehead against Sonya's.

"I just did ask her something, even though I was scared," Sonya confided in her sister.

"Really? What did you ask her?" Anna looked with curiosity at Sonya. "I mean, do you want to tell me what you asked her? You don't have to if it's private."

Sonya leaned forward and looked toward Benji's room before she whispered, "I asked if she thought something happened to Benji in Saskatoon because he just doesn't seem the same anymore. Does he?" Sonya looked up again, worry creasing her forehead.

Anna gently placed her thumbs on Sonya's crinkled forehead before answering, "You're worried too, huh? Me too. Elizabeth too, that's for sure. But you know Elizabeth loves Benji as much as she loves Jacob, right?" Sonya nodded. "And she wants to figure stuff out. She isn't going to start quoting the Bible and saying Benji should behave like this or that because the Bible says so. She's going to try and figure out what happened, if anything happened, and what she can do right now, here, to help Benji get his shit together. Oops, I mean, figure stuff out for himself."

"You swear a lot," Sonya observed and then continued before Anna could respond, "yeah, Mom said she didn't know what was going on, but that she'd try to keep working at it. I don't know what she needs to work at, but she said that, or something like that." Sonya gave Anna another hug. "I'm glad you're my sister."

"You are so sweet, little sister. I'm lucky you're my sister. And even though sometimes it's confusing, or at least one of them is confusing, I'm lucky to have two little brothers like Benji and Jakey too," Anna finished up. She sat down beside Jacob and pulled Sonya down beside them and started a hand-clapping game for the three of them.

"Hey every… what's that smell? Did supper get burned again?" Walter laughed coming in, rounding the corner and smiling at Elizabeth in the kitchen. He saw the supper on the stove, the look at Elizabeth's red-rimmed eyes, and stopped. "What happened?" he whispered. "Where's Jacob? Where's Benji?"

A tear appeared at the edge of Elizabeth's eye, and she wiped it away and came toward Walter. "Come, dear, sit with me in the living room for just a minute, and I'll try to explain. Or at least tell you what happened. I don't think I can explain anything." Elizabeth led Walter to the living room where she sat down beside him on the couch.

Walter took a deep breath and turned his fearful eyes toward Elizabeth. "Is everyone okay?" He took Elizabeth's hands and squeezed them. "Please tell me everyone is okay, Elizabeth." Tears escaped from his eyes and rolled unchecked down his cheeks.

"Physically, yes, everyone is fine, but only physically," Elizabeth started. "I was at the counsellor's office to pick up Benji today. The counsellor, Earl… Earl something… I can't remember his last name right now, seems like a nice man. He said he'd contact us once he's met with Benji a few times so that we can plan strategy together, and he'll give us ideas about what to try, so we can hopefully help Benji become Benji again." Elizabeth paused.

"And the smoke smell? What made that?" Walter asked, taking another deep breath.

"After Benji and I got back, Anna was taking care of Jacob, and Sonya was helping me make dinner when the smoke alarm went off in the hallway. There was smoke coming out from under and above Benji's door, so I burst inside. Benji was sitting naked…" Walter's eyes grew wide, "in front of a garbage can. Benji had taken his clothes off, his jeans and T-shirt were on the floor, but his underwear, some pairs, I don't know how many, were burning in the garbage can."

"What? Burning underwear? Why?" Confusion reigned on Walter's face.

"I'm afraid there's more," Elizabeth continued. Walter looked at the ceiling as if praying for a moment.

"I'm listening," he murmured.

"After I opened his window to let out some of the smoke and smell, took the garbage can and put out the fire in the bathtub, I went back to Benji's room. He screamed at me that I just wanted to see him naked and that's why I had come into his room. I wrapped him in a blanket then, and I tried to speak with him, but he turned away from me and wouldn't say another thing." Elizabeth sighed. "Maybe he'll talk to you, say something to you to make some sense of this. What happened to him in Saskatoon?"

"Dear Lord, give me wisdom! What do I say to my son?" Walter intoned to the ceiling. "Where do I begin, Elizabeth?" She stood up and put one hand on Walter's shoulder. "I used to think I always knew what the right things were to say. Now, more often than not, what I knew doesn't seem to help so much."

"I don't know. Listen, maybe. If he says anything, just listen to what he says," Elizabeth suggested. "Reassure him that it's safe for him to talk, to say something, anything. Somehow, he has to know he is safe here, no matter what he says. We have to find a way to let him know that he can talk to us, to you, and we'll do everything we can to make his life work. And remind him that you love him, that we all love him." Elizabeth squeezed Walter's hands.

Walter stood up, took a step toward the dining room, then stopped. He turned to look at Elizabeth. Tears were finding their way down his cheek one at a time. She took a step forward and wiped his tears for him, then hugged him, pressing her head against his shoulder for a moment. "Just love him, dear. Nothing about punishment. Please, Walter. We can sort out the fire and smoke stuff later. There's something much more important happening inside of him right now."

Chapter Twenty

Elizabeth and Walter sat side by side on the couch in Earl Tilitson's counselling office. He occupied a chair right in front of them. A notepad was flipped open and lay on the floor beside Earl's feet. "Your phone call about the fire, the screaming, and then silence is much appreciated. You've added the most recent details to the story for me to consider," Earl started. "So thank you, Elizabeth, thank you, Walter, for coming in to see me. I have a few questions, a few details I need to clear up."

Elizabeth nodded and Walter simply kept his eyes on the counsellor. "We have no secrets in our home," Walter said. "We'll tell you anything that might help make sense of what is going on."

Earl smiled and nodded. "First question. You mentioned that Benji was burning underwear. Has he ever previously, in any way at all, done anything like this?" Walter looked at Elizabeth and shrugged.

Elizabeth shook her head. "No, and what seemed so strange to me was that it was only his underwear he burned. His other clothes were on the floor beside him."

"Do you make a big deal of him wearing underwear? Might burning it be an act of rejection of your rules, you trying 'to be his mother,' which you've said he reacts against at times?" Earl asked. "I mean, you've said he can be quite aggressive in declaring you have no right to make rules for him or tell him what do to. Could this be an extreme form of rejection of you, Elizabeth?"

"I don't allow my son to..." Walter started before Elizabeth's hand on his knees stopped him.

"You're right about Benji not wanting to listen to me and trying to find ways to reject me. Is rebel too strong a word for an eleven-year-old?" Elizabeth took a breath. "But I've never spoken to him about what he should wear. He was already old enough to be in the habit of dressing himself, and he always wore underwear. And I've made a point never to choose his clothes because he always dressed so carefully."

"That's true," Walter confirmed. "Agatha taught him to dress himself, each layer of clothing he needed, what was appropriate for summer, playing, church, whatever... Benji has dressed himself for years."

"Okay, so rebelling is most likely not the explanation for this outburst," Earl said. He picked up his notebook and wrote down a few notes. He tapped his pen on the paper, then looked at Elizabeth. "You said he screamed 'you just want to see me naked' at you. Have you ever walked in on his bath, in his bedroom when he's changing, and he's protested before? Have you ever seen Benji naked before?"

"He's never been awkward about his body. When he takes a bath, he walks naked from his room to the bathroom, sometimes he even comes into the kitchen to get a drink to take into the bath with him. And it doesn't matter if his sisters are in the dining room, either. He's completely uninhibited," Elizabeth responded. "When I came into his room because of the fire and saw him sitting naked, it didn't even register because he often does that before getting dressed for school, or before putting on his pyjamas."

Walter nodded his confirmation, blushing. "I sometimes wonder if that is acceptable. Do children in other homes walk around like that, are they allowed to be naked? Or is he too old for that?"

Earl looked at Walter and nodded. "Anything and everything you can imagine regarding clothing, for children, for adults, for families, for whoever, seems to be happening out there. I think what matters is that each family find that path for themselves. Body shaming is a very harmful practice, so as long as there is no shame involved, it's fine. But it's not shaming to say you should wear clothes in some situations, as you feel is appropriate," Earl continued. Walter sighed in relief to discover he wasn't being too permissive or somehow inappropriate.

"Three out of the ordinary incidents – exposing himself to girls in the bathroom at school, burning underwear, suddenly being conscious of being naked in front of you, Elizabeth. Those incidents seem like there must be some sort of connection between them. That is what I'll try to discover in my next few sessions with Benji, if he's willing to talk about it, that is. None of that seems like the usual Benji, am I correct?" Earl moved his gaze between Walter and Elizabeth.

Elizabeth nodded, and Walter responded, "Exactly right. That is very out of the ordinary, but then there is the usual trouble too." Walter looked at Elizabeth, who sighed and nodded to Walter to continue. "Before Agatha died, Elizabeth would sometimes look after my children if my wife joined me on a preaching assignment. And all of my children loved her, and Benji probably loved her the most! He often made comments about her, confusing her, mixing her up with Agatha. Maybe that means Elizabeth was there too often, but it's too late to change that." Elizabeth patted Walter's leg.

"When Agatha died, I wanted someone to look after my children, and of course to have a wife. Elizabeth seemed like God's perfect choice for me, so we got married. Almost from the moment we were married, though, Benji was a different person." Walter looked at Elizabeth, who was nodding agreement with each of Walter's points.

"Initially, Sonya wouldn't call Elizabeth Mom, Anna still doesn't, but something changed. I don't remember what, but one night it changed, and Sonya has been good with Elizabeth, calls her Mom all the time. Benji seemed to get even angrier when Jacob was born. He's been quite mean to Jacob many times, and keeping Jacob safe was a concern."

Earl looked at Elizabeth with raised eyebrows, and she nodded confirmation that safety was an issue. Earl scribbled some more notes into his book, then looked up to listen some more. "I've tried to tell them, the kids, from the start, when Agatha first died that it was God's will and that they needed to accept it." Earl raised his eyebrows again, then added more notes. "I told them grieving Agatha's death meant they didn't trust that God had their best intentions at heart." Walter stopped and looked at Earl, who was once again writing in his notebook.

"Once again you have given me some very important information to help me understand Benji. Some of this is beginning to make more sense to me already, but I'll keep working at it. I'll chat with Benji; the first time he saw me he didn't chat too much. He spent more time looking at his shoes, which of course isn't that strange. It was the first time we had ever met, so who was I to him? It will take some time to earn his confidence, I think, before he opens up to me. It does appear that there are some disturbing ideas rolling around that brain of his." Earl closed his notebook. "We have some time, but it seems it is definitely time that we get started. I will plan to see him once every three or four weeks."

"Once a month? That's it?" Elizabeth was startled. "That doesn't seem very often, or often enough. Isn't there any way that you could see him more often? I mean, I don't know about the other students whom you see, but our situation with Benji seems quite extreme, doesn't it? And we could really use some help too, if you have any ideas or suggestions for Walter or myself. Anything that you think we could, or should try, to help Benji find his gentle, happy self again." Elizabeth looked at Walter, then at the counsellor.

"You're right, Ms. Rempel, it really isn't enough. To start it would be best if it was once a week, and then after a few months, once we've gotten to know each other, longer gaps between sessions might be acceptable," Earl said. "Unfortunately, I have only so much time, and a relatively large case load of students to see." The counsellor almost grimaced when he added, "I'm the only counsellor the school has, and sometimes I feel that two, or three, might be needed to address everything that our students are trying to figure out. Your Benji isn't the only student in our school with a complicated life, I'm afraid. I'm very sorry, but I can't see him any more frequently than what I said." Earl tucked his notebook into a briefcase and stood up. "Once again, thank you so much for coming in. Your answers to my questions are very helpful. Have a good evening."

Elizabeth and Walter stepped out of the office, and the counsellor closed the door behind them. Walter looked at Elizabeth. "Did I tell him too much? Is it okay what I said about Benji, liking you, not liking you, not liking Jacob?" Walter paused. "I don't want to say something I shouldn't."

"Those things need to be said, Walter," Elizabeth said, touching his arm. "It's not being honest if we tell the counsellor that Benji has always loved having me and Jacob in the house. He needs to know the truth, and you told it. It doesn't matter how good or bad the truth looks, it needs to be told." Elizabeth kept walking toward their car.

"He thought the school thing, the fire, and his screaming might be connected. But connected to what?" mused Elizabeth. She looked at Walter, who shrugged. "It does seem like there is more than not liking me, or Jacob, swirling around Benji's head. But what is it?"

"Don't ask me," Walter responded. "He says there are many students here with complicated lives, and I get that. I have only a few children in my home, and each of them have their own complications, so much so that sometimes I feel like I can't figure out anything about any of them. Except Sonya, maybe. She appears to be a good student, to know how to live being kind to others no matter what is going on around her." Walter smiled, opened the car door for Elizabeth, walked around to the other side, climbed in, and drove home.

Chapter Twenty-One

(May 2013)

"Thank you for coming," Earl Tilitson extended his hand first to Elizabeth and then to Walter. "I know it isn't always easy to find time during the day, but I thought now that Jacob is in school, meeting in the afternoon meant not having to find childcare." Earl smiled as he waved Elizabeth and Walter into his office.

"Nothing changes in here does it?" Walter murmured as he took the same seat he had taken in previous meetings. "Not that it matters. Having you here for the whole time Benji has been in this school is the most important thing. At least you have been a constant for him, trying to walk alongside him." Walter blushed, thinking he might have caused offence with his initial comment.

Earl smiled. "Next year things will change. I'm getting some new furniture, finally, something more comfortable." Elizabeth and Walter settled onto the couch and laughed. "Maybe more comfortable furniture will open Benji up," Earl segued to the reason for meeting. Elizabeth and Walter nodded.

"In our previous meetings you have offered some ideas, what you called your speculations, that seemed accurate," Elizabeth said. "The idea that being told it was God's will for Agatha to die being hard to digest, well, that made a lot of sense. Walter and I have had many conversations about that term. What exactly is God's will? And can a person's death be attributed to God's will in a way that might make sense to a child? My goodness, I find that kind of statement hard to figure out!"

Walter shot a glance at Elizabeth upon her final statement. "You talked about the fine line between teaching religious ideas and religious abuse. That hit me hard," Walter confessed. "I'm used to just explaining what I think the Bible means, to telling people, and them listening. Not too many adults, and certainly no children, have ever told me that I'm wrong," Walter paused. "Well, okay, Anna has made it clear many times she doesn't believe anything I say," he added. "Sorry, that's not the point here." Elizabeth and Earl looked at him, expecting him to continue.

"I had never even imagined that preaching about sinners going to hell, God's punishment, even God's will, might have such harsh connotations." Walter's face turned red when he realized what he had just said. "Okay, hell and punishment are very harsh ideas. Especially hell. But God's will. I didn't think that was such a harsh idea, until you explained how a child might understand that sort of language."

"Remember, Walter, I'm speculating," Earl said. "Benji has never complained about a single thing you have taught him, or preached about or, you know, told him was true about God, following God or any of that." Earl looked intently at Elizabeth and Walter. "I'm suggesting that perhaps more because of my own analysis of that language, and then applying that to what I know about children's thought processes."

"But it does make sense." Walter nodded.

"I have to tell you again that Benji just hasn't said too much about anything during our visits. I remember our very first visit, when I told you it might take some time for Benji to gain confidence in me, trust me enough to actually say anything." Elizabeth and Walter nodded, remembering that first meeting. "Well, for whatever reason, too much time between meetings, personality issues, just determined not to open up at all… whatever the reason, it's been much more my reading between the lines and trying to make sense of that than anything else."

"Benji's referral came after a serious incident at school," Elizabeth started.

"Right. Exposing himself to some girls in their bathroom," Earl acknowledged.

"Then you thought the fire he started, and his angry shouting at me about seeing him naked, were possibly all connected, but to what?" Elizabeth continued. "And then the profound issue was his seeming dislike for both Jacob and myself. He was angry from the day Walter told his children we were getting married. In trying to figure out how to deal with that, we have interpreted pretty much everything he says or does from that point of view."

"Has he said anything at all about either of those things?" Walter interjected.

Earl shook his head. "He hasn't offered any comments at all. None, in almost three years. You have mentioned that after those very out-there incidents, Benji sort of calmed down, if that is the right way of describing it. Over this past year, although he won't offer anything himself, he has responded with looks and mono-syllabic answers to some of my questions, and that gives me a little to work with. But not much. I have to go with what I'm hearing from his teachers, you, and what I've learned over time working with students.

"I asked him how things are between him and Jacob, and he hardly looks at me. The first year, he would glare at me when I asked that. To me, that appears he isn't as hostile toward his younger brother anymore. Does that match what you are seeing at home?" Earl asked.

"I think it's better," Walter began, "but you're the one who's home with them more than I am, Elizabeth. What do you think?" He turned toward her.

"You're right. The situation at home is much better, really. Well, it's better for Jacob." Elizabeth paused and then explained. "Benji doesn't harass Jacob anymore, that's true. But the reason it is true is that he hardly ever comes out of his room. He comes home from school and goes to his room. I don't know what he does in there. There's no sound coming from the room. When I go in to make his bed after he leaves for school, there's nothing on the floor, nothing visible, to show he's been doing anything while in the room. I don't go through his drawers or his closet, though. I suppose he could have something in there."

Walter picked up the explanation. "Mostly he does join us for supper. And before he'd comment on how much he didn't like the food Elizabeth made, now he just eats some of it, not too much, but enough, I guess, excuses himself, and goes back to his room. And just like Elizabeth said, it's quiet in there for the evening. No sign of anything. He doesn't come out to watch TV, he doesn't ask for video games, he doesn't come sit at the table to play games with the rest of us. We usually play some sort of table games when Anna comes to visit," Walter concluded.

"It sounds as if Jacob is safer," Earl commented, looking at Elizabeth.

Elizabeth smiled and nodded. "Jacob's definitely safer now, for which I'm very thankful. And although there hasn't been any significant incident for what, can it really be almost three years already? So Benji is physically safe too. But I'm not convinced that he is emotionally or psychologically safe." Elizabeth looked at Walter, who patted her leg in agreement. "And that, I guess, makes me nervous. I wish I knew what to do to help him be more emotionally safe."

"Is he still antagonistic toward you, Elizabeth? I know I asked you this a year ago, when you said no, but I need to ask again," Earl said.

"Yes, of course. Ask again, by all means," Elizabeth said. "My answer is the same as last year, and the same as regarding Jacob. He is not as overtly aggressive, or so blatant about shouting out things like 'you're not my mother' or 'you're not the boss of me,' which I guess he used more for Anna first, then for Sonya. He spends so much time in his room that sometimes it's almost like it's only Walter, Sonya, Jacob, and me who live together." Elizabeth put one hand on Walter's knee. "And he appears to be withdrawing more and more from Walter too." Walter nodded. "He used to at least tell Walter that he didn't like me, that he wished Jacob hadn't been born. But now he barely even talks to Walter about anything."

"I see. So more and more he is withdrawing from his family, disappearing inside of himself," Earl observed. "His teachers tell a similar story actually. In his early years here, he was a strong student. He learned to read quickly, and math was never a challenge. Then when Agatha died, he sort of slowed down the pace at which he was learning. Which, of course is understandable. He was grieving, trying to process his grief, and we've talked about how that process might have been affected, right?

By the 'God's will' sort of language." Walter blushed briefly but nodded his understanding.

"Then, when you enter the house, Elizabeth, there's a short-term dip, another one around the time Jacob is born, but he seems to bounce back and do okay in his classes for a while. Grade five and six were pretty steady, no big leaps or drops in his performance during those years. His teachers said he was sort of reserved, that he didn't make an effort to interact with his classmates, and he always stayed as far away from the teachers as he physically could. That was sort of an interesting detail."

"Did any of them ever say why they thought he chose to stay so far away?" Walter asked.

"No, they didn't, and I wondered if it was some sort of anti-adult thing. You know, the same way he was rejecting Elizabeth as an adult, was he perhaps rejecting the authority of his teachers. I don't know, again, I'm speculating," concluded Earl.

"And now, in grade seven? He never tells us how things are going, and we haven't had any calls from teachers, so we assume that it isn't so bad," Elizabeth stated. "Are we wrong?"

"Not really," Earl said, "it's just that while Benji isn't doing badly, or at least not worse, with his results, all the teachers think he's just not doing as well as he could do. They wonder if they should be challenging him more, pushing him to do better work, or if it's okay for them to just let him do what he's doing." Earl looked his notes, nodded to himself, and then looked at Elizabeth and Walter again.

"Any suggestions? Any words of wisdom for his teachers?" Earl asked.

Walter smiled. "We were hoping to get some words of wisdom from you, maybe from one of his teachers who had seen something that stood out. I'm not sure. What do you think, Elizabeth, good idea to push him harder? Better idea to just let him continue being who he is and doing what he's doing?"

Elizabeth nodded. "The second option, I think. And I realize that is my fear, more than anything else, speaking. I don't go into his room in the evenings because I'm afraid I might somehow push him over an edge. An edge that I don't, or can't actually see," she said. "I've never heard Benji complain about school, his teachers, or his work. But then, I hardly hear him speak about anything at all. He's pretty quiet at the table when he's eating, and then he disappears back into his room and is gone for the evening."

"You have a daughter, Sonya, right? She still lives at home. Does she ever talk to him? Would she have any idea about what is going on in his head?" Earl asked.

"You're right that Sonya lives at home. She's fifteen, in grade ten," Walter explained.

"She's often tried having conversations with Benji, tried joking with him about stuff around the house, my cooking, invited him to do stuff with her, like going for walks. But he hardly even responds. Sometimes he grunts, other times he says a clearer no, and mostly he just ignores her and goes to his room," Elizabeth added. "I don't get the impression he hates her, or anything like that, he's just not interested in anything at all, is how it looks. I don't think she'd be able to get any sort of answers out of him about anything."

"You're right, dear," Walter confirmed. "Can I ask you about one more thing, please?" Earl heard a hint of fear in Walter's voice.

"Ask anything. I'll answer if I can," Earl responded, holding onto Walter's gaze.

"Sometimes when Benji comes out of his room for dinner, his eyes are sort of... how do I describe them... glazed. Sometimes he doesn't walk upright, tall, and with strong steps. It's almost like he's had something to drink. But I have never smelled anything on him. So, could it be that... could he be... I don't know anything about that world. I know Anna smoked for a while when she was in high school, I think it was, and I could smell that. But this is different. I don't even know what I'm trying to ask," Walter fumbled.

"Exactly, dear," Elizabeth said, supporting Walter. "It's not just in the evening when he comes out for dinner. Sometimes when he comes home from school, he just doesn't seem like himself. I'm not exactly sure what 'himself' looks like, but you know what I mean? He's just different somehow."

Earl looked at his notebook, flipped back a few pages, read something to himself, nodded, then looked up at Walter and Elizabeth again. "What I'm hearing you ask me is whether or not there is any chance Benji is using any illicit drugs. Am I understanding you correctly?" Earl looked intently at both of them.

Elizabeth and Walter looked at each other, then nodded. Elizabeth reached out to take Walter's hand. "I think that is what we were trying to find words for," Walter said. "Are we way off? Like I said, I know more about the inside of churches, where no one ever talks about drugs, other than that they are a sin to use. I don't know much about why kids might use drugs, or what it looks like if they do."

"Of course. You can't be expected to know everything about everything. And knowing all about the world of drugs and youth who need them is not the right place for everyone. But, thankfully, there are some people who are very aware and very involved," Earl said. Walter started at the words.

"Need them? People, kids, need drugs? I don't understand," he blurted out. "Surely no one needs drugs!" Walter's eyes grew wide, and he looked from Earl to Elizabeth. "Why would Benji need drugs?"

"I understand in a world where morality is the arbiter of right and wrong, maybe people don't need drugs. But I don't judge students for their choices, Walter. For me, if a student is using drugs, and not so many do at this middle school, it's an emotional, or psychological need. It's not just 'for fun' as some people like to suggest. What I try to do is figure out, with them, why they feel they need to be taking, or using, whatever it is that they are using." Earl's voice was calm.

"Need drugs. Wow! Never imagined that," Walter continued. "Elizabeth, do you think Benji needs drugs?"

Elizabeth shook her head. "I don't think Earl is saying the same thing you are hearing, Walter. Earl isn't saying Benji needs drugs like a doctor might when giving a prescription. He's suggesting – am I right, Earl – that Benji can't figure himself out. He's living in his own world of confusion or pain, and that taking something might be the way to finding his path through that darkness. Maybe it is his way of feeling safe or something like that." Elizabeth looked from Walter to Earl. "Am I saying that the right way? Am I at least close to understanding what you mean?"

Earl nodded. "Yes, exactly, Elizabeth. Many people, of all ages, self-medicate. Have you ever had a cup of coffee because you felt sort of tired, but knew you still had a few hours of work to do? Have you ever poured yourself a glass of whiskey, or whatever you prefer, just to take the edge off because you felt a little anxious, or have you ever taken some over-the-counter medication to help you sleep because you were tired but not sleeping properly?" Earl asked.

"Well, the coffee yes," Walter responded, "but the alcohol, no. I don't drink."

"Fair enough, but do you get it about the coffee? As an adult, you think you're tired and want a boost to get you through the work you need to do. So you determine you 'need' a coffee. Does that make sense to you when I say self-medicate?" Earl looked at Walter.

"Yes, it does." Walter nodded. Elizabeth also nodded in agreement. "Me or Elizabeth choosing to have a cup of coffee for a bit of a pick-me-up has never worried me. I guess I know that as a natural, or common, choice. I know lots of people who would do that." Walter turned from Elizabeth to Earl. "And I get the alcohol thing for those who drink too. But those are adults, making adult choices. Benji isn't even fourteen. He's not an adult. He probably shouldn't be making decisions about self-medicating, should he?"

"First of all," Earl began, "we're not sure he is. Yes, what you described could be symptoms, or indications, of some sort of substance use. They could also be a natural reaction to fear, heightened anxiety, stress. Sometimes those look the same. And as you observed, Benji is only thirteen and has not yet developed the same kind of, or range of, self-care and coping strategies that you have."

Elizabeth and Walter both nodded in agreement. "So, maybe he's not using anything. Do any of his teachers say anything that might make you think he was using something? And back to his need to use something, he has been an unhappy kid for a long time," Walter added.

"I checked my notes, and one teacher has made observations, like yours, on a few occasions. Interestingly, it is always the same teacher, and it is the class he has right after his lunch break." Earl looked at Walter. "That means that he could, and I stress that is 'he could' rather than 'he is' doing it. He could take something during his lunch hour, and then his after-lunch teacher is the one to notice it."

"Oh my," Elizabeth sighed. "Saskatoon seems to have disappeared as a cause for anything. Initially we wondered if something had happened to him while he was in Saskatoon visiting his brother, but that's three years ago. The way he's behaving now surely couldn't go back three years, could it?"

"We will keep exploring every and any angle you want, Elizabeth," Earl assured her. "And yes, certainly traumas can happen and have a lingering affect for many years. Three years is not actually a very long time. I remember asking him questions about Saskatoon when we first started meeting. All I remember," Earl checked the first pages of his notebook, "is that his shoulders tightened up, and his neck totally disappeared because his shoulders rose so high." He skimmed a few pages. "Wait, here's a note about his eyes. And it's my interpretation, not his statement. I wrote 'his eyes expressed terror' when I asked him about his week at some camp – he went to some camp for a week, right?"

"Yes, he did. Darrel told us he acted strangely after coming home from that week. Sonya has asked, I don't know how many times, what happened to him in Saskatoon," Elizabeth said.

"Darrel tried to track that down, didn't he?" Walter added. "If I remember correctly, he called somebody at the camp to ask them questions. That person didn't think anything had happened, or at least that he knew of."

"You're right, Walter." Elizabeth nodded. "We sort of just left that because nothing made sense about it. And, as I said before, we saw almost everything he did as an expression of his anger, or hatred, of Jacob and me, because that sort of made sense."

"And it was just one week. What could possible happen in one week at an outdoor activity camp that would have such a long-lasting effect on Benji?" Walter wondered out loud.

"A lot can happen in one week," Earl said. "If there was something really important in that week, I haven't found any way of coaxing it out of him. Not only has he 'missed' quite a few of our appointments, but when he does come, about the only thing he does say is that he doesn't have anything to say to me." He looked down, coughed, then looked up again. "I've thought this for a while and should probably have made this suggestion sooner. Although I have some training as a guidance counsellor, I've tried everything I know, and nothing has gotten through to Benji. I've spoken with the school psychologist, even made a referral, and obviously haven't marked it as urgent enough, as nothing has happened so far. Perhaps you should seek additional support from a psychiatrist, someone who might know about adding medication to Benji's treatment plan."

"Thank you so much for working with Benji," Elizabeth said. Walter nodded agreement. "We truly are grateful. I know it's been a long haul already, but it still all seems so new when thinking about how to respond to Benji. You're probably right, of course. We should arrange for him to see a psychiatrist, and maybe find an out-of-school counsellor too."

"We just want to make sure that you know how much you have helped us, Elizabeth and me," Walter added. "You've helped us walk along a very difficult path. And it appears we still have some way to go."

Chapter Twenty-Two

"Mom! Mom! I need your help, actually, I think Benji needs your help," Sonya shouted from the dining-room window. Elizabeth looked up from the couch where she was sitting with Jacob, a book stretched open between their laps. Elizabeth slid the book into Jacob's lap and came to where Sonya was looking out the window. Sonya looked at Elizabeth and then pointed out the window. "Look. It's like he can hardly walk. He's staggering all over the driveway."

Elizabeth darted out the front door, pausing only long enough to slip on some shoes. She ran down the driveway to meet Benji, slowing down when she was a few feet in front of him. "Hey, Benji," Elizabeth greeted her son, "can I carry your books for you?"

Benji dropped his backpack to the ground and kept walking, not making any eye contact with Elizabeth. He stumbled when his foot caught a rock, and he caught himself before taking a few more unsteady steps. "How was your day, Benji?" Elizabeth asked, staying side by side with Benji, her arms braced and ready to reach for him if he were to stumble again.

Benji offered no response. He paused for a moment, swayed, steadied himself, and took another step forward. "Are you alright? Are you feeling sick?" Elizabeth asked, moving a step ahead of him, as he seemed to be tottering forward rather than sideways or backwards. Elizabeth saw Benji's glazed eyes as he swung his look past her to the house. "You're close now, close to the house. Do you want to lean on my shoulder, Benji?"

Benji took a step, then collapsed to his knees. He bent forward, leaned his weight on his arms, and began to vomit violently. Elizabeth dropped the backpack and knelt down beside him. She put one arm under his chest to support his heaving body, while with the other she stroked the back of his neck then his back. Benji gagged, then wretched loudly, his body lurching forward. Elizabeth wrapped both arms around his chest to support his body from falling into the puddle of vomit on the ground.

Sonya ran out the door toward them and knelt beside Benji, on the side opposite of Elizabeth. "Mom, I'm here. What do you want me to do? How can I help? Oh, Benji! What's wrong, buddy? What's happening?"

"Ummm, I don't think we need an ambulance, Sonya, but we need a driver and someone to sit with Benji. And we need someone to stay with Jacob." Elizabeth was scrambling through her list of names to find someone who might be available to help them.

"Anna! Please, Sonya, call Anna," Elizabeth instructed. "Dad's not in town and won't be until later tonight. We need to get Benji to the hospital right now. See if she and Shelley can come to help. Both their hands would be good." Sonya disappeared inside as quickly as she had appeared.

Benji threw himself onto the ground and curled up into a fetal position. His feet were resting in one puddle of vomit, and his shoulder was in the other. Elizabeth pushed herself in closer, lifted Benji's head onto her lap, and stroked his sweaty forehead. "Be okay, Benji, be okay," she repeated with each stroke.

Sonya reappeared, relief written all over her face. "Mom, you won't believe this. Anna and Shelley were already on their way here, they're almost here. Wait, there's their car." Sonya knelt behind Elizabeth, put her hands on Elizabeth's shoulders. "Is he okay?" she whispered.

A small blue Mitsubishi pulled to a stop near the group on the ground and two doors popped open. "Elizabeth, what's going on? What happened to Benji?" Anna was on the ground beside Benji, then grimaced when she realized that she had knelt too close to Benji and had one knee in vomit.

Shelley stood behind Anna. "Tell us, Elizabeth, how do we help? What do you need from us?" Shelley's no-nonsense voice brought Elizabeth's mind back to the moment. Anna stood up, wiping the vomit from her knee. "Agh, Anna, yikes! Let me get you some wipes to clean yourself."

Shelley turned to the car, reached inside, and pulled out a package of wet wipes, which she tossed to Anna.

Anna wiped the vomit from her jeans, then wiped her hands, balled up the used wipes and threw them to the ground. "I'll try to not kneel in any more vomit." She turned to Elizabeth and asked, "What happened to Benji?" Anna knelt beside Elizabeth and positioned herself to lift Benji off the ground. "You can tell us in the car. We're taking Benji to the ER, right? Okay, Shelley, go beside Elizabeth so you can lift from that side. Sonya, open the back door. Elizabeth, you're coming with us, yes?" Anna took charge of the situation and barked out directions to everyone.

Sonya dashed to open the back doors of the car. "Will you all fit in here? It looks tight," Sonya groaned.

"Always room for close family." Shelley smiled. She had already helped Anna lift Benji and move him beside the passenger-side back door. "Elizabeth, you want to get in first? That way we can sort of lean Benji in against you. At the least he'll feel a human body supporting him. He is breathing right?" Shelley leaned into the car and placed her cheek and ear close to Benji's mouth. After a moment she muttered, "Yup. He's breathing."

Anna picked up Benji's backpack and opened the zipper. She turned the backpack upside down and dumped the contents onto the ground. Sonya's eyes grew wide. Anna didn't look up but stated, "I'm checking for anything in here that might give us a clue to what Benji took. This isn't an upset stomach from lunch." Sonya dropped to her knees and started spreading the contents of the backpack across the grass.

"There, that plastic bag, Sonya, give that to me," Anna shouted, pointing to the bag Sonya was about to toss behind her. Sonya held it forward with a questioning look in her eyes. "Yeah, that one. Look, there's sort of a residue of something. And that little thing, is that from a pill? We can give this to the doctor and maybe it will tell them what Benji took." Anna grabbed the bag Sonya was extending, turned to the car, and got behind the wheel as Shelley closed the back door and got into the front seat.

Anna rolled down her window and stuck her head out of the window. "Sonya, you're going back inside and not saying a word about this to Jacob. Tell him that his mom is taking Benji on a special outing, just the two of them. You can make some macaroni with a can of soup and a can of tuna for the two of you, or three if Dad gets home on time to eat. If you can't do that, make some sandwiches. And we'll be back as soon as we can."

Elizabeth waved at Sonya, then turned her scared face back to Benji. She held his head in both hands as Anna bumped her car over the lawn, turned it around, and then back onto the driveway. "Anna, Shelley, thank you. Thank you for being here, for taking charge of getting Benji off the ground." A sob escaped from Elizabeth. She clapped one hand over her mouth as tears began to flow down her cheeks. "Benji, please be okay," she cried.

Anna slowed when the long driveway reached the street, but only enough to allow one car to pass before she pressed on the accelerator. Gravel flew as she screeched onto the road. Shelley put a hand on Anna's shoulders. "Be careful, we don't want more people in need of the emergency room people." Shelley turned her body to look at Benji and scanned his face, then his chest.

"Look, Elizabeth." Shelley pointed at Benji's chest. "He's breathing. See his chest rise and fall? It's not much. It's pretty shallow breathing, but at least he's breathing." Elizabeth nodded at Shelley and wrapped her arms across Benji's chest.

"Keep breathing, Benji," Elizabeth whispered, "we'll be there right away."

Anna pulled to a stop at a red light, looked around, then once again pinned the accelerator as she squealed through the red light onto Loewen Boulevard. "Spirit of the law." Anna grunted. "No one was coming, so I wasn't waiting." She raced down the street and slowed only enough to navigate the turn onto Henry Avenue, toward the Bethesda Hospital Emergency entrance. She turned into the emergency entrance and hadn't fully stopped the car before Shelley was out the door and running inside.

Shelley returned, pushing a wheelchair in front of her. "Is a wheelchair good enough? Or should I ask for a stretcher?" Anna shrugged and looked at Elizabeth, who also shrugged.

"You've got the wheelchair here. Let's use it to get Benji inside. They can switch him to a stretcher if they need to," Anna said. "Elizabeth, as soon as we've got Benji's shoulders, you get out the back door and get inside and tell them Benji's coming in. Tell them something. I think his breathing is getting shallower. You get them ready, we'll get him inside."

While giving Elizabeth instructions, Anna had half climbed into the car, put an arm behind Benji's shoulders and shifted him forward enough to allow Elizabeth to get out of the car. Elizabeth darted inside as Anna wrestled Benji's body to the edge of the car door while Shelley positioned it so that Anna could swing and drop Benji's body onto the chair. Anna knelt down to put Benji's feet onto the foot-rests and then adjusted his head so it was leaning on his chest.

Shelley was already directing the wheelchair through the doors into the lobby as Anna finished closing the car doors. She dropped herself behind the wheel and rushed the car down the ramp and into the parking lot. "Yes!" Anna exclaimed as she eyed an empty parking spot right beside the stairs leading back to the emergency entrance. She parked the car and raced up the stairs two and three at a time.

An aide with a stretcher met Shelley and Benji at the door. Another aide was running out from behind the closed doors of the Emergency hall toward them. "Ma'am, please brace the wheelchair so it doesn't move," one of the aides directed. The aides positioned themselves near Benji and hoisted him, lightning fast, onto the stretcher. One aide repositioned Benji's head to open his breathing passages more, as the two of them moved the stretcher behind the closing doors into the Emergency ward.

Anna rushed up to Elizabeth, who was staring after the stretcher that had just disappeared behind the closed doors. "Elizabeth, give me the medical card, I know his name, birthday, address, whatever else they need to know to register him. You go with him. Plus, I don't think they will allow all of us back there with Benji." Elizabeth handed the purple medical card to Anna and took a deep breath. A tear rolled down her cheek and she looked at Anna, her lips quivering.

"Elizabeth, hang in there. We're here. The people here will know what to do for Benji. Don't worry." Anna hugged Elizabeth. "He's going to be okay. You go now, go in there. Sit with him. Here's the bag that might be important." Anna fished the plastic bag out of her jeans pocket and closed Elizabeth's palm over the bag. "Go!" She gave Elizabeth a slight shove before turning to the admissions clerk, who had remained seated and quiet throughout.

"Okay. Name. Age. Address of the patient, please. And could I have the medical card too?"

Chapter Twenty-Three

Elizabeth looked at the door securing the Emergency department. She closed her eyes, inhaled for a long time, then stepped toward the doors. She pressed her palms against the bar and the door opened before her. She glanced into an open door but saw only oxygen tanks, a blood-pressure machine, and an empty bed. The next open door revealed only more of the same. Elizabeth wiped her forehead. "Where are you, Benji?"

A head poked out from behind a curtained area. "Are you the mother of this boy?" Elizabeth saw Benji's still body on the stretcher. A tube was coming out of his nose, and an IV was already dripping into his arm. Elizabeth nodded and stepped behind the curtain. She crumpled into an open chair and looked up.

A young woman stepped around the end of the bed toward Elizabeth. "I'm Brittany, the emergency doctor. I need a little information from you before we do anything else here." Elizabeth took a breath, pulled herself into a more upright position on the chair, and nodded.

"I'm Elizabeth, and that is my son, Benji. He's thirteen, and I have no idea what happened to him. He was almost home from school when he stumbled, fell, and started vomiting. My daughter Anna suggested it was a drug reaction. She found this in his backpack." Elizabeth handed the doctor the plastic bag. "I'll answer any questions you have. At least if I can. I don't know anything about drugs. I didn't know my son used drugs, although the school counsellor did suggest that maybe some of his actions at school were beginning to indicate that maybe he was using something."

"Right now his heart is racing, his blood pressure is quite high, not within the natural range for, you said he was thirteen? For a thirteen-year-old," the doctor said. "We've taken a blood sample and have sent it to the lab for a toxicology report. We should know very soon what it is that he ingested. I'll get this to the lab too so that they can determine what it is." The doctor handed the plastic bag to a nurse who had stood silently by to that point. He took the bag and disappeared into the hallway.

"Elizabeth, first, know that we are doing all we can for your son. We've taken his vitals, and in response, have given him something to calm his body, to get his body back under his control. The vomiting, his high blood pressure and rapid heart rate, suggest that he has ingested some drug, very possibly a form of ecstasy. The vomiting probably saved him from a more difficult reaction, as he most likely expelled at least some, if not most, of what he ingested."

The doctor looked at Elizabeth. "You mentioned that the school counsellor thought perhaps there might be some indications of substance use at school? Do you know for how long this has been going on?"

Elizabeth shook her head. "What did that counsellor say? And Walter, that's my husband… Walter! I haven't called home." Elizabeth looked up in shock. "Walter doesn't know where… oh," she sighed, "of course Sonya is at home with Jacob. She'll tell Walter where we are." She looked back at the doctor. "I'm sorry. For how long? Right, that is what you asked? Well, with what Walter said, and the counsellor said a teacher reported to him, I'd say it is at least a few months. But really, I don't know."

Elizabeth stood up and moved closer to the bed. She reached for Benji's forehead and lay a hand across it for a moment. She tilted her head and stroked the side of Benji's face. She looked up at the doctor. "Will he have to stay the night? Or will he be able to come home?"

"He's very young and the good thing is that means he's quite resilient and should bounce back quickly. On the other hand, he's young, and the drugs he ingested appear to be strong ones. When the toxicology report comes, we'll have a better idea of exactly what we are facing. Once we know the answer to that, it will be easier to assess our next steps, or even if any next steps are required. All that to say, I expect we will keep him for the night for observation. So, if you want to take a break and come back in the morning, that's fine. Benji is sleeping and will be for quite a few more hours."

The doctor pulled open the curtain and stepped into the hall before looking back at Elizabeth. "I will be back periodically to check on Benji. Nurses will stop by to check on him too, so he'll be fine. I think I heard you came in with two young ladies. If you want to stay, of course you are welcome to do so. But if you want to take them home, or have them take you home for a while, you have time. Take care of yourself." The doctor turned, pulled open another curtain, and stepped behind it, leaving Elizabeth alone with Benji.

"Benji, I'm going home to get Walter. Don't worry, we won't leave you here alone," Elizabeth whispered into Benji's ear. She leaned forward and kissed him on the forehead then inched her way backward out of the curtained area.

Anna and Shelley, who were sitting hand in hand, leaped up when they saw Elizabeth open the door of the Emergency department and step out. Anna ran to her, grabbed her shoulders, and asked, "What did they say? How's Benji?" Shelley came and stood behind Anna. She looked anxiously at Elizabeth, waiting for a response.

"Anna, have I told you how grateful I am for you? That you are a lifesaver? I don't know how I could have handled tonight without your help." Elizabeth wrapped her arms around both Anna and Shelley. "And Shelley, you too. You're wonderful. Thank you for coming along and supporting me, supporting Anna." Shelley tightened her hug around Elizabeth's shoulders and smiled at her.

"So," Anna started, "Benji. What's happening with my little brother?"

Elizabeth pushed their group toward the door. "Please take me home." She looked at Anna, who nodded. "Benji ingested something; the doctor said it was probably ecstasy."

"Ecstasy! Holy shit!" Anna exclaimed. "What's my little brother… what the hell… he's thirteen! What's he doing with ecstasy?" She stopped and looked incredulously at Elizabeth. "Are you sure that's what the doctor said it was?"

"He's in grade seven, Anna," Shelley said. "He's not the only kid in grade seven using that stuff. It's supposed to make them feel more connected, and how many kids in grade seven don't feel ostracized or out of the loop?" Shelley looked at Elizabeth. "Was this a surprise for you, Elizabeth? Or did you have an idea that Benji was using?"

"This isn't my world. When I was in grade seven, I was trying to figure out if using nail polish would send me to hell." Elizabeth sighed. "Belonging to God was the only thing that mattered to me. As long as I was good with God, I was good. What people said about me didn't matter. I don't know if anyone in my class did drugs until grade 10 or 11 when they smoked a joint. I've never even heard most of the names of drugs that are in schools now." Shelley nodded her understanding to Elizabeth.

"The car's over here, Elizabeth." Anna pointed at her car. She opened the back door for Elizabeth while Shelley got in behind the wheel. "Really? You driving?" Anna laughed and tossed her the key. She walked around the car and got into the passenger seat. She turned in her seat to look back at Elizabeth.

"How are you doing, Elizabeth? What's this doing to you?" she asked, putting a hand on Elizabeth's closest knee.

Elizabeth put her right hand on top of Anna's and looked up at her. "I don't know, Anna. I find out my thirteen-year-old son is using drugs. And why? Usually there is a reason someone uses drugs. His counsellor used a word, he said some kids feel they need them, need the drugs," she said. Then her face wrinkled. "I didn't understand 'they need to use' drugs. Why does Benji need to use drugs? What on earth happened to that little happy boy I used to know?" Tears rolled down Elizabeth's cheeks.

Anna put a hand on Elizabeth's knee for a moment then turned forward in her seat. "We going?" She looked at Shelley. "You can drive, you know, even if I'm talking to Elizabeth." Shelley turned around in her seat to see her way out of the parking spot. She left the parking lot and drove back to the Rempel house.

The car hadn't come to a stop before the house door beside the garage opened and Walter burst out of the house. He was beside the car opening Anna's door as soon as Shelley stopped the car. "Is Elizabeth in there? Where's Benji?" gasped Walter.

"Hey, Dad," Anna said, pushing past him to get out of the car. "She's in the back seat." Elizabeth opened her door and stepped out. Walter ran to her, hugged her tightly to himself, and held on to her.

Elizabeth wrapped her arms around Walter's midsection. "Hi, Walter," she whispered. "We have a bit of time, but we need to go back to the hospital. Benji is going to be okay. He's asleep in emergency. I don't know which drugs made him sleep; the ones he took or the ones the doctor gave him."

Walter pushed himself back a step and looked at Elizabeth. "So Sonya was right? Benji was using drugs? She wasn't sure, but she thought that might be it. His counsellor was right!" Walter's face sunk. Anna came up behind him and gave him a hug.

"Dad, he's not the first kid to try drugs. He's going to be okay," Anna told him from her position behind him. Walter twisted around and gave Anna a hug.

"Hi, Shelley." Walter turned his face toward her. "Thank you for helping Elizabeth, Anna. Thank you too." Walter nodded toward Shelley, then took a step back towards Elizabeth and put an arm around her shoulder before going inside.

"Mom, is Benji alright?" Sonya rushed to Elizabeth, looking for any indication in her face about her brother's condition. "Jacob's had supper and a bath. He's ready for bed. Should I put him to bed, or do you want to do that?"

"Sonya, you never cease to amaze me! Are you really only fifteen? You take such good care of Jacob, and I'm ever so grateful." Elizabeth reached out and gave Sonya a hug. "First, your question about Benji. He's going to be okay. He's not right now. The doctor said that he probably used some ecstasy, that is what made him so sick. Plus his heart was racing and he had super high blood pressure. Hopefully by the time your father and I get back to the hospital, they will know more. When we get back in the morning, I'll tell you anything else that we were told, okay?" Sonya nodded and stepped back.

"When you get back in the morning? Are you going back to the hospital? Can I come? Or maybe I can put Jacob to bed, if you like, and stay with him for the night," Sonya said, looking at Elizabeth.

Elizabeth looked at Anna. "Anna, if I put Jacob to bed, will you tell Walter the story?" Anna nodded and went to sit down at the dining room table. Shelley sat down across the table from her. "Sonya, you're very kind to offer to put Jacob to bed, but if it's okay with you, I will. With all that has happened over the past few hours, I feel I could use some time with a kid who is happy most of the time." Elizabeth touched Sonya's shoulder. "A kid who is usually happy because he has a sister like you who takes such good care of him every day. But yes, please, please stay with him when Walter and I go back to the hospital."

Elizabeth went into the bathroom while Walter joined Anna and Shelley at the table. Sonya followed Elizabeth with her eyes, then also turned and joined the others at the table. She took the chair right next to Anna, who placed her arm around Sonya's shoulder. "You're growing up beautifully, little sister."

Walter stood up. "Shelley, Anna, can I get you anything? Do you want a glass of water? I don't know what else we have. Some milk, maybe? I know that Sonya made cookies this evening with Jacob." Walter smiled at Sonya and looked back at Anna and Shelley.

"Milk and cookies." Anna smiled. "Always been one of my favourites!"

"Dad, I can get it. You sit down with Anna and listen to the story," Sonya said, getting up. She went into the kitchen to get a jug of milk, some glasses, and a plate of cookies. She returned to the table and took a seat to listen.

"Ready for this story?" Anna asked. Walter took a deep breath, began to reach for a cookie, pulled back his empty hand, and nodded.

"What prepares a father to hear that his thirteen-year-old son is unconscious in emergency from a bad drug experience?" Walter asked no one in particular. "Okay, Anna. I'm listening." Shelley, sitting next to Walter, put her hand on top of his when Anna started talking.

"Sonya, correct me if necessary, cuz you were here from the start of the story. Sonya saw Benji walking toward home, still on the driveway, and noticed that something wasn't right with him." Anna looked at Sonya, who nodded her confirmation. "Sonya called for Elizabeth, who then went outside to meet Benji. Benji fell down, throwing up, and Elizabeth was trying to help hold him, but he collapsed to the ground. Sonya came out, Elizabeth asked her to call for help, and she called us. We were on our way over for a surprise visit, we actually still have a bucket of Chicken Chef chicken in the car somewhere. We were going to bring you dinner from your favourite place. Oh well, another day. Okay, surprise visit, yeah… We were practically on the driveway when we got Sonya's call."

"We loaded Benji into the car with Elizabeth and took him to Emergency. The doctor told Elizabeth that Benji is going to be okay. The doctor was pretty sure that Benji's symptoms, or reactions, indicated that he had used ecstasy." Anna leaned back and draped her arm around Sonya again. "And that's it. Except that the doctor said that maybe someone should come back in the morning. Benji might be waking up around five or six."

Walter gasped. "He's thirteen! What's a thirteen-year-old doing with ecstasy?" He appealed to Anna first, then Shelley, with his eyes. "I don't understand. I don't know if I ever did understand kids." Walter dropped his head into his hands. Anna got up and stood behind him, rubbing his shoulders.

"Well, Dad, maybe other parents of thirteen-year-olds using ecstasy might not get it either." Anna draped her arms around her father's neck. "I know you're trying to talk to him. Don't stop, Dad. He probably needs to have someone listen to him too, if he ever gets around to saying something." Anna stood up, tapped Shelley on the shoulder, nodded toward the door and took a step in that direction. Shelley stood up and looked at Walter, took a tentative step toward him, then stopped.

"Come on, Shelley," Walter said, standing up and turning toward her, "give me a hug." Walter extended his arms to her. "I know I have more to learn about than just about a thirteen-year-old and drugs." He wrapped his arms around Shelley, who returned the embrace. "I'm a slow learner, but I'm trying. Please give me some more time." Shelley smiled and nodded.

"I don't know, Dad." Anna grinned. "You might get kicked out of your church, just like Darrel, if you give Shelley or me hugs." Walter shook his head at Anna, then smiled.

"Good night, Anna. I love you. Thanks again for helping," he said. "And Shelley, thank you too." Anna and Shelley turned and walked out, holding hands.

"Sonya, what do you think? Elizabeth fall asleep putting Jacob to sleep?" Walter asked. Sonya smiled, then nodded. "Can we let her sleep for a little bit before we wake her? I bet she's had a scary and difficult day." Sonya walked up to Walter and leaned against him.

"I've been scared for Jacob before. Sometimes Benji has been really mean to him, but I've never been this scared before," Sonya said, looking straight ahead. "I hope Benji is going to find his way back." Walter looked up into his daughter's face. Tears were beginning to trickle down her cheeks. He pulled Sonya into his lap, reached around to wipe the tears away.

"I'm scared too, Sonya. What do you usually do when you're scared?" Sonya leaned her head onto Walter's shoulder.

"Usually I pray, but sorry, Dad, usually that just seems like I'm left alone in an empty room when I do that. I just don't want to be alone right now." Sonya took a breath. "You don't have to tell me everything's going to be alright either, Dad. I know it isn't going to be alright, at least not tonight, not for a long time." Sonya buried her face in her father's shoulder for a few moments before lifting her head again. "What happened to him way back in Saskatoon? I think somehow that must be connected to this." She shook her head.

Walter patted her knee. "That Saskatoon trip certainly marked a shift in direction, didn't it? Or at least marked a hard turn downward. Do you think Benji trying drugs is connected to Saskatoon too?"

"I don't know, Dad. It just seems that even though Benji had some mean streaks to him before that trip, after that trip, well, I don't know. He just changed so much. I've tried to talk to him, but he doesn't ever say anything to me. I feel like I don't even really know him."

A bedroom door opened, and Elizabeth stepped out and walked toward them. She lifted both hands to pull back her hair. She sat down beside Walter and Sonya and put a hand on Sonya's knee. "Sonya, thank you for everything today. I don't know what would have happened without your help." Sonya gave Elizabeth a hug.

"I think I've had enough excitement for one day. Do you want me to sleep in Jacob's room so I can be near if he wakes up? I mean, when you go back to the hospital," Sonya asked, standing up. Elizabeth nodded her thanks as Sonya disappeared into the bedroom.

Walter leaned back on his chair and inhaled. Elizabeth gave him a tired smile. "This is scary," Walter said. "I feel like I'm in over my head. Anna lives with Shelley, and I'm trying not to be scared for their souls. Or for my soul, for that matter, because I'm beginning to wonder about what I've always known the Bible teaches. Darrel keeps exploring more ideas from the world of science, which I always thought was dangerous, but when he talks, maybe when I listen, it all seems to make so much sense. But this, with Benji, this still doesn't make any sense to me." He rubbed his forehead, then looked at Elizabeth. "There was a time, too, when I wasn't sure if you were going to stay with me. I was really afraid that I was going to lose both you and Jacob. I'm glad that we're in this together. Without you, I would be lost."

Elizabeth took Walter's hand and squeezed it. "I think I'm lost too, Walter," she said. "But I'm not afraid of being lost anymore, because there always seems to be another path opening up in front of me for us. And those paths, well, maybe only experience can be the teacher we need to find our way along them. Or maybe, even better, we talk with others who are walking on those same paths. Yeah, I'm glad we're in this together. I can't imagine trying to make it through this alone. There's no rule book for this, is there?"

Chapter Twenty-Four

Just before midnight, Walter parked the car in the lot below the Emergency department entrance but didn't move after he turned off the ignition. Elizabeth looked at him and put a hand on his knee. Walter gasped out a sob, tried to take a breath to regain control, but continued crying. He leaned his head forward, both hands clasping the steering wheel. His body shook uncontrollably while Elizabeth put her arms around him.

"I'm scared too," she said.

"What… what…" Walter gasped, "what if he doesn't wake up, Elizabeth? He's thirteen! Isn't he too young to die? What if the last thing he did was a sin…"

"Walter!" Elizabeth pulled back in her seat. "He's thirteen years old! If God doesn't understand human pain, then Jesus's entire life on earth was wasted! What are you saying? Of course that wasn't a sin!" Elizabeth hissed at Walter, pressing herself against the car door.

Walter took a breath and stared at Elizabeth. "Is it possible taking drugs isn't a sin? I want to believe that too, Elizabeth, but really? The Bible says…"

"The Bible says parents are to love their children, Walter," Elizabeth interrupted. "The Bible says that love is your, our, only job. Love God, love others. That's it! There's no reason to even think of sin at a time like this. Benji needs you to love him, to hug him, to hold him, to listen to him, not to say a word about the Bible or sin or anything. Just hold him. Just love him," Elizabeth's voice grew quieter with each phrase.

"I'm scared, Elizabeth," Walter whispered, reaching a hand to her. She took his hand in both of hers. "I don't know what I'm going to find inside those doors, and I don't know what to… I've never…" Walter took a deep breath. He bent his head forward, knocked it gently against the steering wheel, then straightened up. "Okay, Elizabeth. I'm ready." He took a deep breath, opened his door, and stepped out. Elizabeth got out of her door and came around to where Walter was waiting for her before they ascended the stairs to the Emergency entrance.

"Together, Walter," Elizabeth whispered into his ear, "we're in this together." He squeezed her hand. The automatic door slid open in front of them and they walked in, side by side, hand in hand.

The receptionist stood up and waved them over to her desk. "Hello, Mr. and Mrs. Rempel. The on-call doctor was just here and told me that Benji is still asleep. She will meet you back at his bed and give you more information. You can go ahead through that door. You know where he is, right?" Elizabeth nodded before they proceeded into the hallway. The doctor was standing at the central desk, reading a chart, when the Rempels approached.

The doctor nodded her greeting. "Hello again. Since you left, Benji's heart rate has returned to normal, as has his blood pressure." Elizabeth lifted both her hands to her face, exhaled sharply, and smiled. "Yes, both of those are good signs, aren't they?" The doctor smiled. "I can't offer you a bed, but there are chairs here, beside your son's bed, and there are more comfortable, stuffed chairs in the lobby, if you wish to wait there. Try to get some sleep. Of course, we will send someone to get you the moment he wakes up, if you choose to rest in the lobby."

Walter and Elizabeth looked at each other before Elizabeth faced the doctor. "I think we will stay here with Benji. We want to be beside him when he wakes." She took the same seat she had been in earlier, and Walter moved to another open chair near Benji's head.

"No matter what is happening, we want him to know we will always be beside him," Walter added. The doctor nodded and pulled the curtain closed behind her as she left the room.

Walter put his hand on Benji's arm, which lay above the sheet covering him. He slid it down to Benji's hand and intertwined his fingers with his son's. Tears welled up in his eyes, and his lips began to quiver. Elizabeth got up from her chair and came to stand behind Walter with her hands on his shoulders. He reached back with his other hand and put it on top of Elizabeth's.

"I don't know what's happening around me, or inside of me. I have one son sleeping peacefully now, after a terrible experience with some drug. I've never paid attention to drugs, other than to add them to a very long list of sins committed by people out there somewhere. Now it's not people out there, it's my son. Now I'm wondering for how many of those people out there drugs is their attempt to find a blessing, because preachers don't actually know how to bring God's blessings to them." Walter paused and took a deep breath, followed by a sigh.

"I have a daughter who has lived her life with my displeasure, my constant reminders to her about her sins. She too was looking for a blessing, and I brought her words of damnation instead. What have I done to my children, Elizabeth? Have I driven them away from God instead of drawing them nearer to God?" He dropped his chin against his chest and let out another deep sigh.

"It sounds to me like you're listening, Walter. You're listening to the deepest desires of your heart. You love God, and you're realizing that you love your family too. And isn't that what Jesus says it's all about? Love God, love your neighbour, and then you've done enough? Keep listening to your heart, and it seems to me you cannot bring a greater blessing, give a more beautiful gift to your children. And to everyone who gets to hear you preach too." Elizabeth dropped her hands to her side and returned to her seat. She leaned back in her chair, smiled at Walter, who was wiping away the last few tears from his eyes, and then at Benji.

"I just wish that Benji would talk to us, to somebody. It's so confusing what is happening here. Obviously something deep within him is hurting, hurting so much, but what?" Elizabeth asked. Walter nodded. "What are we missing, Walter?"

Walter shook his head. "Exactly. I missed everything that Anna ever tried to show me about her life. She seems so happy now, and I am happier for her almost every day too. What all have I missed in Benji's life? Why is it always easier to see something in hindsight? I wish I could look ahead and figure this out so I could somehow be more helpful to him now."

Walter shifted in his chair, looked up, and noticed that Elizabeth's eyes were closing. He glanced around the enclosed area they were in and saw a pile of sheets on a ledge above the bed Benji was on. Walter stood, reached up, and took down two of the sheets. He went over to Elizabeth and wrapped one around her. She opened her eyes, smiled, then pulled the sheet tightly around herself. Walter settled back into his chair and wrapped a sheet around his shoulders.

Walter opened his eyes and realized that a nurse was gently shaking his shoulder. "Yes, I was just resting my eyes," he blurted out, sitting upright in the chair and dropping the sheet from his shoulders into his lap. Doctor Brittany was standing between him and Benji, with Benji's wrist in one hand, and looking at her watch. Benji's eyes were barely open. Walter leaped to his feet, knocking over his chair as he tried to find a place beside the doctor. The noise woke Elizabeth, who rubbed her eyes.

Elizabeth sat up, folded the sheet that had covered her, and placed it on the edge of Benji's bed. Benji rolled his head in her direction, saw Elizabeth, and promptly rolled his head back to face the doctor.

"Good morning Benji," Walter started. Benji closed his eyes without responding.

The doctor let go of Benji's hand and turned toward Walter. "Good morning, Mr. Rempel. My name is Brittany. I've been attending to your son. Welcome back, Mrs. Rempel." The doctor turned to greet her. "Benji is doing much better now than yesterday evening. His heart rate and blood pressure are back to normal." She smiled at Benji. "He isn't nauseous anymore, so I think he is good to go home with you now." Benji sat up in the bed.

"Hello, Benji," Elizabeth began. "I'm glad you're feeling better."

"Son, you had us so worr…" Walter blurted out, leaning forward.

Elizabeth interrupted. "Benji, it's been quite a night for you so far. Are you ready to go home with us?" Benji kept his eyes downcast as he sat up, pushed himself forward, and lowered his feet until they reached the floor.

"Benji, the clothes you were wearing last night are right here, on the counter," the nurse said, pointing to the neatly folded pants and shirt on the counter. "We sort of cleaned his jacket, although you'll probably want to run it through the laundry once you're home. It's hanging on a hook just outside this room," the nurse said to Elizabeth.

"Yes, of course, thank you," Elizabeth responded.

The doctor took a step toward the curtain before addressing Elizabeth. "I told you last night that we sent his blood for a toxicology report. We got the results this morning and learned that the ecstasy in your son's system was contaminated with something. We couldn't make a determination what the contaminant was just yet. We should know within a day. When we know more, and whether or not that raises any concerns, we will contact you. Take care of yourself, and of your son," said the doctor, who, with chart in hand, turned and stepped out past the curtain.

"Should I go get the car?" Walter looked at Elizabeth. He shifted his weight back and forth between his feet. He shuffled sideways to get out from behind the bed, then took a few more steps down the hallway before stopping. "You're ready for the car, right?"

"Yes please, Walter," Elizabeth encouraged him. "Bring the car to the door." He disappeared down the hall. Elizabeth turned toward Benji, who was still sitting on the edge of the bed. "I'll step out and close the curtain so you can put on your clothes. I'll be right outside the curtain if you need any help." Elizabeth stood up, pulled the curtain open for the nurse, who also left, and followed her into the hallway, securing the curtain behind her.

A minute later, Benji, dressed in the clothes from the previous day, pushed his way through the curtain, avoided eye contact with Elizabeth, and started walking down the hallway. He paused at the intersection of another hallway, looking right, then left, not knowing which way to turn.

Elizabeth grabbed his jacket from the hook on the wall, darted down the hallway and caught up with Benji, pointing toward the Emergency ward door. She reached around him to push the open button and the door swung outward. Benji walked through the opening with Elizabeth following. He kept his eyes on the floor all the way to the door, where he paused, waiting for the automatic door to slide open. He stepped into the early morning air, looked up at the sky, took a deep breath, and then opened the rear door in the car that was waiting for him.

Elizabeth opened the front passenger door to get in, looked back at Benji, then settled into her seat. She buckled herself in and looked ahead. "Ready, son?" Walter asked. "Buckled?" Not receiving a response, he drove down the driveway, turned left onto the street, and headed for home. "Do you need anything, son? We could stop at A & W for a root beer float. Or maybe at Subway for a sandwich. Are you hungry?" Walter worked to keep his voice calm.

"Honey," Elizabeth touched his elbow, "let's just go home and get some rest." She stroked Walter's arm once and pulled her hand back. She tried to steal a look at Benji in the rear-view mirror, but its angle didn't allow that. She leaned her head against the window and took a few deep breaths. Benji remained sullen in the back seat, kept his gaze on the floor, and offered no responses.

When Walter put the car in park and turned off the ignition, Benji was the first out of the doors. He ran to the house and disappeared inside before either Walter or Elizabeth had stepped out of the car. Walter looked at her and shrugged. "What now, Elizabeth?" he asked. "Does one of us go check on him? Does one of us stay with him in his room?"

"Yes, Walter, one of us checks on him. And that one of us has to be you," Elizabeth answered. "Staying in his room? I don't know if that is necessary, but as long as he is in that room, we have to check on him. I wonder if there is anything we could do to get him to join us in the living room for some time? Or the dining room. He hasn't joined us for table games for ages, so I don't know about that one. Ask if he would like to join us when you check on him." Elizabeth held the house door open for Walter to enter, she followed, then closed the door.

Walter kicked off his shoes by the door and walked toward the bedroom hallway. Half-way to the hall he turned to Elizabeth. "Are you sure it should be me who checks on him? You know his room better than I do."

"Walter!" Elizabeth whispered a shout in his direction. "It has to be you. Yes, I know his room better, but you know how he feels about me. Didn't you see how he avoided all eye contact with me in the hospital?"

Walter paused after each step he took toward Benji's room. He cast his eyes back at Elizabeth after the first step, swallowed, and took another step. He stood in front of the closed door, placed his ear against it and listened to the sounds of silence. He took the doorknob in his hand and tried to turn it but couldn't. The door was locked. Walter took a step back and looked at the doorknob and tried it one more time. Nothing changed.

Walter placed his mouth near the door. "Benji? Benji, this is Dad. Can I come in?" Walter's quiet whisper didn't penetrate past the door. He cleared his throat and tried again. "Benji, are you okay? Can I come in?" This time his voice travelled into the room.

"Leave me alone," Benji called back. "I'm sleeping!" Walter just stood outside the bedroom door looking at the knob, at the ceiling, at the floor, then back at the doorknob. He ran a hand through his hair, swallowed, half-turned his body, then turned it back at the door. He reached for the knob, tried it unsuccessfully one more time, then leaned against the wall.

"Let me guess," Elizabeth said as she joined Walter just outside Benji's room, "the door's locked." Walter nodded. "And you don't want to break it down." She smiled and took Walter's hand. "Really, though, you have to open that door and check on him. Today, I think, even if he is in his room, the door has to be unlocked at the very least, and preferably, slightly ajar."

"You're right. We will need to check on him throughout the day, won't we?" Walter nodded agreement. "What do you use to unlock one of these doors? I've never had to learn how to do that."

Elizabeth reached up and pulled a bobby pin from her hair and bent it open. She pushed the narrow metal rod into the tiny opening in the door-knob, pushed against it, and turned the door handle at the same time. The door opened under her pressure. Walter watched, shook his head, then pushed the door open and went in. Benji was lying on his back on his bed. He glared at Walter for a moment then rolled over to face the wall.

"Hey, Benji," Walter started, standing beside the bed. "Today, that door has to stay open. You can stay in bed as long as you want to, get some sleep in your own bed, but we want to check in on you every once in a while. Once you've slept for a while, do you want me to make you breakfast? Maybe we could watch something on television together?" Benji made no response. Walter sat down on the bed and put a hand on Benji's leg. Benji pulled his leg away from his father's touch and curled into a ball, still facing the wall.

"Where do I start, son?" Walter spoke, almost as if to himself. "I wish I had done some things differently when Agatha died, after I married Elizabeth, after you got back from Saskatoon. I don't know what I should have done differently, just that I wish I had known how to be a better father to you. I'm going to try and do more things right." He paused. "It may not always feel like it, Benji, but I love you. Elizabeth loves you. Your family loves you. We want to do anything you need us to do for you."

"I need you to leave me alone," Benji whispered, with his face pressed to the wall.

Walter nodded, stood up, and walked to the window. "Okay, I'll leave you alone for now. But when you need breakfast, come to the dining room. Or just let me know, and I can bring you breakfast in bed today." More silence was the only response from Benji. Walter turned, went to the door, and started to pull it closed, when he remembered Elizabeth's concern about the closed door. He pushed it slightly open, looked at Benji lying on the bed, then went to the dining room.

Elizabeth was sitting at the table with a cup of coffee in front of her. Another milky cup of coffee sat on the table across from her. "It's not quite as hot as it was, but it's still warm." She smiled at Walter. "Anything? Are you okay?"

Walter dropped into a chair and slumped his shoulders. "The only thing he did was turn away from me and then said all he needed from us was to be left alone." He took a sip from his cup, then put it down again. "I left the door sort of open. We can look in that way, and maybe hear him too if he asks for something."

"How are you doing?" Elizabeth saw the combination of exhaustion, confusion, fear, and love wrestling for control of Walter's face.

"I don't know." Walter lifted his cup to his mouth but put it down without drinking. "I used to see everything in black and white. Now I think seeing in black and white actually means not seeing anything at all. I don't know what I am seeing anymore."

Elizabeth nodded. "In the past, I thought we had lots of time to keep trying to figure this out. Now everything seems urgent. Although, in truth,

Walter, I don't even know what I'm trying to figure out anymore. At first I thought it was Benji's anger, next was Jacob's safety, then Saskatoon, now drugs. What next?"

"Exactly," Walter agreed. "Ecstasy sounds like such a good word. How can it be so horrible? Does Benji think it's horrible, or does he like what it does to him? Why does he need to use drugs? Or is he just trying them, not really using them? Where does this come from? Did we, I mean, did I do something to make him so angry all the time?" Walter poured out one question after another. "What do you think? Has Jacob's life at least gotten a little easier? Do you feel he's safer now? I hope he doesn't need drugs when he's thirteen."

Chapter Twenty-Five

Later that afternoon Anna and Shelley sat side by side, holding hands, on the couch in the Rempel's living room. Two half-empty mugs of coffee sat on the coffee table in front of them. An engraved wooden tray also rested on the coffee table, with a bowl of sugar and a creamer on it. Walter sat on a large, cushioned chair across from them, sipping water from a cup.

Elizabeth came from the kitchen with a plate in one hand and a steaming mug of coffee in the other. "I think Sonya must bake when she's scared or stressed." She smiled at the two on the couch. "She made about five dozen, maybe more, peanut butter cookies last night while we were at the hospital." She put the plate on the coffee table, lifted the creamer, and added some to her coffee. "Mmm, this is exactly what I need after such a short night." She smiled at Anna, then at Shelley, and then took a seat on the foot stool in front of Walter's chair.

"How many nights ago was it that I told Sonya milk and cookies were my favourite? But coffee and cookies is probably even better." Anna laughed, reaching for a cookie.

Shelley smiled and added, "Anytime there are cookies, with milk, with coffee, with more cookies, it just always seems like the right time to enjoy Sonya's cookies." She also reached for one, took two, and stole a glance at Anna.

"Don't look at me. You can have as many as you want." Anna patted Shelley's knee. "Okay, Elizabeth, tell us what happened at the hospital. What did the doctor say after we left?" Anna put down her cookie, took a sip of coffee, and looked at Elizabeth. Shelley put her cookie down and put a hand on Anna's leg.

Elizabeth nodded. "Actually, not much more. The toxicology report showed that the ecstasy was contaminated, but they hadn't identified with what by this morning. She said she would call once they knew more." Elizabeth turned to Walter. "Or did she say she would call if there was something we should know? I can't remember exactly what she said. I was very tired. It was such a short and eventful night!" She turned back to Anna and Shelley. Walter reached his hands forward and rubbed her shoulders.

"I didn't hear any of it," Walter added. "I was getting the car."

"Shelley, you said something yesterday that I would like to ask you about. You said that Benji wasn't the only thirteen-year-old to use drugs. Did you use drugs when you were his age?" Shelley took a sip from her coffee and nodded. "Can I ask you why?" Elizabeth leaned forward, eyes wide open.

Shelley took Anna's hand before beginning. "You know how popular the LGBTQ community is here, right? You know that we get preached at, called sinners, are told we are going to hell, are pelted with stones, with hateful stares. There just aren't so many people who are willing to give us a chance, to see us as people, the same as anyone else."

Walter's hands dropped from Elizabeth's shoulders. She turned to look at him, but he didn't make any eye contact. Elizabeth turned back to face Shelley and nodded her agreement. "So I knew that there was something different about me from quite early on in my life, even though at first I couldn't figure out what it was. I just knew I was different, I had no friends, I was teased, no, harassed, mercilessly at school, and my parents never talked to me, never noticed anything, never helped me in any way," Shelley continued. "I was a lost soul," she looked toward Walter, "to use your language, Walter. From the age of ten I sort of sunk into a deeper and darker hole of depression and despair. I didn't know what was going on with me at all." She paused and took a drink from her cup.

"I don't know how a dealer heard about me, or that I was sad, but one day, a kid from high school came up to me. He said 'I heard you were a really sad kid with no friends. I've got something for you that will help.' He gave me a Ziploc bag with like, oh, what was it, five, maybe six pills in it. 'It's a gift,' he said, and then 'if you like it, I'll find you again, but you have to buy the next ones.' I didn't even know what kind of pills they were. I just knew my life sucked. I don't know if I thought my life wouldn't suck anymore if I took those pills, or whether I just wanted to forget that my life sucked. Anyway, I went home, sat in my room for a few hours just looking at the bag, and then finally I put the bag under my pillow. You know, just in case one of my parents came into my bedroom to check on me." Shelley smiled ruefully. "As if there was any chance of them ever coming into my room to check on me."

She drank some more coffee. "The next day, at noon, I took one of those pills with my lunch. I don't remember anything about the afternoon, but I do remember how I felt that evening. I thought, 'hey, life isn't that bad after all.' So I took another pill after dinner that night, then again the next day at lunch. Then again, and again and again. I stopped using my allowance, my babysitting money, any money I got for gifts to buy useless shit, oops, excuse me, useless stuff, and instead spent it all for more pills from that high school kid."

"Did you feel like you needed them?" Elizabeth asked. Walter nodded from his seat. "Can you say more about life not being so bad after you started taking those pills?"

Shelley nodded. "Yeah, it didn't take long and I was sure that if I wanted to enjoy any part of my life, I needed to take those pills. No pills equalled no happiness in my mind. Taking pills, one or two per day, made my troubles disappear. I mean, they didn't, not really, but it felt as if they did. And that's all that mattered. I still had no friends, I still got teased and harassed, still didn't know what was going on in my body, head, or heart. All I knew is that I felt better, and I wanted that feeling to continue." Shelley popped the rest of her cookie into her mouth. Anna patted her on the leg, then leaned against her with a body hug.

"People have no clue how mean they can be, or are," Anna said. Walter looked at his feet, then looked up.

"I'm one of those people, Shelley. The kind you spoke about, the kind who tells others they are going to hell. But I tell them they are going to hell for so many reasons, not just because they want a same-sex partner. I had never met anyone who was, what did you call them? LGBQ, or whatever the letters are. I knew them only from a distance, well, I didn't know them at all. I knew what I had been told by the church, what I had read in my Christian magazines, what other church people said. We all accepted that LBG people were sinners and going to hell. You're the first person I've ever known that is… Sorry, Anna is the first person I've ever known, and I didn't know it about her either. Or maybe, I just didn't want to know it. Not until just a little while ago," Walter confessed. "It's just one more thing I no longer know what to think about it. I read the Bible now, and it doesn't say what I always thought it said, what I taught it said." Elizabeth turned to smile at Walter.

"Sorry, Shelley, I'm interrupting, please continue," Walter said.

"Sure. I don't have much more to add, though. The drugs made me forget that I was different, that no one liked me. They allowed me to obliviate all my bad, sad feelings, so yeah, I felt I needed them. I sure as hell wanted them. I knew other kids, the same age as me, who also needed drugs for the same reason. I mean, not because they were LGBTQ kids, but because of some sort of thing that made them different. There is so much abuse going on – sexual, emotional, physical. So many unhappy kids who are wanting to escape what their lives are. They are good targets for the sellers."

"Think about it, Dad, Elizabeth," Anna interjected. "Benji has been unhappy, angry, whatever, not in a good space, for how many years already? Ever since Mom died. And life has only gotten worse for him. I mean, I don't think it's abuse, Dad, that you married Elizabeth, or Elizabeth, that you had Jacob, but maybe in a six-, seven-, eight year-old-head, he thinks it is. After being upset for so long, taking some sort of drug can make him forget all of that, and he might even make some friends who commiserate with him because they are unhappy too. Misery loves company, right?"

Elizabeth turned to face Walter. "I think I'm beginning to understand. Benji's been unhappy for so long that he could just be looking to forget everything."

Walter nodded, then added, "But do you really think it is just us? I know that it's so long ago, but I can't forget that he was much angrier, much unhappier, after his visit to Darrel and Marigold in Saskatoon. How long ago was that?" he mused.

"Dad, that was ages ago. He was what, seven, eight, nine? I remember too, he was weird when he came back. Isn't that when he started a fire in his bedroom? And something happened at school right around then too, I think. Yeah, he's just one messed-up kid. Maybe, just maybe, and I know this is going to sound weird, but maybe he doesn't want to be messed up. Taking ecstasy, or whatever it is he's taking, makes him feel like he isn't messed up. Everyone wants to feel as if they are normal or belong somewhere."

"This all makes sense, what you're saying," Elizabeth agreed. "So how do we take this and apply it to Benji?" She looked from Anna to Shelley, and then back to Walter. "If the drugs he's taking make him forget his trouble, like you say, or make him feel better somehow, how can we get him to quit taking those drugs? Once he's using, won't he just want to keep using because he feels better?" She shook her head. "It sort of makes sense, but it also sort of makes me feel hopeless! He doesn't talk to me at all, and less and less to Walter too. He does still talk to Sonya, at least sometimes, but I don't know about what."

"I get why you're worried Elizabeth," Shelley said. "When I was using, I thought the drugs were my friend, that they were making my life better, so all I wanted to do was to take more." Elizabeth nodded while furrows deepened on Walter's forehead. "But the truth is, they weren't my friend at all. The drugs that kids are taking, they're bad news, they're all sorts of trouble that kids just don't realize because they feel good in the moment. Although, feeling good for a moment is all sorts of good for a kid too."

Anna added, "I tried something, don't even know what it was. A pill, a blue pill? A purple pill? Some sort of pill. I tried it only once and didn't like how I felt. But I had tons of friends, all of us misfits and losers according to the cool kids, who used all sorts of drugs, and some of us had all sorts of troubles because of it, while others seemed to function much better because of what they used. Yeah, if there was some way of getting that little brother of mine to lay off, but still feel good about himself, that would be super. But how?"

"Elizabeth, do you know if the doctor sends a report to the school counsellor?" Walter asked.

"Not a chance," interjected Anna. "There are so many privacy rules about what doctors can and can't tell, who they can tell anything. No way they're talking to a school person."

Elizabeth agreed. "You're right, Anna. I think Walter, you or I, should make an appointment to see that counsellor again and explain to him what happened. That way he knows that the teacher's report about Benji being on stuff is most likely true, and maybe he knows someone or some way of helping Benji, or us. Plus, if it really is about not wanting to be miserable, maybe that is an idea to explore. Maybe someone can help him find a way to feel good about himself without using something. I'll call the school tomorrow morning to make an appointment."

"Yeah, Elizabeth, I agree with you. The more help we can get for him, the more accurate help we can get, the better it will be," Walter concluded. "I'm sorry, I have to get to work. I have some papers to sort, just to earn a paycheck and all. See you later, Elizabeth. Have a good day, Anna, Shelley." Walter got out of the chair, grabbed a jacket from the closet, and left out the side door.

Chapter Twenty-Six

Benji sat on a bean bag chair in Earl Tilitson's office. He was twisting his fingers together and then slowly peeling them apart. The counsellor sat on a short chair, so his knees were practically as high as his chest, but his face wasn't much above Benji's. He was looking at a series of papers in his hands. "These are all the drawings you've done for me since we first met, Benji," Earl said. He laid the papers on the floor, revealing a range of what he had called "drawings."

One sheet had a black splotch in the middle, another had a red splotch, one had a bow and arrow on it, another what looked like the map of a city park. "These sort of coloured ones were the first ones you did, Benji. Do you remember why you chose black and then red?" Earl looked at Benji.

Benji held his fingers still for a moment and looked at his shoelaces. Then he continued twisting and unravelling his fingers without so much as acknowledging the question. The counsellor put five more pages on the floor in front of Benji. Each of these pages had drawings of a scrotum and erect penis on them, some pages had one large image to fill the whole page, others had multiple smaller images, all identical. "Any comments about these?" Benji was steadfastly examining his shoelaces once again.

"And these last few pictures, of houses on the edge of town, each one seeming to be closer to midnight as the sky is getting darker and darker. It seems to be getting later and later, what can you tell me about these?"

Earl asked. He placed four more pages on the floor, covering the penis-laden pages.

Benji stole a glance at the night-scapes but said nothing. "How about I tell you a story, Benji, and then you tell me if any part of this story sounds even a little familiar to you," Earl began. "There was a kid, about nine years old. His mother died when he was four, and this really hurt the kid's heart. He loved his mom, and he didn't know if he could breathe properly for a few weeks, his whole body hurt so much. One day his dad came home with another lady, someone the kid had never seen before, and told his son that they were going to get married and that she was going to be his new mom. The kid was furious! When his dad gave the woman a ride back to her place that evening, the son went to the storage closet where his mom's old clothes were. He took them all out into the front yard, got the gas canister from the garage, poured a bunch of gas on the clothes, and lit them on fire. When his dad got home, the fire department was just putting out the fire. Why do you supposed the kid decided to burn all his mom's old clothes?"

"I was six, not seven, when my mom died. And it was my clothes, not my mom's clothes that I started on fire. How should I know why that kid lit a fire? Maybe he likes fires," Benji blurted out. He glared at the counsellor for a moment, then looked down at his shoelaces again. His hands were balled into fists at his sides.

"Okay, so you don't know about that kid. How about this story," Earl continued, after writing a few things in his notebook. "A different kid, a twelve-year-old, a kid who had fights with his mom and dad pretty much every day. He couldn't do anything right in his parents' eyes, and his parents couldn't do anything right according to him. His dad frequently went on business trips, so the kid was left at home with his mom. His mom didn't seem to have any idea about what a twelve-year-old's life was like, just didn't get the kid at all. The mom was a terrible cook, made only grilled-cheese sandwiches, probably four or five times a week, and the kid hated cheese. After a really bad fight with his parents, when he was sitting on a street curb, an older kid came and sat down beside him. Said he'd noticed that the first kid was often angry, sad, depressed, and that he had something that could change that. The angry kid didn't say anything, but that didn't stop the older kid. He handed over a small bag with some pills in it. These will make you feel better, he said. He put the bag on the curb, got up and walked away. What do you think the angry kid did? Or what do you think the angry kid should have done?"

"How stupid do you think I am?" Benji now glared directly at the counsellor. "A young kid's mother died and he was sad. A twelve-year-old is offered drugs. You think I'm going to tell you stuff if you give me a story about some kid, who just sort of happens to be me?" Earl held Benji's glare for a few moments.

"Benji, how long have we been seeing each other? It's over two years," Earl started. "In that time, you have drawn a few pictures that I think are trying to tell me something. I know many boys your age draw penis pictures, that isn't odd or strange. But each kid that draws them has a reason for drawing them. The dark night sky, I can figure out metaphors, or symbolic elements in pictures, but without a conversation, I'm just speculating. I've asked questions and watched you stare at your shoelaces in response, or at your fingers, rather than answer them, so I wonder what you're avoiding, and why you're avoiding it." Earl's soft voice seemed to appease Benji, as he released his fists back into open hands. He looked down at his shoelaces again.

"Your parents, your sisters, they speak about a Benji who was a super happy kid until his mom died. Then a new Benji took over. A Benji who was upset a lot of the time. They also all seem to agree that something happened in Saskatoon one summer that made you change into a more quiet, isolated person, but none of them have been able to figure out what happened, because you don't talk to them either." Earl wasn't accusing, he was just recounting. "The ecstasy event confirmed your teacher's suspicions that you were using something. I can give you a list of at least fifteen reasons why a thirteen-year-old might choose to use drugs, but I don't know which is your reason."

Benji wriggled into a hunched position, with his knees pulled up to his chest. "I know it might not feel this way to you, Benji, but your parents love you, they're worried about you, and they want to help you. But, and it's a big but," Benji looked up at the counsellor with a smirk on his face before looking down again, "ah, yeah, a big butt, I see what I said. Okay, well, your parents don't know what is going on inside your head, so they don't know what to do to help you. They don't know what type of help you need." Earl smiled a little thinking about Benji's momentary smirk. "And in truth, Benji, I don't know how to help you either. Unless you give me something real, I can only speculate, and frankly, that doesn't help. I'm not sure whether there is any reason for me to keep asking you come see me."

Earl closed his notebook, threw it onto his desk, and stood up. He turned toward the window and gazed out at the afternoon sun shining across the school playground. "Wouldn't you be angry if God killed your mom?" Benji asked. Earl turned quickly to face the boy who was still curled into a near-fetal position.

"God killed your mom? I don't understand," Earl said, sitting down in front of Benji again.

"I don't know how many times Dad said 'God has a plan' when he was talking about Mom's death. If God has a plan, and your mom ends up dead, isn't that like God killing her?" Benji looked up, a tear sitting on the edge of one eye. He swiped it away and looked down again. He didn't wait for a response. "And then God puts a different person into your house, someone who isn't your mother, and she pretends to be your mother. Or at least sort of pretends to be your mother. What kind of God, who's supposed to be so smart He knows everything, is so stupid? That's such a stupid plan!" Benji shouted at the counsellor, who shot a look at the closed notebook on his desk, and then back at Benji.

"So you're really angry at God, is that it, Benji?"

"You aren't allowed to be angry at God. Being angry at God is a sin, and sinners go to hell, forever." Benji started sobbing. Earl leaned forward and extended a hand, but pulled it back before touching Benji. "I can't hate God, so I hate Elizabeth instead. She's really nice, but she had a kid, she lives in our house, I see her every day, and every day it's a reminder that God killed my mom, so I hate her!" Benji snorted, coughed, and took a deep breath.

Earl scratched his head. "Okay, so I get it, why you say you hate Elizabeth. But what's the connection to Saskatoon?"

"What did they tell you about Saskatoon? Do they know what happened there? I've never told anyone." Benji wiped tears from his eyes and glared at the counsellor. "You didn't tell them what happened in Saskatoon, did you?" Benji's eyes softened and his voice pleaded.

"Benji, I couldn't tell anyone anything, I have no idea what happened in Saskatoon. All I know is that you spent some time there one summer," Earl said. "But you can tell me what happened if you want to." Benji only met his eyes for a moment. "Whatever you tell me in this office, stays in this office. Unless it is something illegal, or that might connect to self-harm, or harm to others. Then I have to report it."

Benji jerked his head up and said, "You're going to tell my parents what I just told you?"

"No, no, nothing you've said today is illegal or harmful to yourself or someone else," Earl stated. "I just want to make sure that although almost everything you say in this office is confidential, I'll never repeat to anyone, there are specific topics that I have to report, that's all." Benji looked down and started twisting and unravelling his fingers again.

Earl bent his head down toward Benji's, waiting for another comment, anything else that might clarify what he had been speculating and wondering about for almost three years. Benji closed his eyes, pulled his knees back up to his chest, and started rocking. "Can I go now?" Benji whispered. "I want to go now." He kept his eyes closed and kept rocking back and forth.

Earl leaned back in his chair, stretched his arms, stood up and went to his desk. "Yes, Benji, you can go. I'll send you a message through your teacher about our next appointment time, okay?" He picked up a pen and opened the notebook.

Benji stood up, walked to the door, and turned the handle. He turned to look back, stood silently for a few moments, then lowered his gaze. "I think I'm done. I don't want to come back." He stepped through and closed the door.

Earl dropped to his chair and wrote line after line. He looked up at the ceiling for a moment, then wrote some more. He lay his pen on top of the notebook, walked to the window, and looked out at the children who were playing on the wooden play structure. He lifted one hand to his chin, lifted his hand a little further and ran his hand through his hair. "So close, Benji, so close. Maybe next time we'll cross that bridge," Earl said to the window before returning to his desk and closing the notebook.

Chapter Twenty-Seven

Benji was staring at the pages on the desk in front of him. The numbers in the math textbook blurred into black blobs, and the blank page of his notebook showed only the three holes Benji had dug into the pages with his pencil. He propped his elbows on the table and dropped his head into his hands. A deep sighed escaped his lips, and he closed his eyes. He heard the classroom door open but didn't bother to look up.

"Excuse me, class," the teacher's voice said, interrupting the students. "We have a short presentation from Mr. Pinkerton." Benji's head shot up and he stared at the guest standing at the front of the room. His jaw dropped, and his eyes glazed over. "Mr. Pinkerton has just moved here from Saskatoon to take over Steinbach's day camp programs for the summer. He wants to explain what's available for kids of different ages. So maybe you'll hear something you'd like to do, or if you have a younger sibling, something for them too. Mr. Pinkerton…"

Benji's face flushed, then heated to a deep red. He stole one more glance toward the front of the room and saw the guest looking directly at him, without offering a hint of recognition. He kept smiling and talking to the class, interspersing questions to the students about what they liked to do and explaining which day-camp program those interests might align with.

Benji took his pencil in his hand and bored another hole, then another into his math notebook. When the point broke due to the exerted pressure, he grabbed a pen and kept gauging more holes. The day-camp presentation didn't last long, and the guest waved and left the room.

"Well, doesn't that sound great, kids?" The teacher began to walk up and down the aisles giving each student a brochure the presenter had left for them. "Our town is growing, and thankfully with that growth comes more money for youth programming. Of course, you all know about the range of activities available through the Steinbach Arts Council, right? They offer so much to do for both the summer and winter months too. If you're not sure what happens there, ask me, and I'll make sure you get a brochure regarding the winter programs too."

The teacher dropped a brochure on top of Benji's math notebook so did not notice the dark scratches and holes on the pages. She kept moving up and down the rows of desks, making sure each student had a brochure. Benji swiped the brochure off his desk onto the floor, his face still a burning red. "Now, after that interruption, back to math. There are about fifteen minutes left in class to do the questions that are listed on the board. In about five or seven minutes I'll ask some of you to come to the board to show how you solved the problems. Questions?" The teacher looked around the class. One hand was raised, and the teacher walked over and knelt in the aisle beside the student.

Benji glanced at the teacher's back, then wrote "Fing Fred" in big black letters across the open page of his notebook. He reached for his blue pen and wrote over the letters. He switched from one pen to another, scratching deeper into his notebook page with each pass of his pen. Benji tore the page out of the notebook and threw it on the floor.

Next Benji took out his pencil crayon box and fished through it until he found the pink crayon. He started sketching one image after another. Benji was so intent on his drawings that he didn't notice the student sitting behind him looking over his shoulder, nor did he hear his giggles. The student nudged another student beside him and nodded toward Benji's desk. The girl stood up, leaned slightly forward to peek over Benji's shoulder and gasped. Her face turned bright red and she sat down. She frowned at the student who invited her to see Benji's sketches and shook her head before returning to her work.

Benji's face stayed red, and each successive breath became shallower, more rapid and laboured. He turned the page and madly scrawled more images on the next page, then the next page, and then the next page. He didn't look up, didn't notice that some other students around him were attempting to look at his math notebook then either giggle, cover their mouths with their hands, or blush and look away.

"What's happening over there?" the teacher asked, looking toward the students sitting around Benji. All the students instantly became very focused on their own desks, math textbooks, and notebooks. No student offered a response, and as the question seemed to redirect their focus, the teacher left the student she had been helping and went to her desk. "Two more minutes, and then we'll look at some solutions," she reminded the class.

The boy who sat directly behind Benji threw a glance at Benji's back, stood up, and walked to the teacher's desk. "Yes," the teacher smiled, "how can I help you?" The boy cupped a hand to the teacher's ear and leaned forward and whispered something. As he whispered his face turned increasingly deeper shades of pink. The teacher's eyes grew wider with each comment she heard, and she turned her eyes to Benji, who was still busy drawing image after image on page after page. The boy leaned back, pulled his hand away from the teacher's ear and returned to his desk, making sure to walk to the edge of the room first, then to the back of the classroom, and then up his row toward his seat. He sat down, looked up at the teacher, who was staring at Benji, and pointed toward Benji's desk and vigorously nodded his head.

The teacher shook her head, coughed into her elbow a few times, and stood up. "Okay, class. Time to do some math on the board. Who wants to show us how to solve question one?" Hands shot up. "Eleanor, number one please. Come to the front and show your work on the board. Please go as far to the right as you can go so we can fit lots of questions on the board." She pointed to the right-hand side of the board, and then turned to the class again. "Question two?" More hands shot up, some shaking with desire, practically shouting "pick me! Pick me!" Other students tenaciously examined either their desktops, the floor, or suddenly found something outside the window that needed their most ardent attention.

The room filled with the buzz of students writing out their math solutions on the board, other students shouting, "not like that" or "yeah, that's how I did it too," groans from some, and continued attention to the sky outside the window from others. Benji didn't notice what was going on around him, as his focus was on his math notebook.

"Benji." The teacher raised her voice in his direction. He didn't notice or respond. "Benji, hello, Benji!" The teacher raised her voice a little more and took two steps in his direction. Benji snapped his head up, eyes glaring at the teacher. "Benji, can I see you for a moment when the bell goes, please?" He looked down, slammed his math textbook closed, and pushed his math notebook over the edge of the desk onto the floor. A few students near him looked at him quizzically, but upon seeing the expression on his face, looked away without making any comments.

The bell rang and the teacher dismissed the class. "Have a good day, everyone. Remember to finish those questions for tomorrow. See you." Benji stayed seated at his desk, eyes on the floor. The teacher walked toward him and knelt down beside his desk, trying to look into his face. Benji lowered his gaze further and clenched the sides of the desk with both hands.

The teacher reached for the torn paper on the floor, turned it over, and saw the two words and many gouges. She reached for the notebook on the floor, flipped it open, and gasped. She dropped both the single page and the notebook. "Benji!" she cried out and covered her mouth with her hand. She stood up, then leaned down to pick up the two pieces again. "Benji, I… I… what does this mean?" Benji's ears turned red, and he covered his face with his hands to stifle the sobs that began to shake his body.

"Benji, oh, Benji," the teacher said. "I wish I knew what to say or to do, but I don't. I know I can't leave these drawings with you, though. I have to turn them in. Here's what I'll do," she explained. "I'll bring these to Mr. Tilitson. You know him. He's the school counsellor. You've been seeing him," she kept going without waiting to hear a response from Benji. "I think he will know what to do with this stuff. I'll bring this to him, please wait here for me, or for him. One of us will come for you, and then you can explain these to him. I'll tell him it's sort of important to see you right away."

Benji dropped his head and shoulders onto the desk, no longer able to suppress the sobs. His whole body shook violently as he wept uncontrollably. The teacher blushed, extended her hand, and touched Beni's shoulder. He recoiled and looked up, his face wet with tears, and leaped to his feet. "Don't touch me! I hate you!" Benji screamed at the teacher, put both hands against her belly, and pushed hard. She stumbled backward as Benji ran out the open door.

The teacher lowered herself onto the floor and turned the pages in Benji's notebook. Her eyes grew wider as each new page of images increased her alarm. When she closed the notebook after the last image, she wiped a tear from her cheek. She put a hand on the seat of Benji's desk and used it to pull herself to a standing position. She wiped her face one more time and then stepped deliberately toward the classroom door.

When she arrived at the guidance department, she entered and looked for the counsellor. Earl Tilitson's door was open, and she could see him leaning back in his chair with an untouched sandwich on the desk in front of him and a cup of coffee with no steam, suggesting it had been sitting on the desk for some time too. She approached and knocked on his door.

"Kristy." Earl greeted her with a wave of his hand. He motioned toward the chair across the desk from him. "Please, come in and take a seat." When he took a second look at her face, he leaned forward and put both arms on the desk. "Kristy, are you okay? What happened? It looks like something happened to you."

Kristy swallowed, a tear trickled down her cheek, she swallowed again, and she burst into tears. "I think something terrible might have happened to Benji. I think you know the Benji in my class, right?" She burst out as she practically threw Benji's notebook across the desk toward the counsellor. Kristy allowed a few more sobs to escape before she caught her breath. She looked for a tissue box on Earl's desk, and not finding one, searched her pants pocket before pulling one out. She blew her nose and threw the tissue in the garbage before looking back at Earl.

Earl was quickly turning pages, looking at the images and shaking his head. "Is this all one day's work, Kristy? It looks like it to me because there is some math stuff, and then page after page of these drawings. I don't know about the holes gouged into the pages, if they're from one day, or from many. Silly first question… does he do okay in math, or does he hate it?" Earl looked at Kristy, realized she was reaching into her pocket for another tissue, so he quickly opened a drawer and put a box on the desk right in front of her.

"I don't think he hates it," Kristy said. "Although who knows. He is so quiet. He never says anything in class, he never talks to any of the other students, and not to me either." She paused for a moment. "His homework is inconsistent. Work finished some days, others most is done, and others, nothing at all has been started. His quiz and tests are okay. Nothing great, but nothing terrible." She shook her head. "I don't think these drawings are about math, though."

"No, no, absolutely not," Earl agreed. "I just wondered if the holes were connected to the drawings too, or if they were about something else. It could well be that they are connected," he concluded.

"They weren't there the last time I checked his notebook," Kristy offered, "and that was two days ago. His notebook had math, no holes, no drawings." She looked at Earl. "I really don't know him so well because he's so quiet. He just disappears into the class. He's not a troublemaker, and he's not an eager beaver participant. He just is, you know. He's there." Another tear appeared at the side of Kristy's eye. "But this, oh Earl, I can't help but wonder if something terrible has happened to him. Is this his way of telling us? Did you know this already? I keep forgetting that you know a lot more about these kids' personal stories than I do." Kristy wiped the tear away, took a tissue from the box and blew her nose.

"His parents told me that something traumatic must have happened to him, about three years ago, was it?" Earl looked at his ceiling, trying to remember the timing of Walter and Elizabeth's story about Benji's time in Saskatoon. "I'll have to check my notes, as I don't remember exactly when, but his parents said something happened to him in Saskatoon." He pulled open his bottom drawer and began rifling through a collection of notebooks.

"Saskatoon?" Kristy blurted out. "Did you say something happened to him in Saskatoon?" Earl nodded at the urgent question put to him by Kristy. His eyes asked the question for him. "We had a guest in the classroom this morning. Some guy named Pinkerton. He works for the Parks and Recreation Department. He was talking about summer program options for kids. Do you think that my introducing him as someone from Saskatoon might have been the trigger for Benji? But, my goodness Earl, have you ever seen a kid in grade seven draw such sexually graphic images? What is that all about?"

Earl kept pushing aside one notebook after another, finally saw the one he wanted, nodded, and placed it on top of his desk. "Ah, here it is, Benji's book. Excuse me, Kristy, I have to write some of this down before I forget what you've told me. I just glanced at the drawings, and you're absolutely right. Erections, scrotums, well, many boys in grade seven, even some of the girls, are drawing those. But these, it's a veritable Kama Sutra of sexual activity, or at least homosexual activity. Yeah, that's not common! Actually, it's not the Kama Sutra at all; in that book all the sex acts are between adults. This is way different, as it appears to be one adult and one child. I will have to do some more exploring, but in the meantime, I think I need to call in Benji's parents this afternoon for a meeting."

"I don't envy you your job, Earl. I can't even imagine the conversation you will have with the Rempels. Isn't he a preacher? I mean, do preachers even know how to talk about this sort of stuff?" Kristy stood up and walked to the door. At the door, she turned to face Earl. "I don't know what to think or say either, actually. I'm just so surprised, shocked probably, that someone in grade seven would draw pictures like that." Kristy paused, and then added, "Good luck, Earl. I hope it goes well. You'll let me know if there is anything else I should be doing, right? I told Benji that you would probably come looking for him to meet with him and talk about his drawings from this morning. That is when he pushed me over, yelled at me and ran out of the room. He's never behaved like this before, and I was so surprised by all of it. You'll take care of it from here, right? Is there anything else I need to do?"

"Yes, of course, I'll take it from here," Earl said. "I'll head out to find Benji as soon as I call his parents. I'll ask them to come in this afternoon, to see if we can maybe finally piece some of the Saskatoon questions and information into the puzzle that reveals more of its image. I hope, Kristy, that maybe we finally have something that will allow us to help that kid." Kristy nodded and left the office as Earl reached for his phone.

Chapter Thirty-One

Elizabeth could hear Walter's voice coming through the classroom door but didn't hesitate to knock, knowing she was interrupting his class. The voice stopped and Walter opened the door, a look of surprise on his face. "Elizabeth? What is it? Can it wait? There are about fifteen..."

Elizabeth began shaking the moment the door opened and then grabbed Walter's arms. "We have to go see Mr. Tilitson right away. Benji's not at school. Something happened this morning and he's missing. Please, Walter, we have to go. We have to go right now!" Elizabeth tried pulling Walter through the doorway. Initially he resisted, then he stepped into the doorway.

Walter turned back to his class. "Excuse me, but I think I have to leave. We were almost finished for today. Read Philippians five, no, make it ten times, before tomorrow's class. Excuse me." He turned and allowed Elizabeth to pull him down the hall.

"Elizabeth, what did Mr. Tilitson say?" he asked, taking a few quick steps to get ahead of Elizabeth, then turning so he could look into her face.

"He said 'you and your husband need to come to school right now' and then he said 'Benji's missing' and then... and then... he said 'the Saskatoon incident might have something to do with this' and then..." Elizabeth grabbed Walter's hand and tried to force him into a run. "Where would Benji go? He's not at home."

"Today isn't Jacob's kindergarten day. Where is he?" Walter stopped and asked. "Who's got him?"

"He's in the car. Anna said she'd meet us at the school and take him. We have to hurry!" Elizabeth pushed open the doors of the Bible school and pulled open the car door for Walter and ran to the other side to get into the passenger seat. Jacob smiled from his booster seat in the back of the car.

"We're going to Benji's school, Daddy," Jacob explained. "And, once we get there, Anna's going to take me for ice cream!" Jacob smiled into the rear-view mirror where he saw Walter's eyes peering back at him.

"Sounds delicious." Walter smiled into the mirror, then shifted the gears into drive and headed down the school driveway toward the street. He looked to his left, saw the road was clear, and he pulled onto the road without stopping. Two blocks later he turned left for the half block before entering the school's parking lot.

Anna pushed her body away from the car she was leaning against and walked over to the car. She pulled the back door open and reached for Jacob. "Hey, little brother. What's up? Ready to go for some ice cream?" Jacob had already released the seat belt and was climbing out of the car. "Hey, Elizabeth, hey, Dad. Sounded important. What's up?"

"The counsellor wants to see us. Benji's gone missing from his classes. Something happened this morning and he's disappeared," Elizabeth explained.

Walter shrugged. "It's not such a big town. I don't think anything can happen to him here, can it?" He looked at Anna for an answer. Elizabeth took Walter's hand and started to pull him toward the school door.

"He'll be fine, Dad, don't worry. And so will little Jakey." Anna pinched Jacob's cheek and smiled at him. Jacob smiled back at her. "I'll take Jacob for ice cream and then we'll go to a park to play. I'll have him home in time for supper, so don't worry about him." They walked across the school playground toward the ice cream stand.

Walter pulled Elizabeth to a stop just outside the entrance to the school. "Should we pray before we go in to see Mr. Tilitson?" he asked, taking both of Elizabeth's shoulders in his hands.

"This isn't the time for that, Walter. Benji's missing. What's God going to do? Show you where he is? Please, let's go in and find out what's happening.

Then, if you still want to pray, that might be the time for it." Elizabeth pulled away from Walter's hands and opened the door. She looked back at him. "Coming?"

Walter nodded and went through the open door, and Elizabeth followed. "I'm pretty sure I remember that his office is this way." They walked down the hallway looking into classrooms filled with students and heard classroom noises, students opening and closing books, looking out the classroom windows, an occasional student spotting them and waving in the hallway.

"Guidance Department" was written in large letters on the sign sticking into the hallway. "Here it is, Walter. Do we knock or just go in?" Elizabeth paused, and Walter knocked on the door. Earl Tilitson came out of his interior office and waved them in.

"Thank you for coming," Earl said, extending a hand to Elizabeth and then to Walter. "This way, please." He motioned into his office, allowed them to walk in ahead of him, then closed the door behind him.

"Please, Mr. Tilitson, what can you tell us? Has someone found Benji already?" Elizabeth asked one question rapidly after the other. She twisted her hands together in her lap and leaned forward in her chair. Walter grabbed onto the arm rests and also leaned toward the counsellor to hear the response.

"I'm sorry, we still haven't found Benji. The principal and vice-principal are driving around town right now looking for him in each of the parks, the skate park, the drop-in, at the mall, the arena, the baseball diamonds, the soccer park, and basically any place in town that we've ever heard kids talk about."

Earl looked at them. "I want to back up to my conversation with Kristy Newchild, Benji's math teacher, about what happened in her class this morning." Walter and Elizabeth looked expectantly at the counsellor and nodded without saying anything.

"Our Parks and Recreation Department sent one of their new employees to our school to talk to the students about the new day-camp programs available this summer. Ms. Newchild introduced him as someone who just came from Saskatoon, and he does his presentation." Walter and Elizabeth sat up straighter at the mention of Saskatoon. "He does his presentation, leaves, and the kids go back to doing math. Except Benji, he starts doodling these." Earl handed the math notebook across his desk.

A paper drifted out of the notebook and Elizabeth stooped to pick it up. "Fing Fred. Is that someone's name? What does Fing Fred mean?" Elizabeth looked across the desk while Walter opened the notebook. He gasped and grabbed Elizabeth's arm.

"Look at this!" Walter blurted out, his face turning a deep shade of red. He looked up at Earl briefly, shook his head, then turned his face to Elizabeth. She took the notebook in her hand and opened it. She too gasped, her face also turned red, and she looked up at Earl. "We don't allow this sort of drawing in our home," Walter started to explain.

Elizabeth put her hand on his arm and shook her head. "This isn't about what we allow Benji to draw or not draw, Walter. This is about what Benji did draw. Mr. Tilitson, what is Benji trying to tell us with these drawings? Didn't he do some drawings like this before?" Earl nodded and leaned forward toward the Rempels.

"Your first question, Elizabeth, was who or what is Fing Fred. I suspect the intention of that short note was to call Fred, whoever that is, a name, F-ing Fred," Earl explained. "He didn't want to write the whole word. Which I have to say seems a little odd in light of all the drawings he did right after writing that." Earl pointed at the pages of sexually explicit images in front of them.

"When Benji drew some pictures of a penis previously, it didn't really mean that much to me because so many kids draw that exact same image. They're curious, they're grossed out, they want to shock someone, there are many reasons for drawing that. But this doesn't look like shock-value drawing. I mean, yeah, it is shocking, but once again, I suspect Benji didn't draw this to show to anyone else. This was possibly a reaction to hearing the word Saskatoon, and that triggered this response."

Walter grabbed Elizabeth's arm. "What? Are you suggesting that finally we have a clue as to what happened in Saskatoon?" he blurted out. "And today, after all these years of us wondering what happened, it wasn't his anger at me, or Elizabeth, or Jacob?" Walter looked at Elizabeth, who had tears forming in her eyes.

"I don't know what to think, Mr. Rempel, that is why I wanted you both to come. As I said, I don't think he was intending for anyone else to see these pictures, so I don't think it was his intention to tell us what happened in Saskatoon. But now that we have seen what he drew, what he wrote, maybe between the three of us we can make more sense of it and how it might link to Saskatoon." Earl leaned back in his chair. "Those drawings are absolutely clear. Each image is an image of some sort of sex act, and each image is equally clear that there is a bigger person who is doing the sex act to a smaller person. There are so many images, just looking at them, and then thinking maybe this happened, explains so much about Benji over the past number of years."

Tears streamed down Elizabeth's cheeks. "So that first name thing, it is actually a statement about someone named Fred? Do you think that there was someone named Fred at that camp in Saskatoon? Could that really be his name, or just a name that Benji chose?" Elizabeth slid the paper toward the counsellor.

Earl took the paper and shook his head. "Good question, Elizabeth, and unfortunately I don't know the answer. That will definitely be on the list of questions to ask Benji as soon as he is found and joins us in this office. He does have some explaining to do, that is for certain."

"I notice that the name page has many colours of pens to scrawl out those words," Walter observed. "But those pictures, they are all in one colour, pink. What's that about?" Walter looked at Earl and then at Elizabeth. "Lots of boys, at least some boys, say that pink is a gay person's colour. Do you think that because it's a man doing this to a boy, that Benji drew it in pink because he thinks it is a gay thing?"

Earl nodded. "Yeah, a number of our students say exactly that, pink equals gay. Many boys say that when their mothers buy them a pink T-shirt, for example, they will never wear it. So that could be a possible explanation. I mean, it makes sense, right?" Earl looked at Walter. "What do you think, Elizabeth?"

Elizabeth wiped tears from her eyes. "I'm not sure. I get it, I've heard other kids say the same thing, but never from Benji." She looked directly at the counsellor. "Benji has a sister who is a lesbian, and he has heard Anna speak about her partner Shelley in loving terms. I have no idea what Benji thinks about Anna and Shelley, but I've never heard him say anything rude or nasty to either of them, or about their lives. So maybe he's distressed, but he's never shown that before. I'm not sure he'd link pink with gay. But what else could it mean?"

"Oh, how about this?" Earl asked, then continued, "We speculated that this whole drawing reaction could have been triggered by the name of Saskatoon, right? When Benji heard the name of that city again, it brought back all these memories, and this time, for whatever reason, he actually started drawing what happened to him while he was there." Elizabeth and Walter nodded as they followed Earl's words.

"Maybe," continued Earl, "when he heard the name Mr. Pinkerton, that guy who came to make the presentation, he just latched onto the first part of his name and grabbed his pink…" Earl looked across the table at the pained face of Walter. "What?" Earl shrugged.

"Mr. Pinkerton? From Saskatoon?" Walter looked at Elizabeth. "Could it just be a coincidence? Wasn't that the name of the person Darrel called to talk to at that day camp?"

Elizabeth gasped too. "Fred, Fred Pinkerton!" She turned from Walter to Earl. "There was a man who worked at that day camp in Saskatoon. He told Darrel that he didn't notice anything strange in Benji's behaviour at that camp, but if he…" Elizabeth's voice trailed off.

"I know, Elizabeth, I don't even want to think that. But," Walter added, "F-ing Fred. F-ing Fred Pinkerton." Walter stared at Earl. "Is it possible that is what Benji is trying to tell us with this name page and the drawings?"

"I don't want to get ahead of myself," Earl responded, "but it all sounds possible. First, I'll go back to Kristy and ask her what Mr. Pinkerton's first name is. What if his name is Fred? What if he's the same person? It's really important that we find Benji and talk to him. And the sooner we find out where he is…" Earl looked back and forth between Walter and Elizabeth. "Do either of you have any idea where Benji might have gone? Does he have any friends we don't know about at school? We already checked the attendance record, and every student we have ever seen interact with Benji is accounted for, so he didn't leave with them."

"I can't remember him ever asking to go spend time with anyone in the past three years," Elizabeth said. "Walter, are there any church kids, or church adults, where he might have gone?" Walter rubbed the side of his cheek with his hand and shook his head.

"He doesn't protest coming to church on Sundays," Walter said, "but mostly I think he hates church, Sunday School, and pretty much everyone in that building." He shook his head again. "I'm sorry, Mr. Tilitson, but we can't think of anyone. Anna is taking care of Jacob, so she's not at her place if Benji went there. Shelley could be there, I guess, maybe, or she could be working. I don't know her work schedule, do you, Elizabeth?"

Elizabeth shook her head. "No, Walter, I don't. Maybe he's just taking a long walk or something. Maybe he'll come home soon." She looked at Earl. "For so long I wondered if knowing what happened to him in Saskatoon would allow us to figure out how to get into his life again, how to get our Benji back. Now I'm even more scared. Shelley told us she used drugs to escape from being bullied for being a lesbian. When she explained why she used drugs, I got it, but didn't know why Benji would need them. If what we're talking about now is true, I get it. I think if I had been sexually abused at age nine, I'd have needed drugs to escape my conscious nightmares too." Elizabeth shook her head and started to cry. "Walter, we have to find him. Where is he?" She stood up, reached for Walter's arm, and tugged at it.

"Mr. Tilitson, we're going to drive around too, see if we can think of any places to look for Benji that the principal hasn't already gone to. Then we're going to go home. Please call us if you hear anything. You'll call us, right?" Walter begged.

Earl stood up and nodded. "Absolutely I'll call. I'm going to join the search too. Another person looking can't hurt." He reached behind him and pulled a sweater from the back of his chair. "Ah, probably don't need this," he said and threw the sweater back. He followed Walter and Elizabeth out of his office and into the parking lot. He waved to them as they got into their car and drove away.

Chapter Twenty-Eight

"Walter, we better call home first and tell Sonya where we're going," Elizabeth said, turning in her seat toward Walter.

He nodded, looking back over his shoulder and moving out of their parking spot. "And then where to? Where do we go to look for Benji? Where would he have gone?" Elizabeth pulled out her phone and called Sonya's number, but got no response. "She's still in class, not answering. Let's stop at home." The drive home was a silent one, both Walter and Elizabeth sorting through any name Benji might have mentioned, any places he might have mentioned, including places he hadn't been to but might have wanted to see.

Minutes later Walter stopped the car outside their garage and turned to Elizabeth. "Wait here, I'll be right back. I'll write her a note." He got out of the car and entered the house. A minute later he was getting back into the car. "Left a note telling her we'd be home later, that we're looking for Benji. Any suggestions as to our first stop?" He looked at her as he shifted into reverse.

"Uhm, the counsellor said the principals were going to all the parks, so we don't need to go there. How about we just drive around some of the residential sections? If Benji is walking to clear his head, maybe he's walking in that place behind the cemetery." Elizabeth sounded hopeful, although her forehead was creased with worry.

"How about I drive there along Giesbrecht Avenue and maybe up and down Ellice on the way to the cemetery?" Walter asked, turning right onto First Street after passing by the 7-Eleven. Walter kept his speed around thirty kilometres per hour so he could look into backyards, along intersecting streets, and ahead on the street where they were driving. Elizabeth looked into backyards and streets on her side of the car.

Walter stopped at the intersection of First Street and Giesbrecht Avenue, peering in every direction. A horn blast from behind him reminded him he needed to keep driving, so he put on his signal light and turned left. The white Honda Civic behind him squealed around the corner as well and sped past him, while Walter, nonplussed, kept his speed down, and peered into one yard after another.

It was almost nine when Walter stopped the car in front of their garage again. He dropped his head and shoulders forward, slumping against the steering wheel. Elizabeth leaned her head back as far as the head rest would allow and sighed. They both remained silent and motionless, even when Sonya pushed the house door open and stood waiting in the doorway. She leaned against the door frame and started crying when she saw only her parents in the car. A moment later Anna appeared in the doorway beside her lifting her shoulders and arms in petition toward her parents.

Elizabeth took a deep breath, put her hand on Walter's knee, and said, "I'll go in and talk with Sonya and Anna. See if anyone from the school called." She opened her car door and inched her way out. She grimaced and shook her head toward Anna and Sonya. "We didn't find him. We really didn't… don't know where to look for him." Elizabeth reached out her arms when she reached the doorway and drew both Sonya and Anna into a hug. Sonya wrapped her arms tightly around her mother and hid her face in Elizabeth's shoulder. "Did anyone from the school call? Did one of the principals, or the counsellor, find him?" There was a flash of hope in Elizabeth's voice.

Anna shook her head and wrapped her arms around both Sonya and Elizabeth. "Well, yeah, they called. Someone named Tilitson called at around five-thirty, but only to say that they were all going home. No one saw him anywhere. Oh yeah, he also suggested that if Benji isn't home within a few hours, we should consider calling the cops. He said sometimes they tell parents to wait but sometimes they get right on it, if the parents say it's urgent, or something like that. I thought I'd let you make that call once you're ready to."

Sonya sobbed and tried to tuck herself between Anna and Elizabeth. No one had noticed Walter get out of the car and come to stand behind Elizabeth. He joined the circle hug then put his hands on Sonya's shoulders. "Come here, Sonya." He gently pulled on her shoulders. Sonya stepped backward and Walter directed her to the bench beside the garage and sat down beside her. He kept one arm around her shoulders, and with the other, held one of her hands.

"Honey, I wish I had some words of comfort to give you," Walter whispered into her hair. "I wish I could tell you we just saw Benji, he was smiling and skateboarding with some of his friends, and he'll be home soon." Walter paused, let go of Sonya's hand, and wiped away the tears forming at the corners of his eyes, then took her hand again. "But I can't say any of those things just yet. Hopefully I can within the next hour." Walter's voice broke and he engulfed Sonya with a hug. She buried her face in her father's chest and wept.

Elizabeth opened the door, then shot a look at Anna. "Jacob's inside, yes? He's okay?" An edge of fear hung on her voice.

"Yes and yes." Anna smiled. "He's too young to notice how worried Sonya was when we got here. He's watching some show, I don't know what… but don't worry, Elizabeth, it's child friendly." Elizabeth smiled and touched Anna's shoulder. "When Sonya told me you would be back late, I called Shelley. She finished work at five-thirty, so she was going home to pick up some cookies she made." Anna paused and leaned forward to continue in a whisper, "Not nearly as good as Sonya's, but don't tell her that. From there, she went to Chicken Chef to get some dinner for all of us. I called her when I saw your car, so she should be here any minute. I'll go in and set the table. Coming in, Elizabeth?" Anna held the door open and the two went inside.

Walter held Sonya against himself for another minute, then lifted her face toward his. "Sonya, let's go in. We can figure out how to wait for Benji, or wait for something, inside, okay?" He got up. Sonya took his hand and followed him inside.

"Supper will be here any minute," Anna told her father. "Shelley's on her way. Nothing like dinner-to-your-door, or even better, directly to your table." Anna smiled. She went into the kitchen, opened a cupboard, and lifted out the dishes they would need for the meal. "Sonya, you want to help set the table?" Sonya joined Anna in the kitchen and the two sisters took out what they needed, put it on the table, and frequently stopped to hold each other's hands for a moment or exchange hugs.

"Oh, wow, Anna, thank you so much," Walter said. "I'm exhausted. I think I'll just go lie down on the couch until dinner arrives. Yell if you need me." He walked through the dining room, into the living room, and lay down. He kept shifting, rolling one way then another, propped his legs up on the arm rest, curled them tighter to himself, stretched out, and rolled over again. Deep sighs accompanied almost every change in position.

Sonya took the seat beside Elizabeth, took one of her hands in both of hers, and pressed it against her cheek. A sigh followed by a sob escaped from Sonya. She looked up at Elizabeth to say, "I don't think I've ever been this scared before. And I'm not even sure what it is that I'm scared of. Mom, do you have any idea why Benji ran away from school? Why he didn't come home today?" She paused, then sobbed out, "When will he come home?"

Elizabeth turned in her chair to put her arms around Sonya. "I'm scared too, honey. All I know is that something happened at school today, something that seems to have really upset Benji, so he left school without telling anyone where he was going. The counsellor thinks that finally he might have a clue about what happened in Saskatoon all those years ago, and that something triggered all that fear and anger that has been inside him for so many years. The principals and guidance counsellor drove around town looking for him, just like your dad and I did." Elizabeth allowed her tears to run freely down her face. She leaned her head against Sonya's head. "I hope he comes home real soon too," she whispered, wrapping one hand around her opal amulet.

Shelley's small blue car arrived on the driveway and a moment later she walked into the house with a bucket of chicken under one arm and a large greasy paper bag under the other one. She put the food on the counter and went straight to Elizabeth and hugged her for a long time without saying a word. Elizabeth leaned back into Shelley's hug and turned her face enough to kiss Shelley's cheek.

"You're a God-send," Elizabeth told her, letting go of Sonya, pushing her chair back, and standing up all at the same time.

Shelley chuckled. "Can't remember the last time someone told me that God had sent me. Other phrases that began with 'God' but definitely followed by a different word!" Shelley stepped around Elizabeth and hugged Sonya.

"Chicken! I smell chicken!" Jacob shouted, running up the stairs and bursting into the kitchen. He stopped in his tracks when he saw Elizabeth's and Sonya's faces. "What's wrong? Why were you crying, Mom?" He looked around the room. "Where's Benji? Isn't he coming to eat? Is that chicken from Chicken Chef?" He went to the counter and inhaled long, deep breaths from the food containers.

Shelley came up behind him. "Come here, little man! Give me a hug!" Shelley picked Jacob up, spun him around in her arms and tossed him into the air. Jacob's giggles filled the dining room. Shelley caught him, hugged him, and threw him into the air again. When she caught him the second time, Jacob hugged her around the neck before he was tossed into the air for a third time. "My goodness, Jake, you are growing." Shelley set him down on the floor and tousled his hair.

Sonya went into the living room and touched Walter's shoulder. Walter turned to face her, his red-rimmed eyes full of tears. "Dinner's here, Dad," she whispered, her lips beginning to quiver too. Walter sat up, wiped his eyes, and stood up. Sonya took his hand and led him to the dining room.

Shelley came over to Walter and gave him a long hug, which he returned with a tight embrace, leaning his head into her shoulder. "Thank you for bringing us dinner. One less thing for us to think about tonight."

"Of course, Walter, it's my pleasure." Shelley extricated herself from Walter's hug and took a seat at the table beside Anna. Jacob rushed to the open chair beside Shelley and nestled in as close to her as he could. Elizabeth smiled at Jacob and sat in the last empty chair at the table.

All eyes turned to Walter expectantly. He nodded and bowed his head. "God… oh God… please…" His voice broke into sobs and he dropped his head into both hands. Elizabeth reached out to place a hand on his arm.

Anna got out of her chair, stepped behind him, and put her arms around his neck.

"Let me finish the prayer, Dad," Anna whispered. "God," she started, then switched to a whisper, "if you're there, bring Benji home safely."

"Where's Benji?" Jacob interrupted, looking around the table. When he saw the expressions on the faces around the table he burst into tears. "Where's Benji? How come he isn't here?" Shelley pulled Jacob into her lap and held him tightly against herself. His cries calmed to sobs, then to whimpers.

Anna tightened her embrace for a moment around Walter, then returned to her seat. Walter gulped for air, looked up, and wiped at the tears streaming down his face. Sonya stared into her plate, blinked, then placed her hands over her face.

The motionless silence that had settled around the table for a moment was broken by the plaintiff wail of sirens passing on the street leading out of town past the Rempel house. "Chicken, anyone? Fries? Coleslaw?" Shelley broke the dining room silence, reaching for the box of fries and passing it to Anna.

Food made its way around the table. Sonya passed each successive dish along without taking anything. "What? Sonya, you suddenly don't like Chicken Chef or something?" Shelley asked in surprise.

Sonya smiled at her. "Well, yeah, I do. But I'm just really not hungry." She looked around the table. "I'll just wait a minute, and then I'll help myself." Walter reached over, patted her on the shoulder, and nodded his agreement.

"This looks and smells great, Shelley. This is so thoughtful of you, thanks. I'm sort of like you, Sonya, I'm not so very hungry," Walter said.

Jacob had forgotten his fright of a few moments earlier and, still nestled in Shelley's lap, was smiling past the piece of chicken he had inserted into his mouth. One hand held the end of the drumstick he was eating, the other was reaching for some fries. Shelley lifted him off her lap and settled him onto his own seat again. "Here, young man," she said, putting a fork into his extended left hand, "use this for the fries."

Elizabeth took a small bite of coleslaw and set her fork down into her plate. She folded her hands in her lap and pressed her eyes shut. When she opened them a moment later, tears began forming at the edges of her eyes. "Excuse me just a moment," she said, standing up, "I just need to wash my face. I'll be right back." She turned and went to the bathroom, closing the door behind her.

Walter looked across the table at Anna, shrugged, and whispered, "Should I go with her? Or do I let her wash her face alone?" Anna looked at Shelley, then back to Walter.

"Maybe give her a minute or two, Dad," Anna suggested. "It's been a pretty wild afternoon, and she hasn't had any time to sort out her own head. Everything with Benji has been so complicated for her. I think she might just need a minute or two alone." Walter nodded, then put the piece of chicken he had been holding in his hand back onto his plate. He picked up his fork and moved the coleslaw around the plate before putting his fork down again.

"Should I make some coffee?" Sonya asked, pushing back from the table and standing up. "Anyone want some coffee?"

"I'd have some," Walter said, smiling at Sonya. "Anyone else?" He looked around the table. Shelley smiled at Sonya and nodded and then looked at Anna, who was shaking her head. Sonya went into the kitchen and busied herself with the coffee-making preparations for a few minutes, then returned to the table.

"I think I'm ready for a piece. Please pass the chicken," Sonya said.

The bathroom door opened and Elizabeth came back to the table. Her eyes were red, but her face was composed. She sat down, took a deep breath and once again lifted a fork of coleslaw to her mouth before setting it back down on her plate. She glanced around the table to see if anyone had noticed. "Does anyone want some coffee? Should I make some coffee?" Elizabeth asked, getting up from her chair.

"Mom, I'm making some coffee, it'll be ready in a few minutes," Sonya said. Elizabeth settled back into her chair, and for a third time picked up her fork and lifted it to her mouth. For a third time she lowered it without touching the food.

"Elizabeth," Anna said across the table, "it's okay if you don't eat, if you're not hungry. The food will last. I'll put it in the fridge, and it will be there for you when you're actually hungry." Elizabeth smiled back at Anna and pushed her plate forward. "You go lie down on the couch, on your bed, to get a rest. We'll clean up. And then, why don't you let Shelley and I take Jacob to our place for a sleepover? Jake, wanna come with Shelley and me for a sleepover?"

"Yeah, please, Mom, can I?" Jacob smiled at Elizabeth. "I'll be good."

"You're always good, little one." Elizabeth smiled back. "Anna, Shelley, really? If it's no trouble for you. Tonight seems like a good night for that little one to escape this house."

"Come with me, little man," Shelley said, pushing her chair away from the table. "Let's go put together a sleepover bag for you. Pyjamas. Clean clothes for tomorrow. Do you have a favourite book? A favourite pillow? What else do we need to pack for your adventure?" Shelley took Jacob's hand and went to collect the things he would need. Anna got up and started picking up plates and silverware. After taking the dishes to the kitchen, Anna took the food and placed it on the kitchen counter.

"Oh Sonya, I hope Benji is okay." Anna filled some empty containers she had taken from a cupboard and packed each one full of the food that no one, other than Jacob, had been able to eat. "I'll put all this in the fridge." Anna finished filling the containers and finding spaces for them in the fridge, then returned to the dining room to take a seat beside Walter.

"The counsellor thinks that what happened today might explain what happened in Saskatoon way back when," Walter said. "If he's right, something really terrible happened to him. I can't even imagine…" His voice drifted off.

Anna put her hand on his knee, looking at Walter's face, waiting to hear more. Tears formed and began rolling down his cheeks. Elizabeth sat up and came to stand behind Walter, putting her hands on his shoulders. "What if that Fred… how can a person do that to a child?" Anna's face blanched when she heard those words. She turned her body fully toward Walter. "Oh, Anna, what kind of hell has Benji been living in for these past how many years?" Tears began to flow down Anna's face too.

Shelley rounded the corner with a small backpack in her hands. She stopped short when she saw the scene at the dining-room table. "Ah, maybe Jake needs to pack some more stuff," she said and turned around, keeping Jacob from seeing the others crying at the table.

"We didn't know," Elizabeth consoled Walter. "He never said a thing to either of us. Did he ever say something, give any clue, about this to either of you?" She looked from Sonya to Anna. Both shook their heads.

"I'm sorry to say this, Elizabeth, but we all know he acted like he didn't like you. I really thought that was his whole problem, that he didn't like you moving in with Dad, being here, then having Jacob. But I thought he'd grow out of that," Anna said.

Sonya nodded. "Me too, Mom. I thought one day he'd wake up and like you. You are so good to him." Elizabeth patted Sonya's shoulder.

"Me too," added Elizabeth. "I thought if I kept being kind to him, he'd stop being angry at me." She paused a moment. "I keep trying to think of anything… anything at all… that might have been a clue."

Anna's eyes lit up. "Wait, how about this? Do you remember, this was almost right after he got home from Saskatoon." Anna looked at Elizabeth. "You were making dinner, right? And then the smoke alarms went off. You go into Benji's room, and he's sitting there naked, burning his underwear. We wondered why he would burn his underwear but not his other clothes, I think. Well, if that guy did stuff to Benji, like made him undress, just to his underwear, and then did stuff. Or, made him naked, and then did stuff, that might be why he burned his underwear. I wonder if it was all the underwear he took to Saskatoon with him? And then, didn't he yell something about being naked to you, Elizabeth? Do you remember that?" Anna searched Elizabeth's face.

"You're right, Anna, that's how I remember that night too. And I think you're also right, that was a loud scream of horror at what had happened to him, and we didn't get it,'" Elizabeth responded.

"That seemed so weird because he never cared about who saw him naked before. Do you remember he would undress for a bath wherever he was, in the dining room, kitchen, living room, anywhere, and then walk to the bathroom? You must have seen him naked hundreds of times before that," Anna said. Elizabeth nodded agreement.

"He could have yelled that naked comment about Fred, rather than about anyone of us," Elizabeth surmised. "Anyway, all of this is speculation. We need to find Benji, we need Benji to come home so we can talk to him. So we can ask him about Saskatoon."

Chapter Twenty-Nine

Two police cars rolled past the dining-room window and stopped behind Shelley's car. The doors on both cars opened, with officers getting out of each. One of them was carrying a backpack. They came to the door and rang the doorbell.

"I'll get it!" Jacob yelled as he re-entered the room. He let go of Shelley's hand and raced to the door and threw it open and then took a few steps back. He dropped his hands to his sides and looked at the dining room table.

"Hello, may we come in?" called out one of the officers. Elizabeth rushed to the door, picking Jacob up in her arms along the way.

"Please, yes, please come in. How may I help you?" Elizabeth greeted them anxiously.

Jacob wriggled out of Elizabeth's arms and ran to the officer holding the backpack. "Look!" He pointed. "He's got Benji's backpack. How come you have Benji's backpack? Where's Benji?"

The officer smiled at Jacob with a look of sorrow in his eyes. Elizabeth caught the look the officer gave Jacob and took a step back, her face turning white. "Hey, little fella, that's exactly what I'm here to talk to your mom and dad about." He looked up at Elizabeth, noticed her ashen face, gave the backpack to his partner, and stepped up beside her. He put an arm around her back and another under her arm. "I think sitting down in the living room is a good idea. Let me help you." Elizabeth slumped against his arm, trembling, but walked to the living room where she dropped onto the couch.

Sonya started crying and covered her face with her hands. Anna stood up, lips quivering. "Shelley… Shelley… please… can you… would you… downstairs?" Anna's eyes pleaded with Shelley, who immediately acted on the plea. She came up behind Jacob who was looking at the back of his mother walking away from him, at his father, who had slumped over the table, to Sonya's covered face, to the officer still standing at the open door, now holding Benji's backpack.

"Time for bed, buddy!" Shelley hoisted Jacob into her arms. "But instead of a sleepover at our house, Anna and I are going to have a sleepover at your house. Let's go downstairs and build a tent in the guest room. The three of us can crawl into the tent, tell stories, and drift away…" Shelley's voice broke. She let out a sob before clearing her voice and whispering into Jacob's ear, "escape into the stars with our dreams."

"Yeah! We can take the cushions from the couch and… why are you crying, Shelley?" Jacob twisted in her arms to face her. He lifted his hands and wiped away the tears coming from Shelley's eyes. "It's not sad to have a sleepover. We're going to have fun."

Shelley leaned her forehead against Jacob's for a moment, took a deep breath, and smiled. "It's going to be so much fun. Let's go." She looked over her shoulder at Anna as she descended the stairs. Jacob's voice giving instructions about which cushions to bring to the guest room disappeared as they descended the steps into the basement.

Anna got up from behind the table and stepped toward the police officer still standing at the door holding Benji's backpack. "Please, sir, come in. Come take a seat in the living room." She motioned to the living room, then moved behind Walter. She placed both hands on his shoulders, then wrapped her arms around his neck. Walter's body shook with sobs under her embrace. "Come, Dad, come into the living room, okay? We don't know what they're going to tell us yet." Anna's voice quivered.

Walter sat up, wiped his eyes, and stood. He went into the living room and sat down beside Elizabeth, whose shoulders were hunched forward and trembling, her face bowed, looking at her knees. Walter put an arm around her back, and she leaned her body against his. Walter reached out with his other hand and put it on Elizabeth's knee.

"Coming, Sonya?" Anna whispered into her ear and took another step closer to the living room. She turned back, and when she saw Sonya was staying, with her head on the table, Anna returned and sat down beside her where she could see into the living room.

The officer still holding Benji's backpack cleared his throat. "I'm Constable Hiebert," he said, then gestured toward the other officer, "and this is Constable Richardson." Constable Richardson nodded at them. Slowly Constable Hiebert placed the backpack on the floor in front of Walter and Elizabeth. Elizabeth started shaking her head, covered her mouth with one hand, and dug her face into Walter's shoulder.

"Folks, I'm very sorry to inform you that your son Benji was involved in an automobile-pedestrian accident." Constable Hiebert took a breath before continuing. "And I'm even more sorry to inform you that he did not survive the accident." Walter turned to hide his face in Elizabeth's shoulder and wrapped both arms around her shoulders.

Sonya lifted her head to look at Constable Hiebert, hoping she had not heard his words correctly, that somehow there must be a misunderstanding. "Are you sure he isn't just in the hospital? That he's hurt very bad? Mom, Dad, shouldn't we be going to the hospital to see him?" Sonya begged. Then she turned around and threw herself into Anna's open arms, sobs wracking her body. Anna closed her arms around Sonya, put her cheek on top of Sonya's head and let her own tears fall into Sonya's hair.

Constables Hiebert and Richardson sat still in their chairs, waiting for the wave of shock to settle. Constable Richardson broke the silence. "We were able to do a most-likely identification with this backpack. There are books that have the name Benji Rempel on them. And then there is a school-issued ID card with his picture, name, and address. Nonetheless, we will require a formal identification from someone, someone from your family, please. It is not necessary that it is done immediately, but no later than tomorrow, please." He looked at his feet when he finished.

Walter turned to face the two officers, nodding as he wiped his hands over his face. "Can I ask a question?" His voice was barely audible. Both officers nodded their consent. "Was… was it really… an… acci… accident?"

Walter managed between sobs. "Today was a... a... diffi... difficult da... day for Benji," he stammered. "We went looking for him. He ran... disappeared... from... his school this... this morning."

Elizabeth lifted her face from Walter's chest and added, "We have been so worried about him. We had no idea where he had gone. The principals went looking for him, we went looking for him, the guidance counsellor too. We were all so worried, so afraid for him. We think something terrible happened to him three years ago, and today that nightmare was brought back to life for him. We had no idea, no idea..." her voice trailed off.

"I'm afraid I know nothing more, folks. The road has been closed at the accident site, and there are officers in charge of an investigation. Other officers have interviewed the driver of the car, but I'm sorry, I do not know the details of their conversation. We should have information necessary to answer that question soon, perhaps tomorrow, but certainly within a few days," Constable Hiebert answered.

"Mr. Tilitson contacted me this afternoon, just after he met with you," Constable Richardson explained. "He is the liaison between his school and our department, so I've spoken with him on some occasions previously. When he called, he very briefly painted a picture of what had transpired today, and that there was a search underway for your son. He also mentioned the importance of a continuing conversation with your son concerning what may have transpired when he was in Saskatoon three years ago." Walter nodded. "We can have those conversation at a later date. I believe this is enough to absorb for tonight." The two officers rose to their feet.

Walter and Elizabeth stood. "No need to see us out," Constable Hiebert said, "we can find our way to the door. If you have any additional questions, if you need anything from us, please call. I'll leave my card on your table. I will also leave a card for a grief counselling service, should you want that." Walter and Elizabeth dropped down to the couch again. Anna reached out to take the cards and then to shake the officer's hands. They nodded to her and left. The house remained silent as the sounds of the police car disappeared down the driveway.

Chapter Thirty

A quiet crowd sat around tables or stood in small clusters visiting with subdued voices. A large collage of pictures of Benji was hanging on the wall, with a few groups of people standing, pointing at pictures, smiling, crying, and then moving on. Walter and Elizabeth sat at a table near the collage along with Anna, Shelley, Sonya, Darrel, and Marigold. An untouched, full basket of whole-wheat and raisin dinner rolls sat in the middle of the table, surrounded by plates filled with cheese slices and a variety of cold cuts. Another plate was filled with pieces of brownies, lemon squares, and mini-cinnamon rolls. Nothing had been touched.

"Do you know where Abbi and Jacob are?" Marigold asked Darrel, looking around the hall.

"Yeah, Jacob said there was a playground outside and that they were going there. Oh, what is her name?" Darrel pressed the palm of one hand against his forehead. "Jeez, I can't remember her name, but she and I were in school together. She said she'd keep an eye on them. I'm sure they're safe with her." Marigold nodded.

"I wish I was carefree out on a playground right about now too." Anna smiled across the table at them. Shelley leaned over and kissed her on the cheek. Anna took one of her hands and pressed it against her heart. "I'm so glad I've got you." Shelley leaned her head against Anna's shoulder.

Sonya stood up and looked at Walter and Elizabeth. "Do you think it would be alright if I went outside too? I could take over and keep an eye on

Abbi and Jacob." Darrel took a step toward her and gave her a hug. Sonya turned to face Darrel and hugged him hard.

"You are always looking after someone, aren't you, Sonya? You know you're an angel, right?" Sonya looked up with her red eyes and tear-stained face and smiled. "I hope that Abbi grows up to be just like you!" Darrel said, then added, "and just like you to Anna!"

"Be careful what you wish for, brother." Anna smiled. Sonya let go of Darrel and looked at Walter and Elizabeth.

"Of course, sweetie," Elizabeth said. "I wish I could go out there with you and escape this crowd," she leaned forward and whispered to Sonya.

"Soon, Mom," Marigold responded. "Most of the people who came have already left. It won't be much longer before we can, how did you call it, escape." Marigold squeezed Elizabeth's hand.

Earl Tilitson walked up to the table, nodded at the group, and then approached Walter and Elizabeth. Walter stood up to greet him. "No need to stand up, Mr. Rempel," Earl began. "I want to tell you how incredibly sorry I am for your loss." He handed a thick manila envelope to Walter. "These are condolence cards from Benji's class, and also from his teachers." Earl sighed. "I also want to apologize to you for not recognizing the signs that Benji seemed to be giving earlier." Earl bent his head and started to cry.

Elizabeth stood up and put a hand on his arm. "Oh, Mr. Tilitson, that is so very kind of you." She patted his arm. "Sure, we wish you would have figured it out earlier too, we wish we would have figured it out earlier. Who knows if we could have reached into that closed shell and tried to find something helpful, or good, for our hurting Benji." She smiled. "I'm sure there are enough regrets to go around for a long time. But those regrets too will need to be put to rest. I pray I'll never have to try to figure out something like this again, ever, with any of my other children." She took out a clean tissue and offered it to him, then put her hand up to his face and placed it against his cheek. "You, dear counsellor, will probably not be so lucky. You have so many children, so many stories, so many mysteries and heartaches. I don't know if you pray, Mr. Tilitson, or if having someone pray for you is any comfort, but that is something I can do for you." Elizabeth lowered her arm and sat down. Mr. Tilitson nodded at the rest of the family and walked away.

Anna stood up and moved close to Darrel and Marigold. "Constable Richardson told him that there was nothing they could do about that F-ing Fred from Saskatoon. All of the conversation between Mom and Dad and Tilitson was speculation, and without Benji to ask questions, or confirm anything, there's nothing more that can be done. At least not legally," Anna said, recounting the conversation she had with the counsellor two days earlier.

Darrel shook his head and started to cry. Marigold reached over to take one of his hands. "Oh, Anna. I was so young, I had no clue! I was so busy studying chemistry, not children's signals. I had no idea what went wrong with Benji, and then when I spoke with that Pinkerton on the phone, I simply believed him without doing any more checking. He was an adult, Benji a messed up kid, and I believed the adult." Marigold patted his hand and Anna took his other hand in hers.

"None of us got it, Darrel. We thought that just because Benji didn't like Elizabeth being married to Dad, that was the answer to everything bad he ever did, every time he was angry or disappeared into his room," Anna said.

Dave Hoeppner approached the table. He shook Marigold's hand first, then Darrel's, then Anna's. He smiled and stepped closer to the table. "Hello, Shelley, I'm Dave Hoeppner. I don't believe we've ever been introduced, or met, for that matter. I used to be a friend of the whole family. Now everyone's so grown up, and I don't really see them so much anymore. But I am still a friend of Mr. and Mrs. Rempel." He extended his hand to greet Shelley, who stood up, took his hand, and smiled back.

Shelley saw Anna and Darrel's large eyes filled with surprise, smiles spreading across their faces, behind Dave Hoeppner. Dave swallowed and then moved toward Walter and Elizabeth. "Are you kidding me?" Anna choked out. "Darrel, did you see what I think I just saw?"

"What? So some guy says hi and shakes my hand. What's the big deal?" Shelley asked, looking confused.

"That man, Shelley, was a part of the group of people who excommunicated Darrel for getting Marigold pregnant. He's a preacher in Dad's church," Anna blurted out.

Darrel blushed and added, "To his credit, he voted against my excommunication. Dad told me that." Then Darrel grinned. "But to smile at and shake the hand of a super sinner like the two of you are, well, what next?" Anna giggled and draped an arm around Shelley's shoulders.

Dave Hoeppner approached Walter and Elizabeth and sat down beside them. He looked at his shoes for a few moments before he looked up, tears welling from his eyes. He took one of Elizabeth's and one of Walter's hands, held them briefly, then let go. "I have no words. I'm so sorry."

"Thank you, Dave," Walter said. "Thank you both for having no words, and for your condolences."

"Mostly, we don't have words either," Elizabeth added. "Your kindness is what we need to heal, though, so thank you." Dave nodded a few times. "We will welcome you to our place for a cup of coffee, a visit, a cry, or just to come and sit with us. Some days have been so dark, all we need is someone to sit and share the darkness with us." Elizabeth looked past Dave and blinked away a tear.

"There are some dark days around us, aren't there? And who doesn't need another person, sometimes to just sit, or walk, beside them?" Dave added. "Soon," he said, "I'll be by to see you soon." He hung his head and walked away.

"Soon," Walter repeated, then looked at Elizabeth. "Soon," he whispered and sat down. "This is all too soon. I want to go home and help Benji put on his pyjamas again. I want him to laugh and giggle again. I want…" his voice broke into sobs.

Darrel moved close to Walter and knelt down beside him. "So much stuff happens too soon, doesn't it? Agatha left us too soon. Thankfully, soon after that Elizabeth came. I don't know, Dad, we don't get to choose times, do we? But we get to be together."

Walter looked up at Darrel, then across to Elizabeth. "We are in this together, aren't we?"

Acknowledgements

When I was ten, my father bought the card game "Authors" for his children. I didn't just play the game—I was inspired to read almost all the books named in the game and diligently sought out more books by those authors. I became enamoured by authors, by writing, by words, and by ideas, and determined that someday I would be an author too. Thank you, Dad, for inspiring me in that way.

My mother was a storyteller who held children in rapt attention with her heart-wrenching stories (always with a profound religious moral to be learned). She dreamed of writing stories, and about fifteen years ago, she and I began to collaborate on writing one story a year for *The Carillon's* (a southern-Manitoba newspaper) Christmas writing contest. We became authors together and writing with her was always a gift to my soul. Thank you, Mom, for sharing your love of storytelling with me.

Some years ago, Eldon and Shelleen Stoesz suggested that they would love to read my family story, as they knew some members of my blended family and about a few of the incidents that made up our lives. They also suggested they would like to read my take on some of the religious ideas they had faced within the community, about which they had heard me express my views. With their encouragement in place, I hatched a plan to create a fictional family in which the characters could be various iterations of my own faith journey, and I started writing.

Six months and 25,000 words into *The Four Horsemen*, Stephanie Ware, a former student and now friend, expressed interest in my story, and I sent it to her to read and offer feedback (she's a literature teacher, among many other things). My manuscript rested for a full year, and then she wrote asking when I was going to continue writing as she was interested in knowing what might become of these characters. She was the person whose encouragement (gentle but clear) got me back to the keyboard. As I continued the story, and continued to send her a Chapter, or a few Chapters, at a time, her feedback fed my desire to write more. She began to speak about the characters' lives in ways that intrigued and pushed me to develop them more deeply. She made comments connecting some dots in her own life to dots in the plot line and character's lives, which helped me believe that my story was credible. By late August 2020, after writing nearly 15,000 words in a three-day period, I couldn't stay away from my keyboard, as I saw the story unfold in my imagination.

Ralph Friesen, a pastor's son as well, from the same denomination as my father, was one of the readers of my first draft. Ralph, also a writer, offered valuable feedback about my story and characters, and ideas for revisions started.

Cara Hart, another writer and friend, did a deep, rich reading and gave me volumes of feedback that further prepared me to develop the second draft and then the third and fourth drafts. Her insights and encouragement to finish what she called "an important story" helped me to do just that.

I've written many academic papers, a number of short stories, and now I've finished my first novel. And I'm grateful for all the people along the way who encouraged me to turn the dream of being an author into a reality.

Mark Reimer

Printed in Canada